Heart of Silk and Shadows

Fae Isles - Book 0.5

Lisette Marshall

ISBN: 9789083256894

Cover design: Saint Jupiter
Editor: Erin Grey, The Word Faery

www.lisettemarshall.com
www.facebook.com/LisetteMarshallAuthor
www.instagram.com/AuthorLisetteMarshall

CONTENTS

CHAPTER 1

Yet again, the sun rose.

Her first golden rays filtered through the arched bedroom windows as they did every morning, flooding the mahogany floorboards with buttery light and shrouding the red-veined marble walls in an unearthly rosy glow. A sight, Agenor faintly remembered, that had filled him with awe and wonder when he had first moved into this tower apartment at the heart of the Crimson Court, a good six centuries ago.

He barely allowed his gaze to linger on that most familiar of spectacles now, just flicked the thin blankets aside and hauled himself from the overwhelming softness of his mattress before it could convince him not to get up at all.

Yet another morning.

Yet another day.

He suppressed a groan as he got to his feet and sauntered over to the windows, rolling his shoulders to get rid of the stiffness in his limbs and wings.

Below his elegant balcony the island basked in the early light, the rugged mountain range and the densely built towns of the lowlands behind, and finally the pearly white beaches and the frothing azure of the sea. So quiet. So peaceful. So ... tedious.

Agenor wondered, at times, where the sun found the will to climb above the horizon every single morning, knowing the same unchanging earth would yet again be waiting for her.

Perhaps she, too, knew the meaning of duty.

Movement in the corner of his sight pulled him from his mulling. Coral came slithering towards him over the mahogany, still sluggish from the cold of the night. A smile tugged at his lips – a moment of levity in his heart.

'Morning, girl.'

She glared up at him, tongue flicking out as if to berate him. Agenor laughed. Her morning moods were, impressively, worse than her day moods.

'Don't worry, I'll leave you alone. Shouldn't make them wait downstairs, anyway.'

Coral ignored him as she curled the full five feet of her ruby red body below the window, in the spot where the sunlight already had to be warming the floorboards. He resisted the urge to bend over and pet her. Later today, she would appreciate it. Right now, he might find himself with fangs embedded an inch into his wrist if he tried.

The poison wouldn't be the problem; after a century in her company, he was immune to it. But dislodging her from his flesh would take a little while, and the Mother did not like to be kept waiting.

He left Coral to her sunbathing and pulled a shirt from his wardrobe without looking – dark green silk. Fine enough. He didn't expect to need much red magic today, anyway, and if push came to shove, he always had his wings as an extra source of colour.

Something stirred in the chest pocket as he unfolded the piece of clothing. Again Agenor couldn't suppress a chuckle.

'You really have an uncanny talent for predicting my clothing choices, little one.'

Basilisk stuck his small head out, beady eyes bright and alert. Agenor offered him a finger, and the little snake curled around it, resting his head comfortably against the warm skin. Agenor pulled his shirt over his head, then gently stuffed Basilisk back into his pocket before he buttoned his wing slits and then his front buttons. The small weight against his chest was an odd reassurance, like an invisible smile he carried with him.

If the tone of last night's summons was anything to go by, he might need it today.

He carefully stepped over Coral on his way to the balcony, opened the high doors, and drew the briny sea air deep into his lungs. This first inhalation – it was always the only one that made him feel alive. After that, breathing blurred into simple survival for the rest of the day, a matter of unthinking reflex. A matter of duty.

He shut the balcony doors behind him and let himself drop, flaring out his wings in the fall. The air carried him down in a slow slide, around the tower in which he lived, over the large courtyard where the warriors trained, all the way to the high marble arches that gave access to the hall's antechamber. Even that central part of the palace was still deserted around this time, with the exception of a few human servants scurrying past in their frocks and aprons. He neither knew nor memorised their faces; they all looked the same, anyway.

The copper- and ruby-plated gate to the hall stood ajar rather than wide open, confirming his suspicions about the nature of this meeting. He tucked in his wings and slipped in. Counting five heads around the table in the centre of the hall, he shoved the heavy door shut behind him.

At the head of the table, Achlys laughed her silvery laugh. 'Late as always, Agenor.'

He hadn't woken up before sunrise since the War. She hadn't expected him to at this occasion either; the summons to be present at that time had simply told him, between the lines, to come to the hall as soon as possible after waking. He knew. She knew he knew. They'd had the same exchange twice a month for the past century and a half. Why he still made the effort of playing along – he wasn't even sure.

'There was a snake in my way,' he said, examining her quickly as he crossed the distance to the table. Bright blue eyes without a fleck of darkness in the irises. Fully Achlys's own eyes, then, with not a trace of the sister who shared her body. Melinoë, the other half of the Mother, had to be fully asleep, leaving this conversation to Achlys entirely – which meant the meeting could not be *that* exceptional.

As he'd expected.

At the Mother's side, Ophion threw him a quick grin. 'I'm afraid you missed the introduction, brother.'

'I'll manage,' Agenor said, barely suppressing a groan as he sank down beside Thysandra. She granted him a firm nod – a more genuine gesture of affection, he knew, than any smiles or overly pleasant amiability he'd get from Ophion. 'I presume it's about Khonna.'

Achlys pursed her pale lips. 'Ah. You heard. Excellent.'

He always heard. Rumours spread fast through the ranks of his warriors; few fights happened in the archipelago that he wasn't aware of within a day, even if he rarely left this island anymore. News of the rebellion on the island of Khonna had come dripping in over the course of last night. It had been an unremarkable one, of course, nothing to threaten the stability of the empire – just another one of those squabbles that happened every few weeks. He had barely blinked at the first mention of it. But Achlys – or rather Melinoë, as she must have been the one awake as the news came in – had ordered a meeting anyway.

As always.

He wondered if they ever grew bored with it. Sitting in this hall with its bone-covered walls and its bone-covered throne, playing High Lady to an empire that seemed stuck in the same everlasting circles. A senseless revolt here, a fae feud there. The same dances over and over and over again.

He was being ungrateful, he knew. This was what they had fought the War for – peace and stability, unthreatened prosperity, a world in which no one still had to lose their loved ones to alves' swords and phoenixes' flames and vampires' teeth and the occasional human ambush. But peace ... There was a deadliness to it, too.

'I heard,' he said. 'Please continue from wherever I interrupted you.'

On the opposite side of the table, Deiras resumed his unnecessarily lengthy report of his nightly flight to Khonna – the force of the revolt broken, the miners in the frontlines of the fight dead. Thysandra listened quietly, earnestly. Achlys listened with a fire flickering in her eyes

4

Agenor knew all too well – the first sign of bloody revenge to come. Next to her, Ophion sat lounging in his chair, leisurely stroking her wings. He seemed more occupied, as usual, with his position as the Mother's lover than with the tasks he'd fulfilled at the court before she'd taken him into her bed.

Last, two chairs away from the rest of the company, Creon sat staring at the skull-lined ceiling arches, the look in his dark eyes so demonstratively bored that anyone but the High Lady's son would have lost his head for it.

As always.

Agenor forced his eyes back to Deiras's scarred face as the male talked and talked. He felt like they were acting out a ridiculous theatre play of which they all knew the full script already – a performance so old, so familiar, that he could have mimed along with every single word that was spoken. The humans of Khonna, like those of so many towns and islands before them, had thrown themselves into some reckless fight they were doomed to lose. Too much of this nonsense, and the production of food and other resources might become strained. Some punishment had to be enacted, a message to other human islands that this kind of behaviour would not be tolerated. The question was what the punishment would be.

The discussion followed every predictable step. Ophion proposed to kill every single one of the island's inhabitants. Thysandra kindly reminded him that three hundred dead miners wouldn't produce anything useful, and Khonna was one of the court's main sources of coal. Deiras scoffed and grumbled something about making a point. Agenor suggested that a few dozen deaths would likely make a point as well, in a community that small. Ophion made a joke about old age and growing weakhearted. Agenor pleasantly invited the other to join him for a sparring session one of these days to see which of them was growing old, which Ophion jovially agreed to, although they all knew he would never show up.

All the usual nonsense, and yet it took Achlys half an hour to smile and say, 'Creon?'

Her son looked up for the first time at that, still that faint, lazy smile on his face. His lips didn't move, but Agenor knew he was answering their High Lady in silence – the way he could speak to her, and to no one else, since she had taken his voice from him decades ago.

Even that embarrassing scene, somehow, hadn't changed anything about the world. Without a voice, Creon Hytherion was still the same arrogant warrior, the same loyal murderer; if anything, he'd grown more firmly into that role. The Silent Death, they called him on the human isles these days. Khonna, like so many others before it, would soon find out why.

The same circles. The same patterns. Over and over again.

'Thank you, Creon,' Achlys said, with another one of those tinkering, mirthless laughs. 'I have all faith you'll handle it.'

A conclusion she could have reached in five minutes last night, had she wanted to. But the Mother of all fae loved her theatrics and always had. A small price to pay for his peace and life, Agenor was well aware. A small price to pay for his people's wellbeing. And yet he couldn't help that treasonous voice in the back of his head as he left the hall minutes later, ready to resume his daily duties ...

That voice that told him he may not have fought so valiantly in the War, had he known these would be his fruits to reap.

The day was a haze of tedious, mindless routine. There were new recruits to be welcomed to the training fields, all young fae hungry for glory. Some small issues with Deiras's administration of the tributes he'd collected from the human isles. A fight to be solved between two lieutenants, who had unknowingly shared a lover for a year and now blamed each other for their alleged partner's unfaithfulness.

All problems Agenor had seen and solved a thousand times before. Every soothing remark that left his lips, every pointed question, every annoyed command – he could have produced them sleeping.

He spent the afternoon wandering through the academy halls, watching the newest year of fae children practice their magic under the sharp eyes of their instructors. *Red for destruction.* Here and there, a desk broke to splinters as the red abruptly drew from the surface under a student's hands. *Yellow for change.* Wood became iron, velvet became glass; once he had to assist when a reckless young girl changed her teacher's dress into twisting ivy. *Blue for healing.* That part, as usual, was mostly left to the adults running after their pupils, attempting to undo the worst of the damage done to the furniture.

The green shirt he'd put on that morning did come in handy after all. Agenor kept his left hand against his side as he walked, drawing all but the last shred of blue from the silk as he swung blasts of colour at broken windows and shattered chairs and torn clothes in passing to repair them. By the time he was finished, only a golden yellow was left in his shirt. The children stared, he knew, and not just because of the small snake that stuck its head from his chest pocket every few minutes. Even after years surrounded by magic at home, very few of them would have seen powers like those he wielded, or the skill and precision he'd developed after centuries and centuries of training.

He would know. He'd seen their parents learn to control their colours in this same hall, and their grandparents too. He'd taught their teachers and their teachers' teachers.

It took a certain level of talent and skill to survive at the Crimson Court, and he'd survived since before this palace had even been built.

There was a bitterness to it – these excited young faces, this reckless magic. It made him feel impossibly older, a tiredness that reached deep into the marrow of his bones and made the years weigh even heavier on his shoulders. Basilisk's weight against his chest was an anchor now – a reminder that he was still a living, breathing male, not just a relic from some long forgotten age, lingering in a world that had grown up without him.

As soon as he dared to trust no one would be accidentally decapitated or turned into mud, he excused himself and retreated to his rooms earlier than he usually would.

The servants had kept the fire burning all afternoon, as always, to keep the room warm for the snakes. Agenor loosened his shirt the moment he stepped into that clammy warmth, plucked Basilisk from his chest pocket, and tugged the silk over his wings and shoulders. A few hours of calm. Soon Achlys – or more likely, Melinoë – would summon him for dinner. Then later tonight, Thysandra would find him, ask for a private word, and grumble about Creon behaving like a spoiled brat when decisions needed to be made – frustrations she always bottled up after meetings like this morning's discussion. And then he'd step into bed and sleep, waiting for the sun to wake him yet again, for yet another day to follow every predictable twist and turn ...

He swung open his wardrobe door to chuck his shirt back onto the pile of clothes, and stiffened.

His wardrobe was supposed to be a mess. It had always been; he'd told the servants to give up on it centuries ago. But the shirts and trousers and coats lay in neatly folded piles now, sorted by colour and fabric, an organization so thorough he felt almost ashamed about the shirt he'd been about to fling in.

And on top of the nearest pile, the one of shadowy black silk ...

A note.

Someone had left a note in his wardrobe.

Agenor stared at it, his skin tingling with a sensation he hadn't felt for so long that it took him a few blinks to name it – *surprise.*

Twelve hundred and thirty-three years of life, and no one had ignored his commands in the last eight centuries of that time. No one had ever left him notes between his shirts.

The snakes sensed it, of course, his sudden agitation, the incredulous flush of confusion that tingled up his spine. Oleander curled her ink-black body around his ankle, hissing softly as if to warn him when he stretched out a hand and picked the shred of parchment from his shirt. Agenor lifted her to his shoulders without thinking. She curled around his torso, her leathery body tense against his skin, as he sat down on the edge of his bed and stared at the folded note for a moment.

He had no idea what message he'd find inside – not the faintest notion at all. When had that last happened to him?

It was almost a waste to open it. A shame that it would likely be nothing remarkable after all, just a bit of parchment the servant cleaning out his wardrobe had found and wanted him to notice, or ... or ...

With a muttered curse, he shook his head and unfolded the damn thing.

Most Esteemed Lord Agenor, the first line said.

And there it was again, itching up between his shoulder blades – that uncanny, rejuvenating sensation of something unexpected. Something *new*. Because that greeting – it showed none of the usual reverence people employed around him. None of the usual circumspect caution.

It looked like *mockery*.

Agenor rubbed his eyes. The letters stayed in their place.

Until today I was under the impression ancient fae lords were one of the most fearsome forces on the face of this earth. Having seen the (admittedly fashionable) pandemonium you call your wardrobe, I now stand corrected. Nothing could be more terrifying than the utter chaos I found waiting for me there. Had it continued to exist any longer, I'm confident some hellish creature would have materialised from the sheer power of your cumulative neglect to devour us all. You should be grateful I saved you from a painful end at the hands of a bundle of enraged coats.

Speaking of coats, I'm quite sure you can do without the one I took with me as a reward for my hard work. If there are any pieces of clothing in your collection you feel particularly sentimental about, please be so kind as to mark them so I can avoid breaking your fearsome heart when I return to further supplement my own cloakroom.

Yours insincerely,
  A thief

CHAPTER 2

Allie threw a last glance down the deserted corridor, then pushed open the door and slipped into the smothering bedroom beyond, clutching her pile of firewood as if it were an alf-steel shield. No harsh voices greeted her. Nothing moved at her entrance – nothing, that was, except the large red snake that lay basking in the sunlight on the unmade bed.

Allie threw the creature a quick grin and hoped the hiss she received in reply wasn't a warning to get the hell out of the room.

No fae guards to be seen. No Lord Agenor himself, either, staying behind to keep an eye on his belongings.

Could be worse. She'd been prepared for *much* worse.

A fool's plot, Russ had muttered again last night, and of course, he was right. If this entire endeavour didn't save them, it would likely kill her, and perhaps the rest of the family too. But the memory of Inga's frightened sobs, of the cold eyes leering at them last night – it was enough to keep her moving. If she backed out now, she would regret it before the sun set again.

And Inga would regret it far, far more.

Suppressing a curse, Allie tiptoed forward, lowering her logs onto the floor before the hearth. A flaring fire was already burning, hot enough to make her face flush red even in this short-sleeved, knee-length dress they made servants wear around the court. And yet Agenor had ordered more wood, more warmth. How the bastard managed not to suffocate in this heat was anyone's guess.

It would be helpful if he didn't suffocate for a few more weeks, though, or she'd have to start planning all over again.

Leaving the wood beside the hearth, she hurried to the other side of the room, to the imposing wardrobe that covered a third of the marble wall. The snake on the bed followed her with its beady eyes but didn't untangle its long body from the blankets.

No attempts to attack. Only as she unclenched her clammy hands did Allie realise she had expected the snakes to do *something* – follow their master's orders, defend his fort. He *could* probably give them orders, couldn't he? Admittedly, she'd never met anyone who knew what exactly the bond between Lord Agenor and his animals entailed, or why snakes could live for hundreds of years in his company, but it seemed unlikely he didn't control them in some way. At the very least, they didn't seem to bite him.

And yet, no attack.

She wiped her trembling hands on her skirt, clenched her left fingers around the wardrobe's doorhandle, and swiftly stepped aside as she yanked it open. No snake came lurching out to bury its fangs into her neck. Another unexpected pleasure.

The carefully sorted piles she'd built yesterday were still there. But a dark green silk shirt had been added to the nearest one, neatly folded like the rest below, and on top of that shirt ...

A note.

Allie blinked at it. Not *her* note – this sheet of parchment was larger and of much better quality than the page she'd nicked from a fae secretary's office on her cleaning round yesterday. Which meant someone else had put it there.

And judging by yesterday's chaos, few people but Agenor himself ever looked in this place. Which meant ...

He'd written back?

The realisation sank into her thoughts far too slowly. Gods have mercy. That hadn't been the intention of her letter, starting a conversation. Why in the world would he make the effort of replying to a thief mocking him to his face?

She stretched out a hand, hesitating as her fingertips brushed over the smooth surface of the parchment. Had she been too reckless? She'd only intended to prod him a bit, make sure he'd notice the disappearance of one of his coats. Annoy him a little, perhaps. But if he'd taken offense to the point of writing back …

What if it was some deadly trap? A first warning of the horrific punishment waiting for her?

She swallowed, then snatched the folded parchment from the silk and shook it open. No sense in delaying the inevitable.

In a barely readable hand, it said, *Most Wretched Coat Thief.*

Allie blinked again.

Your concern regarding my coat monsters is quite touching. Let me reassure you that, as a fearsome fae lord (of, indeed, respectable age), I've never had trouble defeating the ones that broke from my wardrobe in past centuries. In your place, I would have been more concerned about the possibility of snakes hiding between my shirts. They can be touchy about intruders.

Allie glanced up at the red snake on the bed. It sent a withering glare back at her but didn't slither into motion.

Hadn't he given his companions commands to stop her? Had he given them commands *not* to stop her? The tone of his letter... It didn't seem enraged. Rather …

Amused?

She turned back to the writing, more and more bewildered.

To answer your question – please keep your quick fingers off the shirts with the snake embroidery. They were a gift from my late sister. As a matter of fact, I'd advise you to keep said fingers off my other clothes too, but from the wording of your letter, I'm not too hopeful you'll follow the advice. Which raises the question of your motives. If you are hoping to get rich from your thievery, you should have noticed I own more expensive items than a couple of shirts.

If you're looking for something fashionable to wear, you should realise that burglary will cost you more than buying your own clothing. Unless this is a creative attempt at suicide by fae lord, I must admit I'm unable to fathom your motivations.

So – in true fearsome fae lord fashion – I offer you a bargain. Take one more coat, but give me answers in return. If your explanation is satisfactory, I will consider the matter settled.

Unwillingly intrigued,
A.

An involuntary laugh fell from her lips. It came out too breathless and too mindless for the sensible person she was usually glad to be.

A *bargain*?

Good gods. She ran her eyes along the crawling lines again, trying to make sense of the unmistakable amusement behind his words. *Unwillingly intrigued.* Enough that he would sacrifice another coat just to see his questions answered?

Nervousness churned in her stomach. This hadn't been an option she'd considered when she made her plans – not a risk she'd prepared for. Why wasn't he furious? Why wasn't he threatening her with hounds' teeth and hellfire? As a proud fae male, the Lord Protector of the Crimson Court, and one of the most powerful mages walking around on this entire cursed island, he should have been out of his mind with anger at her taunting. And instead ...

He taunted back?

What was she supposed to do now?

Giving him the answers he asked for was impossible – she *needed* the deception to get him where she wanted him. But flatly refusing to give him the information sounded dangerous, too. Could she simply not leave a letter at all this time? *Unwillingly intrigued.* Little chance he would call it bad luck and blissfully continue his days while his clothes kept disappearing one by one.

Because she was going to keep stealing them. As long as she needed to keep Inga safe – as long as Agenor needed to play the part she was making him play.

So she had to write back. And win time.

With a last cautious glance at the red snake, she sank to her knees and felt for the pencil in the pocket of her apron. Thank the gods she hadn't taken it out after yesterday's visit. Flipping the parchment in her lap, she stared at the empty surface for a moment, then scribbled,

Most Merciful (Although Still Ancient) Fae Lord,

Your mildness surprises me. I expected to find – at the very least – three snakes, a hound, and perhaps the Mother herself waiting for me between your shirts. One would almost conclude you are not nearly so attached to your wardrobe after all. I'm glad for it; I would hate to feel guilty about my newest acquisition. (I'll leave your sister's gifts alone, of course.)

Allie considered that last sentence for a moment. She hadn't fully intended to write it. Her original plan had been to take exactly the clothing he might have tried to keep safe – anything to push him towards acting. But his dead sister ...

She swallowed. No, there were depths she wasn't willing to sink to. Perhaps she should reconsider her morals if this dragged on for too long or if Inga's position grew too dire. For now, there really was no need to.

As to your request for answers – I believe you're being too hasty, my lord. Doesn't the acclaimed philosopher Dephineia state that the hard road brings us more joy than the easy walk? And aren't we taught by Phyron's Treatises that unfulfilled wishes are a far stronger force than even the deepest satisfaction? If we can go by these wise lessons, I am clearly doing you a favour by not answering your questions at once. But I will give you a small piece of the truth: no, I have no intention of earning even a penny from my thievery.

Nonetheless, I'm curious – which item in your wardrobe is the most expensive? (Assuming not all your clothes are gifts, in which case this would probably be a rude question to ask.)

With unabated greed,
  Your coat thief

She folded the note without allowing herself another minute to think, snatched the nearest expensive-looking shirt without snake embroidery from the piles she'd built herself, and left her letter behind where she'd found it. It would have to do. If she returned tomorrow to be caught by three snakes and a hound anyway – well, she'd figure out how to proceed by that time.

Didn't Dephineia say, too, that risks could not be avoided in love and war?

Russ was already waiting for her when she returned home, his grubby shirt torn at the elbow, his nails still dark from the dirt of the construction sites. His smile as she slipped in and closed the door behind her didn't reach his eyes, and it sank from his face with unprecedented speed when she tugged Agenor's ruby red shirt from underneath her apron.

'You took another one?'

Allie decided to pretend she didn't hear the obvious reproach in his voice. 'As announced.'

'He didn't lay any traps for you after yesterday?'

No traps. Only a letter – the last letter she'd expected from an arrogant fae lord. Russ, she knew, would assume it was some dangerous trick and be even less amused by the plan he'd only supported grudgingly in the first place.

'Not a sign of traps,' she said, flinging the priceless shirt onto their bed in the backroom and picking the first pins from her hair. The dark brown curls sprang free as if they'd held their breath since sunrise. 'Where's Inga?'

'Helping with the baby. They came to get Lora for work.'

Allie froze. 'For *work*? She gave birth two days—'

'I know, Al, I know.' He slumped back in his rickety chair, rubbing a hand over his face. 'Mack tried to stop them, but we're not all as convincing as you.' His smile was particularly unconvincing indeed. 'That lady she works for asked for her. Inga's doing what she can.'

Allie bit out a curse. If Mack allowed Inga to stay with the baby, the situation had to be bad. 'Do we know the names of the fae who took her? I'll try to have a word with Leander tomorrow. He at least won't like it if his employees drop dead because of her ladyship's wishes.'

'Mack probably knows.'

'Good.' She stalked to the backroom and pulled her work dress off, grabbing one of her more comfortable linen tunics instead. Her mind was already buzzing with arguments – their healer's prescription of no less than a week of rest, examples of three new mothers who'd succumbed to their work over the past decade, and if none of that convinced them, the favours some fae still owed her ... 'Any other news?'

'There's a new shipment for us. Greyside.'

A shipment – which meant the goods that were smuggled onto the island every now and then by mysterious helpers troubled by the humans' plight. Soap, herbs, and occasionally some extra food ... No one ever knew in advance what it would be or who had left it where for members of the secret distribution network to find. All Allie knew was who came before her in the line and where she was supposed to drop off her goods in turn.

Which meant she or Russ needed to make the walk to Greyside one of these days. Bad timing. She really didn't want to leave Inga alone in the evenings now.

'Well,' she said, suppressing a sigh as she pulled the tunic over her head, 'we'll figure out something. How's the situation with Gil's leg? Any developments there?'

'They sent a physician to evaluate him today.' She heard Russ groan as he got up from his chair. 'Who miraculously agreed with us that he shouldn't be climbing around any scaffolding for the next two weeks.'

Her shoulders relaxed a fraction. Thank the gods. She'd been begging for a second opinion for days, since the first fae healer to visit their neighbours' house had declared Gil perfectly fit to work despite the infection wreaking havoc on his wounded ankle.

'I'll ask Heloise to smuggle some extra woundwort with her from the gardens,' she said, standing still before the rusty mirror to quickly twist her hair into a looser braid. 'I'm not sure if two weeks will be enough, but the least we can do—'

Russ scoffed audibly in the other room. 'Heloise says she isn't going to as long as Marette won't apologise for that mess last summer. Inga says it was a whole screaming match this afternoon.'

'Heloise can poke a stick up her arse and suck at it.'

A joyless chuckle. 'Al ...'

'A man might die,' Allie said curtly, tying her new braid in place and pulling a face at herself in the mirror. Walking back into the main room, she added, 'If she doesn't want to see sense, I'll have a word with her tomorrow. I don't think she wants Rinald to hear about her little fling with that fellow from Greyside.'

Russ raised an eyebrow at her, leaning against the stove. 'How do you *know* all these things?'

'I keep careful track of what I'm owed,' she said with a shrug.

He let out a soft laugh but left it at that. Allie checked the contents of their food baskets – a meagre few onions and peppers, but better than nothing – and grabbed the cutting board. Russ hadn't moved. Unusual. Most evenings, he already had half of the meal ready by the time she returned from the court.

'What's the matter?'

He muttered a curse. 'I think you should stop doing it, Al.'

'Doing what?'

'Stealing from him. Agenor.'

She grabbed a knife and split the first onion in two, perhaps a little more aggressively than needed. 'I'll be fine. He probably hasn't even noticed that first coat is missing yet.'

'And what if he does notice?' He *really* had to be caught up in his concerns. Any other day, he'd have seen through her lie in a heartbeat. 'Fuck's sake, Al, we really can't lose you.'

'So you'd rather give up on Inga?'

'No!' he snapped. 'Of course I wouldn't, but ... Look, can't you find someone else to strip bare? Someone a little less powerful?'

'We talked about this,' Allie said, unable to keep the frustration from her voice entirely. 'He *has* to be powerful. It's the entire point. The only effective alternatives would be Ophion and the bloody Silent Death, and I'm *not* going to sneak into—'

'No, of course you're not—'

'So it has to be Agenor, yes?'

'No!'

She sucked in a breath through her nose. 'Russ, I don't need your permission to go about my day. Unless you're planning to rat on me—'

'I'm your *husband*,' he hissed.

'Oh, like Farran is just your best friend?' She threw him a glare in between her onion chopping. 'Don't pull the husband card on me.'

'That's not what I mean,' he said sharply. 'Look, *they* consider me your husband. If Agenor finds you with your hands on his belongings, he may as well go after the entire family, and then what would Inga do?'

'Die, probably,' Allie said wryly.

'Al ...'

'I'm being careful, alright? And if they ever catch me, I promise I'll tell them you're innocent as a new-born babe, and—'

A shadow fell over the single window. Outside, she realised as she froze, it had become eerily quiet – no screaming children, no chatting mothers. At this time of the day, in the heart of Rustvale, that silence could only mean one thing.

Russ stiffened at the stove, the fight leaking out of him at once. Only grim determination remained, that expression that had won her trust within mere minutes of their first meeting years ago.

'Well,' he muttered, with a glance outside, 'at least it's good to have the damn shirt now, I suppose.'

Allie sent him a wry grin, but felt it slide off her face the moment heavy fists hit the thin wood of the door.

Time to play this game again.

Russ had stopped protesting by the next morning, and Allie sneaked back into that silent corridor with a feeling oddly like *excitement* bubbling below the fear.

It made no sense. She knew it didn't. Agenor may still have hidden snakes, hounds, and fae warriors in his wardrobe at her refusal to answer his questions. He'd be mad if he entertained her diversions for a minute longer than necessary, truly. Why would a fae lord of his age and power put up with some thief sneaking in and out of his room if he doubtlessly had a thousand better things to do?

But there were no snake traps or hounds to be seen when she dropped her wood and opened the heavy oaken doors of the wardrobe again. Just those carefully folded shirts, and a brand new note on top of the leftmost pile.

Had Russ seen how fast she picked the folded parchment from the dark velvet below, he would doubtlessly have deemed it worth a chuckle or two.

But Russ was nowhere around here in the heart of the Crimson Court, and she sank down on the mahogany floor with her back against the heavy wardrobe, running her eyes along her victim's reply.

Most Ruthless (And Unexpectedly Well-Read) Coat Thief,

Once again, your apparent concern for my wellbeing is moving. I should, I presume, be grateful that you're willing to risk the daily confrontation with snakes and coat monsters only to draw out this apparently delightful experience of what Dephineia would call the hard road. Personally, I'm more partial to Chimalis's fables, which tell us that a starved and taunted animal will eventually bite, whereas a well-fed animal will be mellow and harmless. Just a warning, in case you were not planning to feed me more than the meagre crumbs from your last letter.

You are not hoping to get rich through my clothes, you claim. (If you were, however, I would advise you to pick the dark blue coat of Elderburg velvet at

your next visit; it was made on the continent before the Plague and is the last
of its kind.)

So what other explanations are possible? If you were trying to trouble me,
you'd – unwisely – have taken my sister's shirts. If you were unsatisfied with
my style of dress, there would be simpler ways to inform me of the issue. As
you see, I'm still entirely in the dark and strongly suggest you supply me with
more information soon. As Chimalis would say, don't drive me to bite.

Impatiently yours,
   A.

And there were the threats she had expected yesterday – but not as
dire as they could have been. Even while he was threatening, he was
still playing the game. He was still taking her bait. Allie let her eyes run
over the messy handwriting again and felt an impossible, irrepressible
laugh rise in her – a lightness she hadn't felt since those late-night visits
to Rustvale had forced her to come up with this ridiculous, reckless
plan.

Her back hurt from dragging armfuls of wood around. Her feet were
already tired, and she still had hours and hours of work to go. But
here she was, exchanging letters with one of the world's most powerful
mages, a fae male with more than a millennium of life behind him, and
somehow she wasn't losing yet.

She found the Elderburg jacket within moments; it had caught her
attention on the first day already. But a piece this rare, this striking,
would be too recognisable to serve her goals. So she put it back where
she'd found it and made another choice from the first pile of shirts, still
cautiously avoiding everything with snake embroidery.

Her reply came easily this time. She scribbled it down with a smile on
her lips and a dangerous, excited anticipation sparkling just below her
heart.

Most Ominous (Although I Must Say, You Threaten Me Quite Eruditely)
Lord Agenor,

Ah, Chimalis's wolf – I remember feeling quite sorry for the poor creature as a child. In all thieving honesty, though, I must admit I don't feel particularly concerned about your biting. Something tells me you're enjoying the hard road far too much to end it. Your snakes, on the other hand, have been eyeing me with positively hungry looks during my visits. Have they ever been known to nibble on your warm-blooded friends – or for that matter, on you?

As you'll see, I didn't take the Elderburg coat, although it is admittedly very pretty. But blue isn't my colour, and unsurprisingly, a piece of clothing that old can hardly be called fashionable. I choose to steal two shirts in its place, to compensate for its value. You will doubtlessly forgive me in exchange for a slightly more nutritious crumb of information:

Everything I steal from you is stolen for love. Make of that what you want.

Barely intimidated,
  Your coat thief

CHAPTER 3

Agenor brushed the fingertips of his left hand over Coral's leathery scales, drawing a hint of pale red from the snake's skin. The colour ran up his arm with the faint, familiar tingle of magic and swept down all the way to his right hand again, leaving the tips of his fingers in a small, bright spark of red.

The crumpled ball of parchment on his desk was reduced to a whiff of dust. *Red for destruction.*

Wrapped around his bare shoulders, Coral squeezed her long body a little tighter, as if to reassure him, or perhaps to tell him she would bury her fangs into his throat if he used her as a magic source ever again.

Agenor let out a groan. Coral swept the tip of her tail against his ribs, telling him without words not to whine so much, and he nearly groaned again.

Something tells me you're enjoying the hard road far too much to end it, the perfectly regular handwriting of yesterday's letter told him. And by the gods and demons, a hard road it was. He had not the faintest idea what to write. Not the faintest idea what to think or what to expect. He felt like a clueless hundred-year-old again, flailing through the dark and hitting all the wrong spots – an experience buried so deep in his memory, he had all but forgotten what it felt like.

And he enjoyed the hell out of it, indeed.

How long had it been since anyone, *anyone,* had last surprised him? But for three days in a row, he'd walked back to his rooms with no idea what he'd find upon return, only to be utterly brought off balance every single time. He had expected his offered bargain to be met with some relief or gratitude. Had expected his threats to make *some* impression. And yet the thief had shrugged all of it off with a nonchalance that made him burn with frustration and feel like a brand new soul all at once.

He was running after the facts. He was *curious.* It awoke a part of him he'd thought withered and rotten after centuries of simple, dutiful routine – a part that felt ravenous and playful and desperately alive.

And, as it turned out, hopelessly lost for words.

He reached for another sheet of parchment, racking his brain for something sensible to say – something a little more befitting of his status and power than the plea for answers he'd poured out in his last attempt. The thief, he suspected, would not be very sensitive to plead-ing. The reply would probably call him a sorry excuse of an ancient fae lord, and it wouldn't be wrong.

I don't feel particularly concerned about your biting, the letter on the corner of his desk told him.

A challenge. He'd be damned if he didn't take it.

Most Reckless (And Somewhat Numerically Challenged) Coat Thief,

Your letter made a decent attempt to fool me; I certainly noticed, however, that you did not take two, but three shirts at your last visit. In a few weeks, I'll have no choice but to walk around the court naked. I'm beginning to suspect that might be your intention, as I cannot imagine in whatever other way you would profit from these shenanigans.

He paused there, staring at the words he'd scribbled down and repress-ing an urge to obliviate this second attempt, too. Naked. A thought-lessly sketched scenario, meant to be ridiculous enough to guarantee a reaction – but would he have picked this particular scenario if he hadn't so strongly suspected a female voice behind those impressively regular lines and curls of the thief's writing?

Coral hissed a warning as he laid his fingertips against her red scales again, and he muttered a curse and pulled back his hand.

'As you wish,' he grumbled, sending her a quick glare. 'I'll know who to blame if this goes wrong.'

She gave him a tired, unblinking stare. Agenor rubbed his eyes, turned back to his writing, and read through his hasty start again. A risk, yes. If the suggestion of nakedness came across the wrong way, he may be greeted by deafening silence and an absence of letters at his return. Then again, most fae females weren't so easily deterred by nakedness, and these letters in particular didn't give the impression of a female easily deterred by anything.

And it was a risk he quite enjoyed taking, he had to admit.

He dipped his pen in the ink jar and wrote on before he could change his mind again.

As to your question on the snakes – no, they generally don't bite me, although they've been known to kill the occasional visitor threatening me. You might persuade me to tell you the story of how they came to bond with me, but that is confidential information which only a handful of fae are currently privy to. I would trade it only against a secret of similar magnitude. Your name, your motivations, or the current location of my possessions might be a start.

Sharpening my teeth,
  A.

He folded the letter and put it where he'd found the thief's last night, then lifted Coral from his shoulders, dressed himself, and left the comforting, smothering heat of his bedroom.

But even out in the castle, retracing his steps and wingbeats of so many days before, the routine of centuries wouldn't sink back into his bones. He found himself examining every warrior on the training field with entirely new eyes, wondering which of them could have flown up to his rooms every afternoon to leave those defiant letters in his wardrobe. For every fae passing him by, he couldn't help throwing a quick glance at their clothes, searching for silks and colours he would recognise. As he checked the tribute administration of the past days, his mind carelessly skipped over the numbers and calculations and focused on the shapes of the letters instead, desperate for a hand he would recognise.

But the thief didn't reveal herself in the boring scribbles of a cash book, and the recruits on the training field wore nothing out of the ordinary on their bodies.

By the time he made his way to the Mother's hall in the early afternoon, every fibre in his body was buzzing with persistent, frustrated determination. Soon he'd have his duties of the day behind him. Soon he'd return to his rooms and find another letter with – hopefully – another piece of the puzzle, and he'd spend the night wrestling with his words, finding his way on this delightfully unfamiliar battlefield ...

A glimpse of red in the corner of his eye caught his attention.

It was no more than a flash in the throng of the bone hall, just behind the throne where Achlys was lounging in her black silk and velvet pillows at this time of the day. He wouldn't have noticed it on any other day, wouldn't have batted an eye. But today his mind latched onto that flash like a snake sinking its teeth into its prey, with a sensation oddly like a hammer hitting him on the back of his head – because that colour passing by in the edge of his sight, that deep red of the sweetest, headiest wine, was the exact colour of the shirt that had vanished from his wardrobe at the thief's second visit.

The exact colour for which he'd spent the past hours poring over every crook and corner he encountered.

He froze in his tracks, blinked, turned. Through the swarm of limbs and wings, it took him a moment to find it again – a deep, cherry red silk, as familiar to him as the callouses of his very own fingers.

Worn on a male body he knew just a tad too well.

Agenor stood paralysed on the cold marble floor as Deiras sauntered along the bone-covered walls on the other side of the hall, deep in conversation with a giggling fae girl. The Mother's First Emissary didn't seem to realise he was being observed. Didn't even show the slightest hint of reserve or caution about the stolen shirt he was wearing, so damningly recognisable with the hand-stitched silver embroidery that lined the cuffs and collar.

Deiras?

Deiras?

A violent nausea rose in Agenor's throat, smothering the light, lively anticipation that had pushed him through the morning. Gone were the vague images of a nameless, faceless fae female sneaking into his room and leaving those tantalising letters behind. Instead, he could only see Deiras, digging between his clothes with those thin hands, reading the letters he found with a sneer of ridicule on his scarred face and leaving his own mocking replies behind.

That was all?

Just an overly cocky, overly ambitious bastard he'd never liked, humiliating him for an easy laugh and a thrill of power?

Agenor found himself stepping back, away from the damning evidence of his own stupidity, only barely aware of the fae scattering away from him as he burst through their conversations. A hollowness flooded him – a cold that had his shoulders sagging and filled the tips of his fingers with numb, heavy rage. With *shame*. He'd been toyed with and allowed himself to be toyed with. Had been so enchanted by the dream of some beguiling thief lifting the weight of that age-old boredom from his heart that he'd forgotten to be suspicious and sensible.

He felt the tingle of colour in his left hand, looked down, and found his fingers clenched into the black of his trousers, ready to draw out any of the colours mixed together.

Red for destruction.

What had Deiras said in that mocking, gloating letter? *I don't feel particularly concerned about your biting.* Sly, vicious bastard. He had always been like that, hadn't he? Bullying the young recruits on the training field, preferring violent retaliation to justice whenever another human island rebelled ... Truly, Agenor told himself, he should have expected this. If he hadn't allowed himself to be so easily blinded by the unexpected delight of a surprise – *any* surprise – he probably would have.

Had Deiras completed his raid of the day already?

The nausea won ground again. Had the bastard read this morning's letter?

All lust for violence seeped from his bones at that thought – at the image of Deiras's thin lips curling into their familiar smirk at the ridiculously suggestive sentences and the thinly veiled hunger for answers. Agenor pulled his fingers from his trousers, suppressing a curse. How could he move to kill with that image branded into his mind's eye? He'd have to meet the other's gaze again. To see the humiliation in those mocking grey eyes, to admit that defeat in person for even a fraction of a moment – with the dread and disgust still churning in his stomach, he couldn't stand the thought.

Gods be damned. Time to wash his hands clean of this mess and go drown himself in a vat of wine tonight.

He abruptly turned away, scanning the hall for a tanned face and a familiar pair of ink black wings. As usual, he found Creon's black-clad figure close to his mother's throne, sprawled out in a low velvet fauteuil with the usual air of bored, unassailable arrogance around him.

Agenor was already walking, elbowing through the groups of fae he encountered without paying attention to their shocked shrieks and curses. Only at the last moment did Creon look up, meeting his gaze with that blank carelessness that would have killed any mage of lesser power centuries ago. For once, Agenor couldn't care how apathetic his High Lady's son chose to be. The boy could have rolled his eyes at him, and it wouldn't have made a difference. All that mattered now was swift, efficient revenge, and even in his most apathetic of moods, Creon was nothing if not efficient.

A wide empty space had cleared around them by the time he reached that decadent fauteuil. Even the most curious of courtly gossipmongers knew better than to eavesdrop on members of the Mother's inner circle.

Creon merely raised a scarred eyebrow. Before the War, before the loss of his voice, he might have made the effort of asking a question or two. But Agenor knew the Mother's son sensed his agitation well enough anyway, and he really wasn't in the mood to wait for any written messages.

He was sick of written messages for a few years to come, really.

'I need to get rid of Deiras,' he said, voice low. It took an effort not to spit out the name. 'Would you mind handling him?'

Creon didn't even blink at that blunt proposal of violence. Violence was what he lived for – what he had been bred and raised and trained for from the day he was born. A single cat-like motion and he was standing, dark eyes swerving to Deiras's unsuspecting figure at the other side of the hall. Again that eyebrow came up, another unspoken question.

'He's been stealing from me,' Agenor said, his voice as flat as possible. He knew better than to hope his fury and shame would escape those predator eyes, but it was a matter of futile pride – to keep control of himself, at least for any onlooker without magically enhanced senses. 'I don't have the patience to deal with this today.'

A single shrug and Creon stepped past him, scarred hands wandering to the knives at his belt already. Around them, conversations stilled to cautious whispers. The Mother's attendants knew all too well what it meant when her son and deadliest murderer bothered to get into motion.

Agenor looked up. Achlys had sat up straighter on her throne, examining him with those cold blue eyes. Amusement sparkled in her look – the more bloodthirsty kind of amusement, mingled with a hint of approval.

Theatrics. No easier way to appease her.

Agenor nodded and turned away, making for the entrance of the hall. Behind him, the whispers swelled to a storm of rumours, and then Deiras's familiar voice broke through – shocked shouts, followed by pleas for mercy ...

And silence. Deadly, deafening silence.

The Silent Death, indeed.

Agenor did not look back even as a young girl's voice started wailing behind him. He ignored the yelling of some fae male demanding answers and the subsequent sound of a knife sinking into more flesh and bone, of angry screams turning into cries of pain. There were not many fae he'd trust blindly on any battlefield, but the Mother's son was the first of them.

So he just walked, away from his own damn stupidity, away from the explanation Achlys or Melinoë would sooner or later demand for her First Emissary's death. The hall's antechamber was as good as empty. The few lingering fae hurried off as soon as they saw his face; no one disturbed him as he rested his elbows on the marble balustrade and waited, staring out over the court sprawling down the slope of the mountain.

Such a sickeningly familiar sight. He knew every arched window, every sharp-edged roof. Had he really thought walls so familiar could still hide secrets and surprises for him?

If anything ought to be a surprise, it was Deiras's audacity. But even that … Just the same old arrogance, the same old scheming, the same cruel games all over again. He should know better than to let it weigh so heavy on his old bones. He should be relieved that at least he had put an end to this ridiculous charade before the rumours of his humiliation made the rounds at court, should be grateful a coincidental meeting had revealed the truth of those invigorating letters in his bedroom.

But that ridiculous shadow – it lingered nonetheless, darkening even the bright light of the island sun to his eyes.

He had expected Creon to follow him out eventually, and yet the dark shape in the edge of his sight surprised him. Murderer's footsteps – inaudible like a cat's. Agenor didn't turn. He knew the other didn't expect him to.

Even over the disconcerted murmurs in the hall behind them, he heard the scratching of Creon's pencil over parchment. The note that was shoved towards him over the broad marble balustrade was so short it might better qualify as a question.

He was surprised.

Agenor stared at those words for a moment, small sparks of unease firing through the cover of his smothering disenchantment.

Surprised.

Of course Deiras had *pretended* to be surprised, his first thought suggested. It would be unwise to confess to anything when Creon Hytherion was pushing a knife against your throat. But this wasn't just any interrogator with suspicions of his target's intentions. This was *Creon*, whose magic read emotions like others would read a book. If *he* had sensed surprise in Deiras's heart, even in those very last moments, if he found that worth mentioning now, even though his victim was long beyond saving ...

Something was off, indeed.

Deiras had been an arrogant prick for the full eight centuries of his life. Had been boisterous and overly reckless at times. But even the most arrogant and reckless of fools had to know that stealing from the Mother's Lord Protector was a dangerous undertaking. Confronted with his own imminent death, Deiras should have understood his arrogance had finally caught up with him.

And yet those words stood gleaming dark on the parchment. *He was surprised.*

'You're sure,' Agenor said slowly.

It was hardly a question; Creon didn't bother to answer. Agenor considered that for a moment, then added, 'And yet you killed him.'

Creon shrugged, pulling back his notebook. *Never liked him.*

So that was mutual, too. Agenor allowed a curt laugh over his lips – sounding too befuddled, but then again, the other could sense his confusion anyway. If Deiras had been surprised – if his conscience had been clean or, at least, clean enough on this point – then what in hell was going on?

He couldn't bring himself to care much about the useless bloodshed. He'd lost thousands of fae over the centuries of his life, most of them dearer to him than the rash, occasionally melodramatic prick Creon had left dead in the Mother's hall. But if Deiras hadn't stolen those clothes, hadn't written those letters ...

Then someone else had.

Someone whose plans and motivations were, as a matter of fact, still utterly opaque to him.

With a suppressed curse he stepped back, ignoring the flurry of cautious hisses and fluttering wings as every fae within thirty feet flinched away from him. Creon followed him with cold dark eyes, no doubt calculating his next move as Agenor desperately scrambled for his own.

Someone else had written those letters. Someone else had stolen his clothes. And if their motive had been linked to Deiras, they might very well quit once they heard the First Emissary had reached his untimely end on the Mother's marble floor.

Which meant he had to be fast and hope the news hadn't spread too far yet.

He took his decision in the blink of an eye, old battlefield reflexes taking hold of him. With only one chance, grabbing it was all he could do. The consequences – he'd think them through later. He could probably justify his delay to Achlys some way or another.

'Tell her I'll explain myself as soon as I've taken care of matters,' he said, and turned away without waiting for Creon's nod. He knew the message would be delivered. Heartless murderer or not, the Mother's son was nothing if not loyal to the High Lady they both served.

As he was, of course. And she'd get her explanation, of course.

But not before he'd figured out who, exactly, had been playing him for days.

The wardrobe doors were still closed when he stalked into the humid warmth of his room. The note he'd left behind on his pile of shirts hadn't moved. No thief had shown up in the few hours he'd been gone, then.

And Deiras hadn't read that damn letter. Hadn't read any of them, presumably.

So who had?

He considered his next steps for a few moments. Just sitting down at his desk and waiting for the door to open would tell him who had been breaking into his room – but that nameless fae could easily claim to be here for any other reason, and if they were as skilled a liar as their letters seemed to suggest, Agenor might have a hard time proving them guilty. So he'd have to catch them in the act. Which meant staying invisible until the very last moment.

With a sigh he turned to the window, wrapped his left fingers around his thigh, and swung a thoughtless blast of magic into the glass. *Yellow for change.* The colourless crystal shimmered, then seemed to return to its previous state. But when he sauntered to the doorway and stuck his arm around the doorpost, nothing changed about the view through the window. He still only saw the marble balustrade and the island below that he had imprinted into the glass, not the hand he was waving around behind.

He stepped onto the balcony and tested the view the other way around. From outside to inside, the glass was still transparent as he had intended, allowing him to watch the room unnoticed.

Good. That would do.

Oleander slithered out after him, into the open air and the sunlight. Agenor closed the door behind her and scooped her up from the balcony floor, then gently draped her around his shoulders as he sat down. She slipped her head beneath his collar, obviously annoyed about the silk separating her from the warmth of his skin.

Agenor unbuttoned his shirt with half a chuckle, allowing her to rest her head against his bare chest. Then he tucked in his wings, leaned back against the balustrade, and waited.

For a century or two, it seemed, nothing happened.

Some shouts rose from the training field below. A flock of young fae girls flew by on the other side of his tower, giggling so much that for a moment he expected them to show up at his doorstep.

Finally, just when he'd begun to give up hope – a flash of movement inside.

He shot upright, earning himself a vexed hiss from Oleander. But the small figure that slipped into his room wasn't the thief he was waiting for. Just a human servant, an armful of firewood against her chest.

Muttering a curse, he sank back against his marble backrest, watching her as she tiptoed into the room and lowered the logs before the fireplace. Fuelling the fire couldn't take long. She'd be gone in a minute; little chance she would somehow deter the thief through her presence. He'd have to be patient for a few more moments, and ...

The human woman put down her last log. Then turned away from the fire.

Agenor blinked. Was she going to fetch more? Even with the heat the snakes preferred, the supply of wood she'd brought inside should easily be enough to last until late in the evening. And she wasn't walking back to the door through which she'd entered at all. Instead, she was walking quickly, confidently ...

Towards his wardrobe.

Even Oleander had gone very still against his chest.

Agenor stared, shoulders and wings tensing as he involuntarily leaned forward, struggling to make sense of every next observation reaching his mind. A servant. Small and lithe and so very... *human*, crossing the two dozen feet to the wardrobe where his letter lay waiting. To clean, surely? To take out his laundry – to do *anything* but open the wardrobe and ...

She opened the wardrobe.

And with a small, foxy smile on her pale face, plucked out the letter he'd left between his shirts that morning.

Like a male still half-asleep, he watched her open it – watched her sink down on the floor before his wardrobe as if she'd spent years of her life in that spot, resting in his room, reading his notes to ...

His notes to *her*.

He barely felt himself move as he got to his feet. Barely felt Oleander tense around his shoulders, ready for battle, or whatever else he required of her. All his mind was able to take in was the sight of his thief sitting cross-legged on his bedroom floor, in that simple knee-length servant's frock so unlike the clothes she'd stolen, dark brown locks slipping from her braids. Her bright eyes shooting along his writing. The corners of her mouth quivering into a satisfied smile as she read his words.

A human?

A *human*?

CHAPTER 4

Allie couldn't help the smile that crept onto her face as she reached the note's end.

Sharpening my teeth, it said. Good. She needed them sharp – sharp enough that he'd follow her nudges in the right direction without too much hassle. The right amount of frustration, the right amount of shame and humiliation, and if she was lucky, those sharp teeth would sink just where she wanted them ...

She turned to grab her pencil from her pocket. Now it was a matter of the right reply. The right lack of answers. The right loot, even if she'd built a nice supply with the three shirts she'd taken yesterday. And then—

A lock snicked on the other side of the room.

Allie froze.

A lock, her thoughts reiterated with odd, detached calm. Snicked. Which meant movement. Which meant *someone* moved. Which meant—

Only then did the panic burst free, a sudden rush of fire through every vein of her body. With a shriek, she jerked around, yanked the letter below her back as if *that* would save her, and jumped up, searching for anything that might be an innocent servant's chore. Clothes. Folding clothes. No one could blame her for folding clothes, could they? She grabbed the first handful of silk her fingers could find, her heartbeat a pounding drum in her ears—

'I didn't interrupt you in the middle of anything important, did I?' a soft, jarringly pleasant voice said, far too close behind her.

Oh, gods have mercy.

Allie stiffened, hands buried in the pile of shirts. Stiffening was all she could do to avoid sinking to her knees and pleading for mercy – the surest way of proving her guilt. That voice, that lethally amused, painfully familiar voice ...

She knew it a little too well.

Lord Agenor had returned to his rooms.

Knowing exactly what she'd done. What she'd been about to do. Had this been a trap, after all? How had she been reckless enough to miss it?

She swallowed, her throat dry as pumice. She'd be a fool to think he would buy into any excuse she could come up with now. *He could kill you,* Russ's voice echoed in her ears – words she'd discarded so easily this morning. Her breath quickened. *He could kill you, and no one would bat an eye – is that what you want?*

I'll be cleverer than that, Russ ...

And here she stood, mouth dry and hands shaking, and barely knew the meaning of that word anymore.

'Turn around,' Agenor said, his words still so dangerously quiet.

So close, there was a disconcerting weight to the deep bass of his voice, a shimmer of ancient power that sent shivers up along her spine and turned her guts to a quivery mush. She pulled her hands from his clothes, making desperate attempts to stop their trembling. Why would he want her to turn around? So he could see the fear in her eyes in these last moments? So she could watch the red draw away below his fingertips in the last heartbeat before she died?

Nothing good could come from following his commands. But disobedience could only be worse.

Bracing herself, she turned.

The court's Lord Protector stood barely three feet away, a towering wall of slender muscle and wide wings locking her back against the heavy oakwood wardrobe. Chiselled face a mask of inhuman indifference. Green-gold eyes narrowed in what could be fury or curiosity. An ink-black snake wrapped around his shoulders, slithering over bare, bronze skin where he had unbuttoned his shirt.

Allie felt her eyes drop to the ridges of his muscular chest and swallowed again. *In a few weeks, I'll have no choice but to walk around naked*, his letter had said. For a fraction of a moment, that prospect seemed a sensible motive to fling the contents of his wardrobe out through the nearest window.

Then he smiled. It was a smile that seemed designed to remind her of those teeth he may or may not be planning to sink into her throat.

She snapped her gaze back up to his. A hint of oddly polite amusement twinkled in his cat green eyes now.

Amusement.

That was at least better than murderous intentions, wasn't it?

Allie parted her lips, closed them again, and cleared her throat. Still no flashes of red magic followed, no snakes lashing out at her face. Steeling herself, she opened her mouth again and managed a cautious, 'Good afternoon?'

He tilted his head a fraction, expression unchanging. 'Is it?'

Was he *joking*, now? If he was, his deep voice remained impressively flat. Allie somehow found the nerves to throw him a brisk glare and said, 'I suppose there are worse ways to spend the hours than peacefully collecting laundry.'

'Collecting ... laundry,' Agenor repeated.

'Yes?' If the old gods still existed, this was about the moment they should come to her rescue. 'What else should I be doing?'

He considered that for a moment. 'Looking for coat monsters?'

Oh, good gods. He couldn't be fully serious, could he? She swallowed, unsure what to make of the unbreakable civility on his face. Was this his usual prelude to brutal murder – jokes and witticisms? Or could it be – was it possible – that he wasn't planning to kill her at all?

Or at least not yet?

She took her decision in a fraction of a second. Damn her shaking knees and clammy hands. If her letters amused him – even if it was the dangerous, merciless amusement of an arrogant fae lord momentarily entertained by a diverting new pet – that was the best chance she had. Better than angering him. Better than folding to a heap of pleading, crying misery at his feet.

'I'm always on the lookout for coat monsters,' she said, jutting up her chin a fraction as she met his eyes. 'They're a vastly underestimated danger, in my personal opinion. As opposed to ancient fae lords, who seem to be quite an *over*estimated danger so far.'

Agenor merely raised his eyebrows. 'Deiras might have disagreed with you on that point.'

Her mouth fell shut. *Deiras*? Such a pleasant conversational tone to his voice, and yet ...

A shred of fearful hope flickered to life inside her chest. *Might have.* As if Deiras was currently unable to agree or disagree with anything – as if that ancient anger had already claimed the first of its victims today.

Had she managed, then?

Was Inga safe?

Agenor must have seen the flash of relief that slid over her face. His smile turned even more polite in the same moment, so very pleasant, so very *beautiful*, and yet oddly resembling the predatory glare of the snake resting his head on his shoulder.

'So.' He barely moved, and yet it seemed to her that he was closing in on her – driving her back against the wardrobe, eclipsing the sunlight with those wide, imposing wings. 'I would be most grateful to hear how, exactly, Deiras met his untimely end. I have all faith you'll be willing to enlighten me on that point.'

Untimely end.

Her knees nearly buckled. So he *had* killed the bastard. Deiras was gone – wouldn't come knocking on their door tonight, wouldn't de-mand his price for another twenty-four hours of peace.

'I see,' Agenor said, his voice even lower now, 'that the matter doesn't leave you unmoved.'

'Clearly,' she muttered, 'you have not the faintest idea of his reputa-tion. Or of your own, for that matter.'

He didn't take the bait. 'My reputation isn't what I'm curious about at the moment. What is your connection to Deiras?'

Allie gulped down a breath, thoughts grasping for an escape, *any* escape. Curious. He was *curious*. Had kept her alive so far because he wanted answers to his questions – because she was a diverting riddle and he was not the kind of male to enjoy his own ignorance.

Which meant she was of value to him as long as she knew more than he did. And not a moment longer.

'I don't see,' she said, picking her words with painstaking care, 'why my connection to Deiras would be of any concern to you, Lord Agenor.'

He tilted his head again. 'Are you refusing to answer me?'

'Not at all. Merely asking questions in return.'

'The thieves I catch in my bedroom don't ask me questions in return,' he said, still so pleasantly conversational except for his eyes narrowing a fraction. 'And human thieves certainly don't.'

Bastard. Allie scowled at him and said, 'Most humans don't clean your wardrobe, write you letters, or steal your shirts either. I'm not sure why you expect me to follow your rules on this particular point.'

He raised his eyebrows. 'Has it occurred to you that I could kill you?'

Somehow her voice remained level as the sea on a windless day. 'Has it occurred to you that a corpse is not going to answer your questions any more than I'm currently doing?'

"What are your feelings on torture?' he pleasantly retorted.

'As far as I've heard, you rarely dirty your own hands with that kind of work,' Allie said coolly. 'Am I to believe you'd hand me over to your Silent Death or any of his colleagues so I can tell them all about those lovely letters you wrote me?'

For a moment, he stood motionless – not frozen, not stiffened, but simply motionless, watching her with an expression of what looked like ... *interest?*

Then he stepped back, so abruptly that Allie imagined the cold air rushing to fill the space between them. His wings tucked in, folded over his muscular back like a reassurance, as he turned around and sauntered to the balcony door through which he'd entered.

Allie stood backed against the heavy wardrobe and didn't dare to move, didn't dare to speak. Was he letting her go? Giving up? Or merely preparing himself for a first round of excruciating torment?

At the window, Agenor gently lifted the black snake off his shoulders and lowered it onto the floor. The animal curled up on the sun-streaked mahogany, looking content in a way Allie had never imagined a snake could.

Only then did he say, 'What is your name?'

The question took her by surprise, so much so that it didn't occur to her to lie. 'Allie.'

'Father's name?'

'Of no importance,' she said bitterly. 'I was brought here as tribute payment. He's still on the island where I was born.'

Agenor turned back to her, his face still equally impassive. Bastard. 'Where do you live?'

'Rustvale.'

'Not a lot of philosophy books to be found in Rustvale, presumably.'

She clenched her fists. 'My father was a teacher. I used to read a lot before your people took me.'

'Ah,' he said, nodding as if that rather pleased him. 'He is of some importance after all, then.'

Her self-restraint wavered. Letters and shirts and even Deiras – she could handle those. Home, on the other hand ... Not if *he* was the one listening, pleasant and polite and unfathomably powerful. Not if he might well take every single crumb of knowledge she offered him and turn it, still equally pleasant and polite, against her.

'And what is the intention of this interrogation, if I may ask?' she said sharply.

'I'm trying to converse with you.' He leaned back against his desk, crossing his arms over his half-bared chest. 'But do tell me if you prefer the torture.'

'I'm to believe the Lord Protector himself is wasting his time conversing with some human servant?' Allie said, uttering a joyless chuckle. 'You're just hoping I'll talk, aren't you?'

'Oh, you will be talking in the end,' he said, looking pleased again. 'I'm currently working out under what circumstances.'

Torture or – or what? Allie took an uncertain step forward, away from the wardrobe. As soon as she told him the truth, he might just fling her off the balcony and be done with her. If she *didn't* tell him the truth, he would sooner or later stop being pleasant about the matter. Fleeing was useless, now that he knew her name and village. Which meant ...

She had to be very damn clever, indeed.

'Did you consider asking me?' she said.

'Asking you what?'

'Under what circumstances I would talk.'

He picked up a letter knife from the desk, thoughtlessly turning it between his fingers as he examined her. 'Please continue. I'm all ears.'

She wasn't sure if the undertone shimmering through his voice was laughter or cold-hearted fury, but hesitating wouldn't make anything better. So she cleared her throat and said, 'I'm not necessarily opposed to talking. I just have some wishes of my own I'd prefer for you to grant first.'

The letter knife stopped spinning. Agenor stared at her, the expression on his inhumanly perfect face torn between scorn and a burst of merriment. 'You have *wishes*.'

Allie shrugged. 'Is that a surprise to you?'

He raised his eyebrows. Entertained rather than enraged, it seemed. 'You're a guest on this island and a burglar in my rooms, and you think you're in a position to make demands?'

'A – a what?'

'But by all means,' he continued, waving that interruption away, 'surprise me again. What—'

'A *guest*?' Allie interrupted, loud enough to silence him at once. She stumbled forward half a step, then came to a befuddled standstill in the middle of the room, gasping for words, *any* words, that could even begin to throw that blood-curdling insult back into his face. 'You're calling me a *guest* of this court?'

The way he leaned back was a challenge. 'I sense some disagreement?'

'Oh, for fuck's sake.' She didn't know if it was her or her rage blurting out words now; perhaps they were the same person in the end. 'Are you that delusional? To think I came knocking on the doors of this place as a fourteen-year-old and you were merciful enough to let me in? Do you think I *wanted* to leave – to leave ...'

Her sentence drifted off – words she had barely been able to *think* for a decade. Home. Family. Friends. Her small village on Furja, surrounded by wheat fields and sheep meadows.

They wouldn't even know. If she died here, obliterated by fae magic or fallen to her death from some pretty marble balcony – no one would ever tell them.

Agenor stood watching her, like a lion observing a harmless lamb, wondering where it would jump next.

'Do you think I want to spend the rest of my life here?' she whispered. 'Surrounded by the bastards tyrannising my people?'

The corners of his mouth trembled up a fraction. 'Those are strong words for our attempts to protect you, wouldn't you say?'

'*Protect?*' Her voice soared up again. Perhaps she didn't even care if she died. Deiras was dead. Inga was safe. Perhaps this might be worth it, giving a life for the chance to throw her truth into that uncaring face for a few glorious heartbeats. 'You think you're *protecting* us? This is what you call *help?*'

'I've seen the madness humans come up with when no one keeps an eye on them,' he said, still in that vexingly light voice – that tone that made her want to punch a fist through his skull, consequences be damned. 'There's a reason they lived under the protection of the gods before the War. After most of the gods were gone—'

'Because *you* killed them.'

'I most certainly didn't,' he said with a small smile. 'Although I'm flattered you seem to think me capable of—'

'I'm not flattering you!' Her words burst from her lips like arrows fired. 'You honestly think we *need* you? You think we're *helped* by forced tribute payments and ruthless murder and—'

'You're exaggerating,' he said, standing up from his desk and turning his back to her with such nonchalance that she wished she had the weapons to make him regret it. As he shoved the letter knife back into some drawer, he added, 'Every governance system in the world's history has employed some taxation policy or another. And you can't blame us for intervening when the general peace in the archipelago is threatened, be it by humans or by—'

Allie spat out a bitter laugh. 'Who do you think are living in peace, exactly?'

He turned back around. 'You, for example.'

'You have no idea! You have not the faintest idea of ...' She gasped for breath, taking another half-step forward. 'Do you want to know why they took me? Why they—'

'Insufficient tribute payment, I take it?'

'We had the tribute! We all but starved ourselves for months, but we *had* the grain and gold the usual rates required!' Tears clouded her sight, welling up in frustration rather than grief. She had long since given up on grieving. 'But the bastards who came to collect the money decided they wanted half of our flock of sheep too, and when my father told them he'd sent complaints to the court itself, they took both the sheep *and* me. Is that what you'd call benevolent protection?'

Agenor ran his eyes over her, a slight line between his brows. 'That would be a violation of the protocol, if it's true. If you have names for me, I—'

'Oh, damn your protocols – do you think *anyone* out there gives a damn about them?' She let out something that was half scoff, half sob, her voice rising again. 'They're all the same. You have to know they are. There's no way you can be so oblivious as to think—'

'Seems a bit hasty to call every single fae a murderous fraud based only on your experience with a handful of them,' he said mildly.

'Oh, gods help me – you *are* oblivious.'

He chuckled. 'How old are you again?'

Allie considered setting her nails into his eyes. Considered snatching one of the logs from the floor and bashing him over the head with it until she'd magically slammed sense into him. But she would be dead a moment later, and he would still be an idiot.

She clenched her jaw and muttered, 'Twenty-four summers.'

'A respectable age,' he said dryly.

'Old enough to know injustice when I see it.'

'And yet you consider me young enough to miss it?' He settled back against his desk again, running a hand through his short dark hair. 'I was there when a human city decided to kill a god's son over some minor grievances. Left on their own, your people are capable of escalating some squabble into a divine war at any moment. And you wonder why I'd rather keep an eye on them?'

'It was barely an entire city,' Allie said through gritted teeth. 'I may not have been there, but I've read the books. A handful of idiots decided to kill him. Didn't you say something about drawing conclusions from just a few examples?'

That small smile built again. 'I could come up with a few more.'

'And their grievances can hardly have been so minor,' Allie snapped, 'considering that the other gods sided with them, too. Or are you arrogant enough to believe that you were the only one who could see the truth though a handful of gods could not?'

'Are you arrogant enough to believe you understand those events better than those who witnessed them?'

It could have been a taunt and came across rather like a challenge – a question to which he expected she'd have a reply. He was *enjoying* this, wasn't he? Poking and prodding to get a reaction out of her, an entertaining little human hurtling insults and accusations at his face – an enjoyable little diversion, and he wouldn't lose a minute of sleep over it.

Damn him. Damn every last one of them.

Allie folded her arms and coolly said, 'Judging by the nonsense you're spouting, I'm quite sure I've spent more time observing humans in my twenty-four years than you have in your however many centuries. So yes, I think I'm as qualified as you are to have a perspective on whatever the hell those humans were doing.'

'You seem to be thinking a lot.'

'Perhaps you should take that as a reason to stop smirking so smugly at me.'

If anything, his smile turned a little more satisfied. 'Don't take it personally. But you can't possibly believe the knowledge any human gathers in their lifetime will somehow match the centuries of experience most fae have in this world.'

'Or,' Allie suggested sharply, 'perhaps humans just learn faster and don't need centuries to get new information through their thick skulls.'

'A refreshing hypothesis.' His trembling lips told her exactly what he thought of it.

'You can laugh at me all you want,' Allie said, narrowing her eyes, 'but you *didn't* expect me to be human, did you?'

That, for the first time, hit home.

He faltered only for a moment. No more than a blink, a flash of stiffness around the corners of his lips. But a hesitation it was, and she knew she'd guessed right.

'Most humans don't cite Dephineia in their letters,' he said.

Allie scoffed. 'Not in their letters to *you*, perhaps.'

'Hardly relevant,' he said, sounding annoyed for the first time now. How very fae. All jokes and games until his own failures were the subject of discussion. 'You weren't writing like most humans would write. Of course I wouldn't expect you to be—'

'Oh, but that sounds very relevant to me,' Allie said briskly, planting her hands on her hips. 'If I can imitate fae well enough to fool even your centuries of lived experience, then what's stopping you from assuming I can use my brain as well as any fae?'

He let out a laugh *just* not convincingly careless enough. 'Imitation is not quite the same as identicality, is it?'

'Isn't it Dephineia, too, who claims that a perfect imitation is an indication of—'

'How much did you read before you turned fourteen, exactly?' he interrupted, his dark wings flaring out a fraction behind his shoulders.

'Enough.' She sent him an icy smile. 'See what I mean about humans not needing those centuries?'

'I'd hardly consider you an average human.'

'And you'd call yourself an average fae?'

The amusement returned. 'Are you resorting to flattery? I expected better from you.'

'I don't need flattery to make my point,' Allie said, rolling her eyes. 'You're being an arrogant, prejudiced bastard, and you know as little about humans as you know about folding shirts. If you'd ever made the effort to look a little better, you'd long since have realized humans can do everything fae can, perhaps more. Your turn.'

'*More?*' His smile broke into an open laugh. A dangerous kind of laugh. Where his smiles were all mild composure, all ancient self-restraint, that grin was a different creature entirely – a flash of *life* on his sharp-jawed face, of almost boyish delight. 'Just when I thought we'd reached the peak of the madness.'

'Prove me wrong,' Allie said.

A demand – a *command* – and he barely even seemed to realise it. His amusement didn't falter.

'With pleasure, if you're willing to make a bargain with me.'

Bargains. Oh, gods. She should have known it would come to this. Dangerous fae trickery – and then again …

If the stories were true, bargain magic was one of the few things more powerful than the colour magic they wielded themselves. A bargain, once closed, could not be broken by either party. So if she could convince him to promise he'd keep her alive and unharmed, at least he couldn't fling her off that balcony as soon as he figured out the truth of how she'd played him.

Was it so bad, really, to bind herself to him if it might save her life?

Her eyes slid down to his hands, lying loosely around the edge of his desk. 'This is the moment where I negotiate, isn't it?'

'For most people, it's the moment to be quiet and take what they get.'

'I wish you'd stop assuming I have anything to do with whoever most people are,' Allie said, throwing him another glare. 'But fine. Tell me what you suggest. I'll see what I think of it.'

He didn't stop smiling as he leaned forward, pressing his fingertips together before his bare chest. 'You give me a task. I give you a task. We'll see who of us fares better. Also, you tell me what in hell Deiras had to do with any of this.'

Damn it. He hadn't forgotten Deiras yet. Allie drew in a deep breath and cautiously said, 'I can tell you about Deiras.'

'Within the hour,' he added dryly.

The bastard may have closed a thousand bargains in his life. No sense in trying to trick him – he had to know every ambiguity, every loophole already. Allie bit away a curse.

'Fine,' she said, feigning confidence. 'My demand is you won't cause any harm to me. Whatever I tell you. Whether I win this test or not.'

He waved that away. 'Of course. I play fair.'

'Good. And ...' She hesitated for a fraction of a moment, unsure how far she could push. This all seemed far too easy. She'd won her safety already; with the bargain, she'd survive, even if he was unhappy with her thieving trickery, even if she lost whatever challenge he'd come up with. It was more than she should have dared to expect.

But she didn't *want* to lose.

She didn't want the bastard to return to his soft bed and his silk shirts, unbearably content with his own immortal superiority, and all the more so after having proven his point to the pesky little thief challenging him. She didn't want him to think her something inferior, barely more than a piece of cattle. He wasn't stupid, was he? He could see what was going on?

And if she had to *make* him see it ...

'We could use some assistance,' she blurted out. 'My family and I. So as long as you haven't finished your task – I want you to help us when I ask for it.'

Agenor raised an amused eyebrow. 'You're asking for a lot.'

'You could also just throw me off the balcony,' Allie said, sounding braver than she felt. 'Then you won't have to help anyone. But you can be assured I'll die in the staunch conviction that I *would* have beaten you.'

Again that dangerous grin. There was a fierceness to it, an almost mischievous allure – a sight that made the blood flush hot to her face. This wasn't the Lord Protector as she knew him from the shadows, ancient and stately and imperturbable in the most ominous of ways. This was a male who *felt* things. A male who perhaps ...

He extended a bronzed hand before she could finish that thought, fingers beckoning her closer in a silent but unmistakable command.

Allie didn't move.

'More wishes?' he said dryly.

'Are you – are you saying you agree?'

'With some specifications.' He still didn't lower his hand. 'No help that is detrimental to my own wellbeing, and no help that directly leads to the harm of anyone else. Apart from that ...' A dangerous challenge twinkled in his eyes. 'The task you give me should be doable for humans, just as my task for you should be doable for fae, and neither task should endanger any lives. If you manage to trick me under those conditions, I might as well offer some assistance.'

He was mad, Allie decided, stark mad, and somehow it hadn't killed him for twelve centuries or so. Why in hell would he indulge her in her ridiculous requests? Didn't he have better things to do – an empire to rule, meetings to attend, warriors to train?

'Well?' he added when she remained motionless. 'Anything to add?'

'You've been rather thorough,' she managed. 'It's as if you've closed bargains before.'

'A couple.' The undertone in his voice didn't make the sight of those inviting fingers any more reassuring. He knew every single trick, it told her, every clever trap. If he wanted to deceive her, she might not even notice until it was too late.

But no matter how often her thoughts ran over his conditions, she couldn't find the hole in them. And she shouldn't make him wait – not if impatience may well drive him to rethink this entire, unusual show of mercy.

She stepped forward. And laid her hand in his.

His fingers were firmer than she'd expected, gripping hers as if she was an anchor securing him to the world of the living. And yet there was a gentleness to his touch, to the cautious way he pulled her closer and examined her smaller, paler hand in his.

'We're in agreement, then?'

Allie didn't expect her voice to come out at all, but her words were loud and clear as day. 'We're in agreement.'

47

A small spark of light heated up where their palms were pressed together.

She hadn't known light could be dark. Hadn't known fire could burn black and yet bright at the same time. But the glow that spread from their intertwined hands was a brilliant shade of soot, a flame of night and shadow – dark enough to shroud their skin in twilight and yet fierce enough to light through flesh and bone.

Power – chilling, marvellous power – crackling at her fingertips.

She couldn't look away. Not when an ice-cold heat built in every spot where her hands met those tanned, slender fingers, trailing down from her palm to her wrist. Not when wisps of smoke slipped out from that brilliant darkness, wrapping around their fingers like shreds of morning mist. Agenor's sculpted beauty became a statue of ancient power in the glow of his magic, his room a temple of the night. Small and helpless and painfully mortal, Allie could only stare and marvel and wonder how in the world she would still be alive tomorrow...

A sting of pain shot through her wrist, and at once the darkness vanished.

Barely suppressing a curse, she yanked back her hand and turned it, expecting a trickle of blood on the inside of her arm. But all she found ...

Her breath hitched.

A small, dark gemstone had broken through her skin, lodged into her wrist like a scar turned to glass. It was as black as the bargain magic, an inky onyx absorbing even the sunlight that fell on it and leaving only dull glimmers on the surface.

'Ah,' Agenor said, and when she looked up, that disconcerting smile was once again playing over his handsome features. 'I see I finally managed to surprise you, too.'

CHAPTER 5

He was quite starting to enjoy the way she wrinkled her nose at him – a scowl that without exception announced the arrival of yet another outrageous statement, yet another surprise to wipe the weight of the centuries off his heart.

The more dutiful side of him was well aware that he shouldn't enjoy this ridiculous game so much. He should have put an end to it the moment she started making demands, should have sent a few of his people to trace Deiras's movements of the last days and be satisfied with the answers they would doubtlessly find. But this human girl ...

He couldn't make sense of her, couldn't predict her, and the surprise was an addictive, intoxicating drug he couldn't stop craving. He found his heart leaping a fraction every time she opened her mouth, every time she sent him that foul glare defying all his power and authority.

Damn the duty, for once. He could waste a few hours indulging in this madness instead.

'You knew this was going to happen,' Allie said, the accusation heavy in her voice as she glanced at the bargain mark at her wrist again.

'You didn't?' It surprised him, he had to admit. If she'd read Phyron and Dephineia, what were the chances she'd never come across a detailed account of bargain magic?

'Most fae don't offer me bargains,' she said coldly. 'They just shout commands at me. Does it disappear when the bargain is fulfilled?'

'Yours will when you've told me your story and completed your task, or admitted defeat.' He couldn't help smiling as she glared at him again. Admitting defeat would take her a while. He couldn't say he minded. 'Mine will be gone when you die, presumably. I didn't specify an expiry date to my promise not to harm you.'

Allie blinked, her blue eyes dipping to his own wrist. He saw her count the marks in his skin – nine of them, most of them smaller bargains he'd have fulfilled within a year or two.

'Well.' She sounded a little dazed, with the worst of her anger dissipating. Realising only now, it seemed, what extraordinary protection he had offered her. 'That could have been worse.'

'You may have to reconsider your assessment of my heartlessness,' Agenor said dryly. 'I'm a vicious monster only when I choose to be so.'

'And a thief running off with your clothes is not enough of a reason?'

'Not when the thief in question writes me such pleasantly entertaining letters.' He gestured at the bed, then realised that was probably not his best bet, despite those thinly veiled glances she kept stealing at his unbuttoned shirt, and instead shoved his chair from beneath the desk. He could take the bed himself. 'Sit down. You have a story to tell me.'

She didn't move until he sank down on his mattress; then she tiptoed forward and settled herself on the very edge of his chair. Her gaze wandered from the mark at her wrist to him, then to the snake basking in the sunlight some five feet away from her. Estimating, calculating. So very clever for a human her age, and so very careful.

Which made it all the more remarkable that she'd taken the risk of stealing from him.

'I wouldn't recommend you wait the full hour,' Agenor said, resting his elbows on his thighs. 'If telling the story takes you longer than expected, that mark may make the experience very unpleasant.'

Another glower. 'I don't need the mark to make this an unpleasant experience, Lord Agenor.'

He almost laughed again. He shouldn't have offered her that protection, duty whispered again. He really shouldn't have. But she was so small and yet so fierce, her tongue so sharp in every amusing way ... He just wanted more of this. More of her. If he wasn't going to hurt her anyway, he might as well make sure she knew it.

At least it would make this conversation significantly easier.

'Better to get it over with, then,' he said. 'Tell me about Deiras.'

Her face darkened. 'Did you consider yourself a friend of him?'

'I don't usually kill my friends without asking questions first,' Agenor said, raising an eyebrow. 'He was a colleague. Not my favourite one.'

'Oh. Good.' She glanced at Oleander again, hands fidgeting in her lap, and blurted out, 'He wanted my sister.'

'Your – sister?'

She heard the surprise in his voice, it seemed; the next look she sent him was a positively scorching one. 'A girl I consider my sister, if you must know. She ...' An unnaturally level breath. 'When I came here on my own, a woman with a foster daughter younger than me took me in. She died a couple of years ago. I've been taking care of Inga since then.'

Of course she had. Fierce and proud enough to argue with fae mages – he should have known she'd be loyal to the death, too.

'How old is she?' he said.

'Fifteen.'

Agenor almost cursed. For fuck's sake. Deiras could at least have shown the grace not to go after a girl still nearly an infant.

'I see,' he said instead. 'And so you resolved to stop him?'

She met his eyes without reluctance this time – a hard gaze that took every trace of human vulnerability from her delicate face. 'If you really want to know, I resolved to stick a kitchen knife between his shoulders. But since I'm a powerless little human' – her smile at him was a whiplash – 'that required a few workarounds.'

And at once he understood.

A plan so reckless it was closer to suicidal – but a plan that could achieve her impossible goal, too. A plan that *had* achieved her impossible goal. Those taunting letters, meant to add fuel to the fire of his displeasure, her loot consisting only of clothes not obviously recognisable to the rest of the court, Deiras's oblivious surprise. Gods and demons. She *had* played him, indeed. She'd played both of them.

But how had she managed to trick Deiras into her game?

'I begged,' she said coldly, reading the question on his face 'Told him those shirts were all I took with me from home, my savings to buy my freedom one day. He enjoyed peeling them from my hands while I made a show of sobbing at his feet, if you want to know. Enough for him to give us a day of respite for every shirt he took.'

Bastard. Agenor rubbed his face and said, 'You don't strike me as the begging kind.'

A flare of fury broke through the cold in her eyes. 'Do you think *anyone* is the begging kind if they can avoid it? You learn to play the part soon enough in this place.'

'We're not all like Deiras,' he said, a little offended despite the source of the insult. 'I have no intention of making you beg for anything.'

'And doesn't that make you a paragon of kind-heartedness?' She let out a mirthless laugh. 'Do you have any idea how long he's been doing this? Preying on women from our villages? I could give you five names from the past decade alone. It's never occurred to you to stop him?'

'If I'd known, of course I—'

'See? Oblivious.' She fell back in his chair, wrinkling her nose at him again. 'Glad we've proven that point, then.'

Agenor opened his mouth, unusually unsure of what to say for a moment. Oblivious? For hell's sake, there was nothing oblivious about him. He couldn't be expected to keep an eye on every single fae male on the island every minute of the day; he was busy enough dealing with fae trying to maim and murder each other. Overseeing their interactions with humans – that had never been his responsibility, and ...

His thoughts faltered there. Not his responsibility, no – but if he thought about it for a moment longer, he wasn't sure who else should carry the blame in his place.

No one really kept an eye on the humans' safety apart from their direct supervisors. Leander for Rustvale. Others for the other villages. If they didn't do their job ...

Well, then what? It wasn't oblivious to expect people to do their job, was it?

'So,' Allie briskly interrupted his thoughts, and he gave himself a mental kick in the shins. What was he doing, getting his brain all tangled up over some servant's accusations? 'What else did we have to prove? I think you're supposed to have a task for me.'

A task. Yes. He swept those nonsensical doubts back into the shadows of his mind and forced himself to focus on the matter at hand – some way to make his point. Not too unpleasantly, of course. She had enough to deal with, he couldn't deny that; he wasn't going to put her in danger only to prove himself. But he wasn't going to be weak-hearted either. He wasn't going to give her a chance to *win* this bet.

There was plenty humans couldn't possibly do, of course. Fly. Use magic. But that would be a childish point to make, and they'd both know it; she hadn't been talking about the means but rather the goals they could achieve. Even if she had unwisely omitted that point from their bargain, he wasn't going to abuse that oversight. Any victory worth claiming had to be fought on fair ground.

So what did he have?

Patience.

It was the main difference – the *relevant* difference – behind the superficial matters of magic and wings. Fae lived longer. They didn't need to be impulsive and rash like most humans he'd known. They made plans unfolding across three human lifetimes; they recognised patterns and connections over centuries rather than decades. It was that quality, more than any other, that enabled them to rule an empire so much more effectively than any human would – unfortunate exceptions like Deiras notwithstanding.

It was her sense of strategy he should be testing, her planning and patience. That was where the important differences were to be found. She'd played him once; she wouldn't manage again.

Although, he had to admit – he wouldn't mind watching her try.

When he looked up, he found her studying him, a small frown etched into her forehead. Again, he was struck for a moment by that gleam in her eyes, looking so very little like a *human*.

'Well?' she said.

'Well.' He took his decision in the blink of an eye. 'You seem to like stealing things. Let's see how you fare with the key around my neck.'

'The ...' Her gaze fell to his chest and then a few inches farther down. Then dragged back up to his face, a hint of a blush on her pale cheeks now. 'You want me to steal that key?'

'Without me noticing,' Agenor added, a little more amused than he should have been. 'I take it that won't be a problem at all?'

She pressed her lips together, aiming her glare at his face with a determination that made him suspect it took an effort not to look down again.

'Fine. Prepare to wake up without it soon.'

'I'm looking forward to it,' Agenor said dryly, and again that fleeting hint of red flushed over her face. Human morals – how very interesting. 'So. Do you have a task for me too, or am I to—'

'I do.' She spoke faster now, her voice stumbling over the words for the first time in their conversation. Her mastery of his language was excellent – uncannily excellent, really, knowing she had likely spoken a human tongue for the first fourteen years of her life. 'I'm challenging you to do something kind without selfish motives.'

Agenor stared at her.

She snapped her mouth shut and glowered back at him, that defiant, challenging scowl he could feel burning just behind his ribs.

'Something *kind*,' he repeated.

'Yes.'

'That ...' He let out a laugh, unable to suppress a sting of disappointment. A surprise, again, but not of the positive kind. He'd wanted a challenge. He'd wanted to *work* for this victory, inevitable as it was. And yet, after tricking Deiras, after tricking him – this was the best she could come up with? 'That's not hard.'

She cocked her head. 'Isn't it?'

'It ... No.' He stood with another befuddled laugh and walked six long strides to the file cabinet next to his desk. Allie followed him with her eyes but didn't move as he pulled open a small drawer and plucked out a purse of gold coins. He weighed it in his palm, then shoved it towards her over the smooth tabletop, turning away as he did.

'Give that to your sister.'

He heard her pick it up as he sauntered back to the bed; her breath caught for a moment. 'Are you sure?'

'You should know I won't miss it,' he said wryly, sinking into the blankets again. Her eyes were a little too wide. He liked that, he realised – surprising her. A shame she'd made it so easy for him this time. 'Call it an apology for my carelessness with Deiras. And I think that should settle the first half of our bargain.'

She ran her gaze over him as she slipped the gold into the pocket of her apron with quick, clever hands. Something like a smile quirked the corners of her lips – the first true smile he'd seen from her.

'So it seems,' she admitted, jumping to her feet. 'A shame. I could definitely have used some help at dinnertime tonight.'

Agenor blinked. She was suspiciously quick to concede. Had this been her plan all along – had she just wanted him to offer her money, and had she estimated that would be the first option he'd think of? But how was he to align that with her passionate argument of minutes ago?

How was he to align *anything* about this woman with the rest of her?

'Well,' he said, pushing away that thought. He'd have time to ask questions later. They weren't done yet. There was still her task to be fulfilled – or, more likely, to be attempted. 'In that case, the outcome of our argument depends on your thieving skills, I believe.'

'Yes. We'll see each other soon, then.' Again that smile – disconcertingly bright for a woman facing such swift defeat. 'Very soon, perhaps.'

And before he could work out if this little human of barely two dozen summers was *threatening* him, she was gone.

He didn't mention her to Achlys when he returned to the great hall to explain himself.

He should have, once again. The High Lady was entitled to a full account of anything that happened at her court; she should know, too, what exactly had happened to the male she'd trusted with the human tributes since the end of the War. But he knew what she'd do to a servant playing with the lives of her inner circle, and that ...

In general, he reminded the sliver of discomfort that ran through him, he agreed. Of course he did. They couldn't just let anyone plot murders at this court, fae or human; that would destroy their hard-won peace very quickly. But this wasn't just any human, and Allie hadn't made her plans for the pleasure of it. A fifteen-year-old girl – he wasn't going to punish her for saving a child from Deiras's hands.

So for the first time in centuries, he found himself lying to the Mother of all fae. Spun a story of Deiras's thievery and his human accomplices, and made it dramatic enough for her to accept it without further hassle.

And didn't regret it. Not for a minute.

Gods and demons. What had the little vixen done to him?

He tried to resume his usual routine – training field, offices, meeting rooms. But the restless curiosity of the past days had moved over for an equally restless discomfort, an impatience for something he couldn't name himself. He watched the innocent sparring of his warriors, the maps and plans and strategies, the imperial administration and the hustle and bustle of the court, and somehow heard that brisk, light voice in the back of his mind again.

Who do you think are living in peace, exactly?

She was. Agenor knew she was, even if she didn't realise it herself. She hadn't seen the utter destruction the War had brought, the stark white battlefields emptied of every last fleck of colour. She hadn't known the chaos before the Conquest either, before Achlys and Melinoë united them, when the fae were still warring amongst each other. The world was better now. He *knew* it was better now, and he wasn't going to doubt that just because she'd shouted at him with tears in her eyes ...

You're oblivious.

No, he wasn't. Who did she think she was?

He shouldn't be thinking about her. A human servant, for the gods' sake. But he'd been thinking about her for days, and knowing her face didn't make it easier to shake the habit; it just gave a voice to the letters he'd read and a blistering blue-eyed stare to accompany them.

Prove me wrong.

No human had ever spoken to him like that, all but ordering him around. And instead of fury, all he felt was ... confusion?

For years – *decades* – he'd craved a change, *any* change. Now it was here, and he had not the faintest idea how to handle it.

His routine shattered, he wandered around the court until the sun sank to the horizon and the halls and corridors quieted. Soon he, too, would retreat to his rooms to eat a silent dinner there, and—

A searing stab of pain shot through his arm, like a burn wound deeper than his bones.

Agenor nearly stumbled over his own feet as he grabbed his wrist with a hiss of pain. The burning sensation flared a last time under his fingers, then waned slowly – too slowly, though, for him to be relieved.

What in hell? He knew that pain, had felt it often enough when he was younger and reckless and altogether stupid.

But he wasn't violating any bargains now, was he?

He stood still in the silent corridor, blinking at the nine small gemstones buried in the skin at his wrist. Eight of them were not the problem. They couldn't be. He had been excruciatingly cautious in negotiating them; there was no way they would suddenly catch up with him after months or years.

But the ninth one ...

Gods' sake. Had he made a mistake somewhere?

He'd bargained not to harm her, but he wasn't harming her. Apart from that, there had been his promise to help her if she asked for it, but only as long as he didn't fulfil whatever task she gave him. And he'd handled that task hours ago – hadn't he?

I could have used some help at dinnertime.

Oh, gods.

Had he?

Agenor threw a quick look around. Not a soul to be seen in this deserted corridor. Carefully, still clutching his wrist tightly, he turned in the direction of his bedroom and took a single step forward. Another sting hit in the same moment, not nearly as painful now that he was prepared – but painful enough to know he'd regret walking farther.

What in the world?

We'll see each other soon. Her voice hit him again, with that suspicious undertone of smug triumph. *Very soon, perhaps.* As if she'd expected his mark to cause trouble. As if somehow she and the magic knew something that had entirely escaped him. What had he overlooked? Giving that sister of hers a heap of gold hadn't been intended to buy her loyalty or to buy off his nagging conscience; he'd just wanted to help, and to—

To make a point.

To win that bet.

He could just hear Allie snickering at him, nose wrinkling as she sent him another glare. *Winning, Lord Agenor, is not a selfless motive.*

Oh, fuck.

Perhaps ... Perhaps he had slightly underestimated her again.

He bit out a curse as he turned around, stalked towards the nearest open window, and unfolded his wings. The faint, throbbing pain in his wrist abated at once, leaving only a memory of hurt behind. A deceptive kind of bliss, he knew. As soon as he stalled again, or worse, turned back, every moment would be agony until he obeyed her request for help again.

He had underestimated her, indeed. Dangerously so. It was high time he stopped being amused and started being slightly unnerved.

He flung himself out of the window, too agitated to pick a more dignified option. Decades had passed since he'd last left the court in the direction of Rustvale, but the rugged mountain slopes that slid by below him as he flew westwards hadn't changed a speck. The village itself still looked like it had always done, too, small and proper, some three dozen houses gathered along the road that led through the small valley. Peaceful, his mind suggested.

Who do you think is living in peace, exactly?

Gods be damned. He had to stop thinking of her as if she actually made sense – as if her trickery would somehow give her words more weight.

Children were playing between the houses below when he approached. They vanished as soon as he began his descent, though; by the time he landed in the yellow sand of the main street, the village could have been deserted a decade ago.

A door slammed open behind him.

And an all too familiar voice said, 'Changed your mind, I see?'

Agenor whirled around. She stood in the doorway of a low house built from black bricks and weathered wood, arms crossed over her chest, chin jutted up high. Her hair was bound into a sloppy braid, loose brown strands framing her freckled face. A simple short-sleeved tunic had replaced the servant's frock, and her legs and feet were bare and a little dusty. Looking so thoroughly, undeniably human ...

And yet the breath stopped in his lungs for a heartbeat.

What was he *thinking*?

He forced himself into motion, twenty endless strides to that rickety hut where she stood waiting for him, her face a beacon of cold, sharp triumph. An expression that should have left him furious. It was clear enough she detested him. She'd humiliated him and now gloated about it; he should be fighting back with all his might, making sure she regretted tricking him as much as he regretted being tricked by her.

But he didn't *want* to fight back. It was as if he was behind his desk again, wrestling with the letter she'd left him – desperate to change her mind and utterly clueless how in the world he was going to manage.

'You're looking a little befuddled, Lord Agenor,' she told him, stepping back inside but leaving the door open for him. 'Come in, if our little human abode isn't too humble for you.'

Behind her, Agenor heard a male voice say, 'Al?'

'He's coming to help,' she said, switching to a human language. Agenor knew the dialect – or had known it a century ago, and still recognised enough of the words even through the changes they had undergone. 'We need someone to take a look at Gil's ankle.'

'What have you been *doing*?' the man sputtered.

Agenor entered, ducking a little in the low doorway. The room was small and dark but spotlessly clean, sparsely furnished with a table and a few patched-up chairs. A tall human man stood at the small kitchen counter, blond and broad-shouldered and a little pale as he glanced back and forth between Agenor and the woman between them.

'Won a bet,' Allie said, waving that question away. 'He's harmless.'

'*Harmless?*' Another one of those harrowed side-glances. Only then did Agenor realise they didn't expect him to understand their language at all. His voice lower now, the man added, 'Have you gone mad? What's the next step – are you going to invite him for dinner? We barely have the food to—'

'I doubt his lordship is going to stoop to eating onion soup and old bread,' she said sourly, then whirled around and effortlessly switched languages again. 'Take a chair. Inga should be here in a moment, if you want to meet her. And this is Russ – my husband.'

Agenor almost choked on his own tongue.

Her *husband?* He threw the blond man another look as he sank down in his chair, to be met with a glare as sharp as Allie's own. Her – it took him a moment to make himself accept the inevitable facts – *husband.*

Why did that word make him feel like punching the fellow in the face?

Russ looked decent. Steady and reliable. A man with the fists and wits to protect her if the need arose. That was all quite positive, wasn't it? Had he wanted her to wither away as an old spinster, with only her sister to keep her company?

'So,' Allie interrupted his thoughts, stalking to the kitchen counter and nudging her husband aside with a gentle hand in his side. Again Agenor found himself swallowing something ... bitter. Something that shouldn't be there at all. 'Something to drink? Tea?' She glanced over her shoulder. 'I'd offer you food, but we'd have to starve ourselves for the hospitality, and I'm not *that* fond of your face.'

He managed a grin, glancing at the reed baskets beside the primitive sink. 'That doesn't look like a meagre dinner to me.'

'Shame that it's our supply for the rest of the week,' Allie said with a snort, and suddenly the humble pile of onions, peppers, and half a cabbage took on an entirely different appearance.

'A *week?*'

'Five more days.' She pulled a face as she plucked a mug off a shelf, grabbed a nearby jug, and poured him a splash of water. 'But at least it's peaceful, hmm?'

Next to her, Russ still stood glaring at Agenor as if he'd be glad to wrap those large workman's hands around his neck. Allie either didn't notice or didn't care as she crossed the six feet to the table, all but slammed the full mug down, and added, 'Leander started weighing us every year. If someone gets heavier, he limits their food distribution.'

'He – *what?*'

She shrugged and fell down in the chair opposite Agenor's. 'Probably one of your beloved protocols again.'

'It ... No? No, it isn't.' *Weighing* them? Even their cattle wasn't treated like that. And she thought he'd known about it – she thought he'd *approved* of it?

Good gods. Should he have kept an eye on the humans' supervisors after all?

'I'll have a word with Leander,' he added in a spurt of something desperate – for what, he wasn't sure. 'If he tries this nonsense again, let me know.'

Allie blinked. Met his eyes. And for a single frozen moment, the staunch aversion was gone.

That, he realised, was what he'd needed.

Her blue eyes darted over his face for two silent heartbeats – looking for mockery, or insincerity, and finding none of it.

'You ... Really?'

That sudden crack in her voice, revealing something far softer, far more vulnerable below the icy fury – it shouldn't have hit him the way it did. And perhaps this could have been a selfless offer of help a moment ago. Perhaps he could have intervened from the goodness of his old, tired heart. But now, he knew, there would not be any selflessness about it – hell, he'd do the same and five times more just to make her look at him like that again.

Like perhaps she didn't hate him. Like perhaps the woman who had written those taunting, amicable letters might be real, not just an act meant to drive him towards violence.

So he said, 'What else did you need my help for, then?'

'Oh.' She blinked and brusquely turned away. Leaning against the kitchen counter, his broad shoulders stiff with self-restraint, Russ only gave her the smallest, curtest nod.

'The neighbour,' Allie said, sagging in her chair. 'His ankle – it's really very bad. Some infection. He has to get back to work soon, and it might honestly kill him. So I was thinking – if you could do some magic, that would—'

The door opened, interrupting her.

A tall girl slipped inside, all limbs and movement, half a mile of ash blonde curls dancing over her shoulders. She made it three steps inside before she noticed Agenor at the table, froze, and blurted out a curse that didn't fit that wide-eyed, innocent face at all.

'Oh, evening, Inga,' Allie said, impressively unaffected. 'We have a visitor. Could you go get water for dinner?'

The girl was lightning fast as she snatched the nearest bucket from the floor and bolted for the exit again – but not fast enough. Agenor caught a last glimpse of her as she flew out and around the corner, into the light of the sunset, curls fluttering back over her shoulders.

Between the mess of her hair a slender, pointed ear stuck out.

Oh.

Fuck.

Half fae? Was *that* why Deiras had gone after her?

He opened his mouth to comment on the observation, then caught Allie's withering glare and thought better of it. He had no idea of the history, no idea of the circumstances of the girl's conception. If her father had been a male of Deiras's kind – well, he wouldn't blame the family for avoiding the subject.

And Allie ... He really had no desire to see those blue eyes cool even further.

'So,' he said instead and managed a pleasant smile, 'where were we? The neighbour, you said?'

CHAPTER 6

'Well,' Allie said, sitting barefoot on the countertop, 'you have to admit that could have been worse.'

Russ grumbled something in that low voice that meant he was looking for objections.

'Gil's ankle really looked a whole lot better after he was done,' Allie hastily said before her husband could make too much progress. 'And if he was speaking the truth about talking with Leander, that might actually—'

'Al,' Russ interrupted, halting his pacing between the door and the table. 'Please. I don't care how many ankles he heals. I still trust the bastard about as far as I can throw him.'

Rightly so, she knew, and yet ... 'He's our best chance to improve anything here.'

'And why would he make the effort?'

'Because I made a bargain with him. He doesn't have a choice if I—'

'And why,' Russ said, voice rising as he swung a fist in the direction of the Crimson Court, 'did he make that damn bargain with you? He didn't need to. He could have killed you just as easily, did you forget?'

She hadn't forgotten. She'd wondered the same thing in silence all day. Her letters, her insults, her challenges – but why in the world would a male of his power and status bother with any little human's challenges? Shouldn't he be spending his time lounging around in the Mother's damned bone hall and having lavish dinners with half-naked fae females, as half of that court seemed to be doing all day?

'Don't know,' she said, rubbing her face. 'Perhaps he just woke up in a good mood.'

'He might be brooding on some very indirect revenge plan.'

'Bargain wouldn't let him.' She jumped down, landing lightly on the coarse wooden floor, and added, 'And anyway, I don't think he'd want to.'

Russ remained silent – a deep, sceptical silence.

She wasn't sure what to say, so she slipped into the back room instead, where Inga already lay sleeping. In the darkness, she found her clothes by touch alone: her court frock, her coat against the night cold, her boots. The rummaging in her cloth basket at least distracted her from the whirling of her own mind for a moment – from that question Russ would doubtlessly ask as soon as she emerged from the bedroom again.

Why in the world would she trust Agenor's good intentions?

Something was off with his helpful suggestions. Had they just been helpful suggestions indeed, the bargain would already have released him, and she'd seen the grimace of pain on his face when she'd asked him to come back tomorrow and he'd hesitated for just a moment too long. So there had to be selfish motives of *some* kind, and who was she to believe some arrogant fae lord would be at all benevolent towards her after she'd stolen from him and forced him to do her bidding?

But he had looked so lost at the dinner table when she'd told him about Leander's policies. So ... eager?

As if he truly wanted to be helpful. As if he wanted to win that bet between them as desperately as she did.

Something hardened in her chest. It could just be another fae act, of course. Well, if he thought he could play her heart and weaken her resolve, he'd be wrong. She was going to win this game, uncanny fae emotions or not. He was welcome to come cry in her arms when he could acknowledge she had just as capable a brain as his dear immortal friends.

That was to say – not in her arms, of course. She shook that thought off very quickly. But she could perhaps be persuaded to pat him on those muscular shoulders once or twice.

Russ had sunk into his usual chair when she returned to the front room and quietly closed the door behind herself. His eyes narrowed at the sight of her clothes.

'Are you going out?'

'Off to steal a key,' Allie said lightly, hoping against her better judgement that he'd forget to take interest if she sounded like there was nothing interesting about her announcement.

'You ... Al, it's past midnight!'

'Yes,' she said, stripping off her home tunic to don her servant's frock instead. 'That's the idea. If I'm lucky, he's sleeping.'

'You're going to sneak into his *bed*?'

'Don't sound so scandalised, Russ.' She scowled at him as she emerged from her stiff linen frock. 'Just because you have no desire to see me anywhere near a bed doesn't mean I should avoid all horizontally oriented furniture for the rest of my life.'

He paled. 'Please say you're not planning to—'

'No! What do you think I am?' She snatched a handful of hairpins from her pocket and began to snap them into place. 'I'm just going to sneak into his room, hope the snakes don't eat me, get his key, sneak out again. Worst that can happen is he wakes up, and then I'll just try again another—'

'Worst that can happen,' Russ said sharply, 'is that he wakes up to find you in his bed and decides to make good use of the occasion.'

'He's not *that* kind of a fae male, Russ.'

He scoffed. 'Bastard shot me some damn unpleasant looks when you called me your husband.'

'Oh, did he?' Where did that tingle of satisfaction come from? She shrugged it off. 'Well, in any case, he made a bargain not to harm me. He'll make his own life pretty unpleasant if he tries to put a hand on me.'

Russ looked unconvinced.

'I'll be fine, Russ.'

'That's what you said last time,' he grumbled, 'and before I knew it, you were dragging bloody Lord Agenor himself into the house for tea.'

'And then he fixed Gil's ankle,' Allie said, pulling her coat over her shoulders. 'So I don't think we have reason to complain so far. Say hello to Farran from me.'

She knew he meant to complain some more, but she was out before he could open his mouth, slipping into the dark night of the mountains.

Most of the Crimson Court was silent on this night, its inhabitants either fast asleep or gathered around the Mother's bone hall. The few fae she encountered between the gleaming orbs ignored her. Humans, after all, were as good as invisible.

A dangerous fact, most days; a servant could disappear without a trace, and no one would ever have seen or heard anything. Tonight, though, Allie was grateful for the protection it offered her. At least no one would notice she was not one of the humans usually making her rounds at night.

Up the many, many stairs, through gallery after gallery. His room had never seemed so far removed from her. When had she started wishing him closer?

No – not him, of course. Only the key around his neck, the road to victory.

She'd made the walk so many times before, and yet she was almost surprised when she finally arrived – as if it had taken her both twice as long and twice as short as usual to reach the tower floor where he lived. With a final glance through the deserted corridor, she sucked in a breath and tested the door.

Unlocked.

A pleasant surprise. Allie hoped it was not a first sign of an ambush waiting for her, a snake about to sink its fangs into her ankle if she stepped inside.

She edged the door open a few more inches and slipped through without allowing herself another moment to think. He probably hoped she would cower away from the task he'd given her. Expected her to be a little human coward, a weakling without the spine to rule even a single city, let alone an empire.

He could go step on a nail and dance around with it. She wasn't going to shrink back from a challenge.

The room was dark, and cooler than she'd ever found it by day. As her eyes adjusted, Allie could distinguish no more than the outlines of walls and furniture at first. Gradually, she got used to the mere shred of silvery moonlight that fell between the heavy velvet curtains, and more and more details revealed themselves to her – the gleaming, leathery form of a snake on the floor to her left. A silk shirt carelessly thrown over the desk chair. Agenor's muscular shape in the bed on the other side of the room, his magnificent wings spread out around him, his chest rising and sinking on the rhythm of his slow breath.

Asleep.

The second surprise, even more pleasant than the first.

She tiptoed forward, carefully scanning the mahogany floorboards to make sure she wouldn't trip over yet another snake. Her rustling frock was the only sound disturbing the eerie silence of the night – that and Agenor's breathing, sounding so oddly peaceful for a fae warrior who had lived to see gods perish and empires crumble.

A bitter taste filled her throat. And he truly believed it, that they were living in peace indeed.

No need to think about that now, either. They could discuss his naïveté after she had claimed her victory.

Tiny step by tiny step, she crept up on him, every sinew in her body tense as coiled string. Just three feet to go, now. Two. In the faint moonlight, she could just make out the lines and planes of his upper body – taut muscles that really didn't show their years, or rather, their centuries. His velvety wings lay loosely over the blankets on either side of his torso, gleaming softly in the silver light.

Allie swallowed, her throat suddenly dry. It had been a while since she'd looked at any man in a state of undress. And those innocent flings from years ago certainly hadn't looked like *this*.

Why couldn't he be a wrinkly old man grumbling at her through a toothless mouth? That would have made it so much easier to feel the aversion she should have felt as she finally stood still at his bed and bent a little closer, peering at the key's chain in the dark. It would have made it so much easier to focus on the task at hand, rather than on the slender muscle gleaming at her in the dark, the surreal beauty of his sharp-jawed face in the shadows of the night.

Focus. Wasn't this just the trap he'd laid for her?

His thin silver key chain ran around his neck like a scar, the key itself invisible in the hollow between his neck and shoulder. No choice but to try and pull it out. It wouldn't do to wait here until he turned in his sleep – that moment may not come for hours.

Holding her breath, Allie bent farther and stretched out her hand. Too far away. He slept in the middle of his broad bed, his far side a good arm's length away from where she stood. If she were to lean over far enough to get her fingertips on that key, she might well lose her balance and tumble on top of him like a blundering child.

The idea of lying sprawled over that hard, sculpted chest – best not to think about it.

Calm, gradual movements, then. Carefully, like a mother trying not to wake an infant, she rested her knee on the soft mattress and slowly transferred more and more of her weight to that leg. The mattress dented equally slowly. Agenor's breath didn't falter.

Time for a second attempt.

She reached for his unprotected throat, wishing for a moment she'd brought a knife – not to hurt him, but rather just to make a point. Alas, the theft of his key would have to be enough for today. Leaning just a fraction farther forward, she lowered her hand. Her fingertips brushed over soft, vulnerable skin as she felt along the silver chain – over his collarbone, down a muscular shoulder—

68

Something wrapped around her waist.

Something warm and strong and tight like an iron chain.

Allie cried out as that something – that *arm* around her waist – tugged her down and she lost her balance after all, collapsing over his naked chest with flailing arms. Darkness closed around her. A *wing* closed around her. The world was reduced to soft blankets and warm, bare skin and the scent of male nearness washing over her –

And the body below her. Tall and hard and – oh, gods – awake.

'It seems I always underestimate how soon we'll see each other again,' Agenor muttered, pinning her against his chest as if he owned her. Allie tried to wrench out of his grip but found his arm unmoving as a steel bond. 'An admirable attempt, I'll be the first to admit it.'

'You *bastard*,' she managed through her half-panicked panting. Yes, panic. It was certainly panic that had her heart rattling in her throat like that, and not at all the sensation of his powerful body pressed against hers, skin separated from skin only by a thin blanket and her simple dress. 'Take your hands off me, or I – I ...'

A silent rumble shook his chest. Laughter. He was *laughing*. 'Or you'll do what? There's not much left on me to steal at the moment, little thief.'

She froze, her attempts to escape forgotten as those words came through. 'Are you *naked*?'

'Did you expect me to change my sleeping attire just for the possibility of thieves sneaking into my bed?'

Oh, gods have mercy on her soul. Naked. The muscular thighs pressing against hers. The – was she imagining it, or was there a slight bulge pressing into her lower belly?

'Did you expect me *not* to sneak into your bed,' she managed between the sparks of panic firing in her mind. Panic and – no, surely there was nothing else to it? Surely it could be nothing but humiliating to lay here tousled and sprawled in his hold, subject to his every whim?

Agenor chuckled. 'I expected your husband might object.'

'He's barely my husband,' she blurted out, and now he was the one to go still beneath her.

'You introduced him as your husband.'

'He is, he is. Officially, I mean. He ... we ...' Hell. Why was she even betraying this secret? The perfect rejection of whatever his advances were, and yet her mouth wouldn't stop moving. 'Look, we've been friends for ages. And when Resa died, I needed someone who could keep the men off my back, and Russ's family was nagging him to get married, and he needed a wife who wouldn't mind him spending his nights in his best friend's bed, so ...'

Agenor burst out laughing.

The deep sound of it rolled through his body, shaking her against his chest. Again Allie tried to squirm away, to no avail. If anything, the arm around her waist held her tighter. Exasperated, she clawed her nails into his bare chest, only for his laughter to turn into something suspiciously like a moan.

Oh, gods. Warmth stirred between her legs at that sound, unwelcome as a fever. No. No, she had to keep her head clear, statuesque body below her or not. Struggling for some last dignity, she managed a brisk, 'And none of that means you're supposed to keep holding me. Are you finally letting me go?'

'Do you want me to?' His voice had become a purr.

'Do I give the impression I'm comfortable here, Lord Agenor?'

'You surely make an effort not to,' he admitted, and the fingers in her side drew a slow, small circle over the cloth of her dress. Goosebumps rose wherever they passed, no matter how hard she willed her own body to behave. 'Do you know what's interesting, though?'

'Your impertinence?' she suggested between clenched teeth.

'My bargain mark isn't burning.' His hand shifted up over her back, trailing closer to her spine – a maddeningly demanding touch, soft and seductive, leaving her incapable of moving or objecting. 'And yet I should be incapable of harming you. Are you sure you find your current predicament so unpleasant?'

She drew in a cold breath, unable to quench the flames flaring below her skin. Was she sure? Locked against the rock hard contours of his fae body, surrounded by the scent of heady arousal and a dark wing that seemed to promise quiet, conspiratorial secrecy – how could she be sure of anything? She hated him. Had she forgotten she hated him? But his fingers on her skin promised easy pleasure, such a welcome escape, and bargain magic was not so easily fooled ...

What was she *thinking*?

'All the pleasant predicaments in the world are of little use if I can't fathom the reason for your sudden interest,' she forced herself to say. 'Whatever game you're playing, I'm not—'

'So distrustful.' His breath brushed the side of her cheek, and she shivered. 'Is it such an unfathomable idea that I might simply find you attractive?'

The warmth below her navel bloomed hotter. *Tighter.* It would be so easy to believe him. So easy to give in to the silent temptation of those fingers playing over her back and shoulders, reminding her at every turn and twitch of the hard warmth pressing into her stomach.

But no – oh, no. She was better than that, falling for easy flattery.

'Attractive?' she jeered, lowering her voice to meet the hoarse, hushed sound of his. 'A stupid little human? You stoop to approve of me, lord fae?'

He stiffened below her. The caresses of his fingers faltered, then vanished as he abruptly released her and came up on his elbows, his breath irregular. Allie hastily rolled off him, fighting a nonsensical sense of disappointment as she huddled in his blankets and tried to ignore the phantom fingertips still skimming over her shoulders.

'You're not stupid.' His voice was his own again, but that smoothened edge of politeness was giving way to something rough, something chafing. 'I never said any such thing.'

'You told me I was incapable of handling myself without a bunch of fae looking out for—'

'I wasn't talking about *you*.' She'd never heard him so agitated. So *defensive.* 'Just humans in general, but that doesn't mean—'

All lingering arousal was gone at once. 'So what about Russ? What about Gil? Did any of them strike you as stupid cattle?'

'No, of course not, but—'

'And fae like Deiras, flaunting some stolen shirt without even wondering where it came from? Does that strike you as the most brilliant—'

'Allie,' he snapped, and the sound of her name on his lips shut her up. It was tinged with frustration. With *disappointment*. 'You're making a point about a few people while—'

'You've been convinced of the same nonsense for a millennium because of a few people!' Her voice grew louder. 'How is that any different?'

'Do you want to know, then? Do you want to know what happened?'

In the darkness, she could only make out his silhouette as he sat up, his shoulders tense, his wings quivering in the silver moonlight. Allie drew in a deep breath, suppressed the urge to shove away from him, away from that ancient fury in his voice. Reminded herself that she was safe.

'Tell me,' she said.

His shoulders loosened a fraction. 'Where do I start?'

'At whatever the beginning was.'

'The beginning,' he said sharply, 'was a little feud so common and so unremarkable that no historian ever bothered to give it a name. It did kill both my parents, though.'

Allie's breath caught. 'Oh.'

'This was before the Mother's Conquest. The three fae peoples weren't yet united.' His voice was a soft, deep rumble. 'Everyone was fighting everyone. It happened all the time.'

'How old were you?'

'About as old as you are now.'

Twenty-four – but twenty-four in fae years was something entirely different. He'd still been a child. No better prepared for an orphaned life than she had been when the fae took her to the Crimson Court.

'They found me and the other survivors,' he continued quietly. 'Achlys and Melinoë. Before they were High Ladies of anything. They were just trying to stop it – the bloodshed. So I helped.'

Before they were High Ladies, the sisters who sat on the Crimson Court's throne these days – before they became the Mother, through whatever ungodly magic allowed them to live as two souls in a single body. Allie wanted to ask if they'd already been so inhumanly pale back then, that empty colour of exhausted magic. If they'd already shown such a preference for bone thrones and useless violence. But perhaps this was not the moment.

'At some point,' Agenor said, and his voice sounded miles away now, 'they decided to ask the gods on the continent for help. Korok was living closest, so they asked him first. That turned into ...' He groaned. 'A somewhat messy romance. But he did help.'

'Between him and both of them.'

'Yes.'

'And then they decided they might as well become one person?'

'It was a little more complicated than that,' he said wryly. 'With a god by their side, they became a threat to the ruling powers. We had assassins showing up every other night. Sharing a body, one could be awake when the other slept, which reduced physical risks significantly. Also, the sister awake could draw from the powers of the sleeping one, which rather strengthened their magic.'

Allie swallowed. That magic, yes. Rivalled in strength only by her son's powers, and the Silent Death would be the last to harm his mother.

'Korok also ...' Agenor hesitated. 'He taught them some of his own powers. How to bind the magic of others, mostly – making it impossible for people to use their magic against her. Which was of great help during the Conquest.'

'What?' Bind magic – like human servants were bound to the island, made incapable of ever leaving the shores again after they arrived? 'Do you mean – did she do that to everyone she conquered? Limit their magic that way?'

'She bound me too. It's the safest way to—'

'You let her *bind* you? Are you *mad*?'

'Don't make it sound so dramatic,' he said sharply. 'I didn't give up my powers. I simply guaranteed I wouldn't use them to harm them, which I wouldn't do anyway – a damn small sacrifice to bring for the peace they were giving us. It was all perfectly well after the Conquest, do you understand? Korok built the courts, the feuds and fights had stopped, everyone was peaceful and prospering, and *then* ...' His voice had become a knife's edge. 'Then Korok's humans got jealous of the time he spent at the courts and killed their son. And everything was ruined again.'

'And so,' Allie said, hugging her knees against her chest, 'you decided all humans must be idiots?'

'Who in the world kills a god's son over some jealousy? We'd fought for centuries. We were finally safe. And then they—'

She interrupted his rising voice. 'Was it truly about jealousy, though?'

'What?'

'You've been telling me humans shouldn't be left on their own. Were they jealous, or was their community actively suffering in Korok's absence?'

He scoffed. 'Then they should have let him know, rather than—'

'And also,' Allie added, speaking faster now, 'are you very sure the son himself wasn't the problem and those humans weren't just trying to protect themselves? Wasn't he harassing them the way you fae seem to enjoy doing here?'

'What?' Another joyless laugh. 'Of course not. I've never had reason to assume—'

'Just like you didn't have reason to assume Deiras was violating women left and right?'

'Don't be ridiculous.' He was leaning closer now, his voice biting and cold. 'Someone would have told me if that was the case. I never heard—'

'Did you hear anyone vouch for his outstanding character, then?'

'He was beloved enough at the courts, if that's—'

'Yes,' Allie said, snorting, 'and the *fae* weren't the ones who killed them, were they?'

'You're just spouting theories now,' he snapped. 'Did you ask the humans of those days what in hell had gotten into them?'

'Did you?' she retorted.

The silence told her all she needed to know – heavy, panting silence. The air between them throbbed with frustration. She was leaning forward, Allie realised, hands clenched in his blankets. His face – it was far closer than it had been a moment ago. Close enough to distinguish the lines of his fury, his tight lips, his heaving chest.

'Did you?' she repeated, softer now.

'I ...' He parted his lips twice, thrice, before the rest of the sentence followed. 'I didn't.'

'So who's making assumptions, then?'

His heavy breathing was her only answer. She saw him look away in the darkness, shoulders tensing and releasing in an irregular, twitching rhythm. They key around his neck gleamed in the moonlight, and for a moment she was tempted to try again, see if he would notice through the turmoil of his thoughts. But it would distract. Weaken her point. And this argument – it may be more important than winning any bet in the world.

'Agenor,' she said quietly.

No title. He didn't seem to notice. The gleam in his eyes was a plea for mercy as he looked up to meet her gaze, his pupils unnaturally large in the darkness.

'What are you doing to me, little thief?'

His voice was a hoarse, harrowed whisper. A shiver trailed through her.

'I'm not doing—'

He moved so fast she never even saw him coming. A blink and his hand had locked around her wrist, yanking her closer, into an embrace of limbs and wings and blankets. Allie shrieked, grasping for freedom and finding only his naked body under her fingertips. Rock hard muscle and feverish skin and those powerful arms pulling her into his lap, trembling with fury or desire or something else entirely.

'Let me *go*!'

'I wish I could.' A hoarse growl, so close to her face, sounding nothing like the sophisticated fae lord of mere minutes ago. 'I wish you weren't ensnaring me the way you do, I wish you weren't so gods-damned clever and so gods-damned *complicated*—'

'Agenor—'

'Why did you write those letters?' he hissed. His hands were roving over her back, her hips, with desperate, claiming touches. His muscular thighs strained below her bottom, promising abandon. At once the arousal was back, burning and throbbing, as if he'd never let go of her. It took all she had not to moan, not to wilt in his arms – not to wonder what he would feel like inside her. 'Were you just trying to spite me? To mock me?'

'Why else would I have—'

'Because you enjoyed them. Did you, Allie?'

'I ...' She couldn't think, enveloped in his scent. Could only feel his strong hands on her hips, her thighs, clawing into the little softness the Rustvale diet left on her. Fiery throbs of want burned through her, of *need*. 'I – I don't—'

'Do you hate me?' His fingertips moved up the inside of her thigh, his other hand still locking her in his lap. Still no burning bargain mark. Because she wanted this. Because she couldn't help but revel in every forbidden caress, every tempting whisper. 'Be honest with me, little thief. Do you really loathe me as much as you're telling me you do?'

No. Yes. Maybe. Was this hate, this intoxicating feeling burning bright enough to wipe the sense from her mind? Somehow her fury only stirred up the flames, making her feel like punching him and kissing him both at once. She didn't want to think about those letters, didn't want to admit how much she'd enjoyed them. She wanted to throw him back into the blankets. Wanted to tear this damned dress off her. Wanted to ride him until he lost his mind with pleasure and begged for release, power and age be damned – was that hate?

'Why do you even care?' she managed between struggling breaths. 'Do you want every human at the court to fawn over you now?'

He wrapped his fingers around her chin and pulled her closer, close enough for his breath to warm her lips. 'Do I want every human at the court to be mine?'

His.

What?

She stiffened in his hold. No. She was nobody's property. She was nobody's prize. *His* – was that what this was all about, then? An attempt to secure his hold on her? To seduce every hint of revolt back into line?

She was not going to change her mind about him if she was to be a *triumph*.

'Allie ...' he breathed.

'Get off me.' She blurted out the words like a stumbling drunk and scrambled back in the blankets, away from him, away from his claiming fingers. 'And don't ever *think* those words again. Don't ever—'

Too late did he lurch forward to stop her, biting out a curse as the bargain flared to hold him back. '*Allie.*'

Her feet hit the floor. She dashed back, staggering blindly through the darkness, towards the door. He flicked out his wings, then grabbed for his wrist again with another barely suppressed curse.

'Please,' he ground out. 'Allie – what did I say? What did I ...'

It was worse to hear him beg. She shouldn't be the one to feel guilty. She wasn't the one claiming every pretty little diversion as her own like this court claimed its humans as possessions ...

'And honestly,' she heard herself say, her voice a shard of glass, 'you're very easy to hate indeed, Lord Agenor.'

And she ran.

CHAPTER 7

He was an idiot.

A stumbling, dull-minded fool, and he wasn't even fully sure why.

Agenor lay in the smothering darkness of his room, listening to his own ragged breathing, and tried to make sense of the past five minutes, the whirlwind of memories and impressions Allie had left behind as she slammed the door behind her slender back. They tangled into an agonising knot in his chest, frustration and fascination and a blinding arousal that left him hard as steel even with her last words still echoing in his mind.

Very easy to hate.

He should have kept his hands off her. Shouldn't have given in to that unexpected temptation of waking with her small body so close, her hands roaming over his skin – should have been the wiser one despite her body moulding to his, despite the bargain mark's silence. What in the world had gotten into him? She was pretty enough, yes, but since when did he lose his mind over a pretty face?

And then there was everything she'd said, questions no one had ever asked him ... outrageous, ludicrous questions – so why did they only make him want her more?

He had allowed his confusion and frustration to take over. Had let himself go like some infatuated youth, begging for answers and affection – admitting how badly, how *desperately*, he wanted her close. And that ...

Very easy to hate.

He muttered a curse into the darkness. Idiot.

It was time to put an end to this madness. She wanted nothing to do with him – that much was clear. She'd used him as a tool to protect her sister and written her letters to that effect – a cold, calculated act – and he should know better than to look for anything else behind her words. He had no reason to linger on the thought of her. It couldn't take him *that* long to fulfil the task she'd given him, and if he was lucky, she'd simply avoid him from now on; soon this would all be a thing of the past, and life would return to its old state of blissful, thoughtless routine ...

Dread clenched his stomach, so violently he almost gagged.

Back to the days droning on, endless hour after endless hour. Back to solving petty squabbles and playing his part in the Mother's theatrics. Back to the bland, boring grind of insufferable peace ...

Who do you think is living in peace, exactly?

Perhaps he wasn't, either.

He squeezed his eyes shut, impressions crowding him from the shadows of his mind. The triumphant tone of her voice as she declared him oblivious, an arrogant bastard. The way she'd glared at him in that shoddy hut, how her gaze had softened for a single, short moment. Her quick fingers and her bright blue eyes, the weight of her lithe body over his, and the way she unwillingly softened in his hold.

She was movement in a world of stillness. She was a song breaking that deep, lethal silence of his existence. Even bewildered and frustrated, he felt *alive* for the first time in decades – like perhaps his time wasn't over yet.

And he wanted her so much he could taste it.

He drew in a deep, shuddering breath and tried to think. Tried to make sense of what he'd said and done. *Mine.* Too fast, too blunt, too reckless – or was there something else he was missing? He knew not the faintest thing about human romance. He'd never bothered enough to find out how they worked or lived or loved.

Another groan escaped him. Idiot.

She should be here now, in his bed, in his arms. The image came to him far too easily. His hands peeling that dress off her, that plain servant's frock no one should ever have forced her to wear. Her naked body emerging in the moonlight, pale skin and small breasts and pebbling nipples pleading for his attention – her voice moaning his name as he caressed her hips, her thighs. Until she'd beg for him to take her, wet and willing beneath him. Until he'd spread her legs and claim her, his little thief, his living miracle …

He almost moaned as he wrapped his fingers around his pulsing erection and began to stroke, imagining that it was her warm tightness around him, that it was her panting breath he heard. Let him be mad, then. Let him lose his mind. Let him run after a human woman like a lover under a spell – because no amount of senseless, infatuated insanity could be worse than the tedious normalcy he left behind.

He came in a roar of agony, milking himself until every last drop of madness was spilled. Even then, his hunger for her wouldn't go. He lay awake for hours, tossing and turning and craving the touch of those delicate fingers, until he finally slept and dreamt of accusing blue eyes and a voice like sweet hoarfrost.

For the first time since the War, he woke well before sunrise, feeling battered and floundering, and yet oddly resolved at the same time.

It had been a long time since he'd last planned any battle or military campaign; his days as the empire's main strategist had been over since the defeat of the human army and their magical allies. But he felt a spark of that old rush return to him as he lit the fire for the snakes and sank down at his desk with Basilisk wrapped cosily around his wrist – of that slow, methodical process. He had his goals. He had his forces and assets. He had his opponent – a small, alluring, and utterly unpredictable opponent.

And that he somehow had to work with.

He sat at his desk until the sun rose, his attempts at meticulous thinking disrupted by fits of frustration and overwhelming urges to throw all caution to the hounds and just fly to Rustvale to demand an explanation from her. He held back. Confirming all her worst opinions of him wouldn't win him anything.

Instead, when he finally brought himself to move, he made for the adjacent wing of the palace and found Leander in his rooms. Rustvale's supervisor seemed to have spent the night in the company of two scarcely dressed fae girls, who vanished without objection when Agenor kindly suggested they might prefer not to witness this conversation.

It took no more than half an hour to make his point, perhaps a little more convincingly than necessary. All he needed was a made-up story of a fainting servant, a mention of Leander's food policies, and a few pleasant reminders of the various fates that had befallen others who wasted the Mother's money and resources through their incapable management. By the time Agenor left the other male alone again, Leander had turned a worrying shade of green and got nothing but muttered, incoherent apologies over his lips.

A satisfying result – but not enough. It was only Rustvale. There were seventeen human villages on the island, and somehow he suspected Allie wouldn't be impressed if he ignored the other sixteen entirely. So he made a round of visits to the different supervisors over the course of the morning, pulled their administration records from their shelves, and made some pointed comments about their lack of accountability, reliability, and basic decency.

He should have kept an eye on the fools, indeed. Why had no one else ever bothered to tell him about the havoc they were wreaking among the human population of the court?

And if no one had ever told him about this problem, how many others had he missed?

Her voice was a constant presence in the back of his mind, commenting on every step he took, every word he spoke. *Oblivious.* Until mere days ago, she'd thought he knew. Now she believed he hadn't cared enough to know, and that was even worse ...

Because it might be true.

But he *wanted* to care. He *wanted* to know. He hadn't survived this entire damn war to become the next violent evil in the world, the very same thing he'd started out to fight. And if that was what doing his job and following his duty had made him, he needed someone to tell him how to make it right.

He needed *her* to tell him.

He'd been determined to wait – to give her time until his mark reminded him of last night's promise to come by again. But he found himself making for Rustvale mere minutes after the day servants' hours had ended, unable to stay away, unable to stand the tedious and ever familiar movements of the court a moment longer. Even cold blue eyes welcoming him would be preferable to this mess of not knowing, of realising something was happening out of his sight, and having no idea how to catch even the faintest glimpse of it.

Allie's door was still locked when he arrived; his knocking went unanswered. Right. She had to make the walk back home on foot, of course.

He should have thought about that complication. Nothing about humans came instinctively to him; he had lived with gods, visited alves and nymphs and phoenixes, but met the humans of the archipelago mostly on the battlefield. They'd never seemed interesting enough to justify further attention.

Drawing conclusions from just a few examples.

He had, hadn't he? How many Allies had he missed over the century?

There had to be others in the village, children and the neighbour with his healing ankle, but Agenor didn't see a single living soul as he leaned against the black brick wall and waited, his resolve weakening with every minute passing by. Russ arrived at the other side of the main street, sent him a heartfelt scowl, but disappeared into another house before Agenor could explain himself. Perhaps that was better. He still wasn't entirely sure how to justify his presence even to the woman who'd requested it, let alone to anyone else.

Half an hour waiting for her, and yet he wasn't prepared when she finally emerged between the houses, her face cold and the look in her eyes nothing short of murderous.

Perhaps it was that lethal glare that made the breath hitch in his lungs for a moment. More likely it was the *realness* of her, his feverish dreams appearing in the flesh before him – that slender body he'd held in his arms, that smart mouth he kept thinking of for all the wrong reasons. Even the look in her eyes was a reassurance. Still furious, yes, but it seemed an entirely different kind of furious compared to the glares she'd given him yesterday. Then she'd hated him for being fae and powerful. Today she hated him for being *him*.

At least the night hadn't left her unaffected, then.

She stalked up to him with her chin held high and her back stiff like armour. Making admirable efforts to look nothing like the sensual creature melting in his arms last night – but he caught her glances at his hands, his torso, and couldn't help another small sting of grim satisfaction. They would see about that indifference later.

First he had some questions to ask.

'Well,' she briskly said as she approached him within hearing distance. Such a cold, level voice. As if she'd never seen him naked. As if she'd never lingered against him just a little too long, softened under his caresses. 'It's you again. Afraid the bargain would kill you if you showed up a minute too late, Lord Protector?'

He closed his eyes for a fraction of a moment. 'Just Agenor will do.'

She'd called him by his name in the moonlit darkness, in that hushed, gentle tone. Perhaps the memory returned to her equally easily; her voice was even colder as she said, 'I thought you made a point of me showing fitting respect to my *hosts* on this island.'

For fuck's sake. Whatever he'd said last night – it had been very, very wrong.

'Allie—'

She interrupted him as she pulled a rusty key from the pocket of her apron, turning away from him to open the door. 'We suddenly had a load of food delivered this morning.'

There was no gratefulness in her words. All Agenor could make out was thick, heavy suspicion.

'I talked with Leander,' he said.

'I concluded as much, yes.' She stepped inside without looking back and didn't hold the door for him; if not for his battlefield reflexes, it might have knocked him in the face for all of Rustvale to see. 'Why?'

Agenor blinked, hesitating in the doorway as she stomped through the front room. It was quite miraculous how much noise that delicate body could make.

'I promised I would,' he said. 'It seemed the decent thing to do.'

She impatiently clucked her tongue but turned towards him, yanking hairpins from her thick brown locks. 'Tell me you won't help me.'

'That I – what?'

'That you won't help me.' An impatient gesture. 'If it pleases you to do so, of course, Lord Agenor.'

It was the obvious contempt in her voice he couldn't stand. Anger – he probably deserved that much. Suspicion – he understood that, too. But that biting mockery that laced the syllables of his name and title ... It stung. Deep.

'I suppose ...' He cleared his throat. 'I won't help you, if you—'

A flare of pain interrupted him. He swallowed his words, barely suppressing a curse as the fire burst through his wrist and lingered there, burning below the bargain mark like embers glowing just beneath his skin.

At the dining table, Allie smiled for the first time – a grim, wolfish smile.

'Just as I thought.'

'What was the use of that?' Agenor managed, rubbing his wrist. 'You knew that would—'

'—hurt. Yes.' She turned away again, untangling the ribbons of her apron as she spoke. 'If you were just trying to be a decent person from the bottom of your heart, I'm pretty sure that would count as selfless kindness. In which case you'd be absolved from your obligation to help me now. Since you don't seem to be, we'll have to conclude you have underlying motives for your unusual show of helpfulness. So.' She threw the apron onto the bed in the backroom, then sent him a narrow-eyed glance. 'What are they?'

For the bloody gods' sake. So much for his attempts to be halfway prepared for this confrontation. His talk with Leander should have been an argument in favour of his good intentions, a proof of his word – and somehow that unpredictable mind of hers had turned it into yet another secret, yet another lie to tell.

He knew his underlying motives. He wanted her to call him by his name again. Wanted her to speak with him again. Wanted her to join him in his bed again. Somehow, he didn't think any of that would further his case.

'Trying to impress me?' she said sharply before he could come up with anything better to say. By the way she wrinkled her nose at him, denying would be useless.

'Well ...' Agenor started, feeling like a fumbling school boy.

She scoffed. 'Oh, spare me your excuses. Is this a new way to get me back in line? If you can't convince me or intimidate me, you'll just charm your way in?'

'Back in line? What makes you think I'd—'

'Do you think I didn't *hear* you last night?' she snapped, stalking to the kitchen corner and snatching the kettle from a shelf with such violence he thought she'd throw it at him. 'If you want to be secretive, try not to let your dick speak for you next time, Lord Agenor.'

The body part in question reacted a little too enthusiastically to her mention of it. If she'd been looking his way, she might have seen him wince.

'Allie.' He was balancing on a very thin edge, now. He'd made one mistake – he might be able to recover from that. A second time, and she may well fling a kitchen knife at his face. Which would be daunting enough if he'd known what exactly he'd said wrong yesterday, and was altogether terrifying if he had no idea what words he should avoid now. 'What is the problem, exactly? That I consider you attractive?'

'The problem is I consider you an idiot,' she flung back, slamming the kettle onto the stove. 'I don't give a damn what you think of me, I don't care that you're trying to screw me – but what in hell made you think I'd be happy to play your possession?'

Agenor stared at her. She scowled back, lips trembling with a fury she only barely held back.

His possession.

Mine.

Oh, gods and demons.

'I ...' He opened his mouth, closed it again, uttered a bewildered laugh. 'No. No, wait. That's not what I—'

'And a coward too,' she interrupted, planting her fists on her hips. 'Of course it's never what you meant. Spin me a story, then, Lord Agenor. How else should I interpret your claims – as a marriage proposal?'

Not the moment to point out fae didn't even practice marriage. He swallowed and weakly said, 'You think I'm trying to constrain you.'

'Has any fae ever wanted anything else from me?'

Oh, gods and demons. They took her from home. Bound her to this island. Starved her and silenced her. Agenor closed his eyes as the understanding seeped into his mind, with a heavy feeling of shame. An idiot, indeed. He could have known, should have known.

As with *everything*.

'I see,' he whispered, averting his eyes as he sank down in the nearest chair at the dinner table. 'I'm sorry.'

Deafening silence answered him.

When he looked up, she still stood in the same spot by the stove, her blue eyes sparking with confusion. In the dusky light of this small house, she looked barely real – a pale, beautiful dream of a woman, about to vanish into nothingness if he spoke one more poorly chosen word.

'What?' she said.

'That's not what I intended to say. Not what I intend to do.' He pressed his lips together. 'But the wording was ill-considered indeed.'

Her face was a mask of cautious suspicion, but she didn't call him a fool again and still didn't reach for the kitchen knives. Agenor looked away, aiming his gaze at the bright blue sky behind the single small window. He was exhausted, all of a sudden – tired of wondering and worrying, of running after the facts and arriving nowhere at all. Of trying too hard and lying.

She'd defeated him, and she may not even know it. He didn't care about winning any damn bet anymore. How could he work to prove something he wasn't sure he still believed himself? All he wanted now was to understand.

To understand – and to be understood.

'I have no desire to constrain you,' he muttered. 'None at all. Honestly, the opposite.'

He heard the rustle of her dress, saw her fold her arms in the edges of his sight. 'You want me to grab a torch and set this entire cursed place on fire? Because truth be told, that's the first thing I would do if no one were holding me back.'

Agenor couldn't help the twitch at the corners of his mouth. 'Please spare my tower. I'd hate for that perfectly organised wardrobe to burn.'

'You think I'm *joking*?'

'I don't think you're joking at all. I just – I didn't expect you to say that.'

'Does that make it funny?' she said sharply.

'No. Just ...' He hesitated. 'Just a relief.'

'*Relief*,' she repeated, sounding like she still expected him to be joking. 'For what, exactly?'

'Age. Boredom. Slow decay.'

She stayed silent now, and he needed a moment to gather his courage.

'I've lived for ... a long time,' he said quietly, 'such a very long time, and if I'm honest, the years are blurring for me. The *decades* are blurring for me. It's the same things over and over and over again, same stupid fights, same stupid mistakes, same stupid conversations, and I stopped caring about all of it. I've barely known why I still bother to get out of bed in the mornings for a century. If I hadn't felt obliged to, I don't think I would have.'

He didn't hear her move at the stove – didn't even hear her breathe.

'I'm stale and rusted and as good as dead already,' he managed. Words he'd never dared to speak to any living soul. Words he'd barely even dared to *think*. 'And then you shoved that bloody letter into my wardrobe, and that was ... new. So very new and so very surprising. Like you pulled my brain straight from its grave.'

'Agenor—'

'And you don't stop,' he said, looking up with a brusque, uncontrolled movement. She still stood at the stove, staring blankly at him. 'Everything you say – every *single* thing you say – turns my mind inside out all over again, do you realise that? I thought I'd seen it all, and now you're telling me the world I thought I knew never even existed. You – you ...'

She just blinked.

'You change everything,' he whispered. 'And I can't stop revelling in it – can't stop craving it. I can't bear the thought of going back again. So yes, I want you. Desperately. But not constrained – never constrained. Surprise me. Scandalise me. But for the love of the gods, please don't ever surrender to me.'

A plea.

It hung in the air between them like a cobweb, fragile and vulnerable. The Lord Protector of the Crimson Court, reduced to pleading. But Allie's blue eyes had widened, the lines around her mouth softened, as if he were a stranger at her table, a male reborn before her very eyes.

Her lips parted. Her fingers clenched white around her upper arms, as if she had to physically stop herself from reaching out to him.

'Oh,' she whispered.

'So.' His voice had gone hoarse. He didn't dare to speak louder in the quiet, small confinement of this room – as if he'd startle her like some frightened deer. 'Feel free to throw me out. But don't do it because you think I—'

'I'm not throwing you out.'

The words came out so hard, so brusquely, that he found himself flinching at their impact. At the stove, Allie froze with him for a moment, then abruptly turned away, hands suddenly everywhere but by her side. Gathering herbs for tea. Taking mugs off their shelf. Everything – *anything* – to not look him in the eye again.

'Allie ...' he started.

'I can't tell what you expect me to do now,' she interrupted, fingers fidgeting with the potholder. 'Am I supposed to feel honoured? Frightened? Sympathetic?'

'I've stopped supposing anything where you're concerned.'

'Well.' She pressed her lips together as she poured two mugs of tea, her eyes focused on the whirling steam. 'In that case, I hope you won't feel too disenchanted when I tell you you're spouting utter nonsense, Lord Agenor.'

Not what he'd expected. He had to give her that.

'What do you—'

'You're making me into something unique, aren't you?' she said, turning around with quick, nymphic movements. Even as she handed him his tea and sank down in the chair opposite his, she didn't look him in the eyes. 'As if I'm some mythical changer of worlds, some heroic defier of expectations. That's horseshit. There are five more humans like me in every dozen you look at.'

Agenor managed something like a chuckle. 'I've never noticed them.'

She snorted. 'Let me ask the usual question.'

'Did I look for them?'

'Mm-hmm.'

He groaned. 'Not very thoroughly, I presume.'

'Thought so.' Somehow there was no smugness in those words. 'That's the only difference. I've been pushing it right under your nose, and they haven't. You couldn't obliviously gloss over me even if you tried.' A chuckle. 'Which is your problem, isn't it? You only ever see what you expect to see. No wonder you're never surprised.'

Agenor stared at her. She still kept her eyes focused on her mug, even as she parted her lips in hesitation, closed them, and parted them again.

'Stay for dinner,' she said.

'Stay ... What?'

'For dinner.' She shrugged, a wry smile playing around her mouth. 'We have enough food to feed an extra mouth, by some happy coincidence.'

'Yes, but—'

'It's not an *invitation*, Agenor,' she said and finally met his eyes to scowl at him. A different kind of scowl. Almost ... sympathetic? 'It's a challenge. We have neighbours coming over tonight. So stay and eat. And for once in your life, just try to *see*.'

CHAPTER 8

This evening was, by far, the strangest of Allie's life.

There was food – such an abundance of food. Russ was smiling. Inga was singing. Her heart was a pounding, fluttering mess in her chest, and the Lord Protector of the Crimson Court was sitting at her dinner table, holding polite conversations with her fellow villagers as he ate onion soup and somehow found it within himself to look like he enjoyed it.

Impossible. But every time she pinched herself, the scene was still there.

She'd told Gil and Marette that he was here to investigate Leander's mismanagement of the Rustvale community, because that sounded better than whatever the full truth was. A decent lie – except that she'd underestimated the attraction of a chance to complain. Soon enough, several other neighbours had come knocking on the door under the guise of surprise visits that had nothing at all to do with the fae male sitting in her living room. Their shows of astonishment were unconvincing, and their apologies all too flimsy, but Allie didn't have the heart to complain. More visitors, after all, meant there was more for Agenor to see.

And so she found herself in a crowded room with sixteen other villagers and her fae guest and listened to the stories, the jokes, the memories. Tragic deaths and ridiculous rules. Wistful laments of homes left behind and quiet accusations of the fae taking them. Agenor never flinched, rarely even blinked – but she caught his gaze wandering in her direction every other minute, and dared to hope that unaffected mask was not a matter of indifference.

I thought I'd seen it all, and now you're telling me the world I thought I knew never even existed.

She couldn't stop seeing that look in his eyes. That lost, brittle shadow, grasping for any relief, any reassurance. She couldn't stop hearing the hoarse despair in his voice, even through his composed conversations on court protocols and broken laws. Had she misjudged him? Was she supposed to *trust* him now, the male who'd fought the Mother's battles for her and shaped the empire that had destroyed so many lives?

She shouldn't. Rationally, she knew that much. But then there was her heart, twisting stubbornly from her mind's grasp ...

And perhaps that was the strangest part of all – the tingle of *sympathy* that fluttered through her chest every time their gazes met for the shortest of moments.

Or at least, she hoped it was just sympathy.

I want you. Desperately.

The tingle returned in entirely different places as his hoarse, raw voice echoed in her ears. She swallowed, fighting the heat flushing her cheeks. That, too, didn't make sense. She was too sensible for desperate longing, too practical for star-crossed romance. But even a sensible mind wasn't immune to the ravenous glances of inhumanly gorgeous fae lords, it turned out, and the memory of his words mingled effortlessly with the memory of last night's madness, his fingers clawing into her flesh, his hard body beneath her—

For the bloody gods' sake. She was sitting in one room with half the village and her husband. Not the moment to lose control of herself.

So she stayed in the kitchen, distributed soup and bread, and listened as the conversations slowly turned away from fae crimes and towards the current affairs of Rustvale. More and more small circles of visitors forgot to speak in Faerie and turned to the village dialect instead, that strange mish-mash of seven different human languages made to live together. Agenor still didn't make any move to leave. He sat quietly in his corner, his green-golden eyes moving from Rinald's passionate argument on vampire biology to Marette's description of her newest composition.

Listening.

It hit Allie a moment too late – that he *knew* the language.

Oh, hell. What had she said to Russ, yesterday? Nothing too flattering, she was sure of that – but still his eyes wouldn't let go of her for longer than a minute, returning to her quiet corner again and again as if he'd wither and die if he let her out of sight for a heartbeat too long.

She tried not to look back. Tried not to blush. Tried to figure out what to feel about the unexpected admiration of a fae lord centuries her senior, and failed hopelessly at all her attempts.

Finally, the visitors began to leave, reminded of the time and tomorrow's early work hours. Russ went last – and only after she had reassured him five times – to slip into Farran's bedroom as usual. Inga vanished to the backroom with a timid goodnight and a last cautious look at Agenor's winged figure at the table.

He hadn't spoken for at least an hour, but he did wish Inga a good night. Allie caught a glimpse of burning cheeks and bulging eyes as her sister shut the door behind her.

Then it was just the two of them, in a room that hadn't been so empty for hours and hadn't felt so small yet.

She stared at his feet – at the hem of her work dress – at the dirty dishes piled up in the sink – anywhere, really, but at his face or the hands that had touched her so frantically last night. Dirty plates wouldn't make her blush. Dirty plates wouldn't make her imagine the movements of his lips ... *I want you. Desperately.*

A blush rose on her face anyway. Damn it.

She expected a smug remark or, at the very least, one of those pleasant, perfectly polite observations. But when he finally cleared his throat, all he said was, 'Would you fancy a walk?'

Allie jerked up her head, meeting his gaze despite all her determined resolutions to do no such thing. A smoulder was burning in the depth of his eyes – an unnervingly patient smoulder.

It would have been so much easier if he'd just lunged at her and torn her dress off. At least she'd have remembered to hate him that way. Now, out and alone with him in the dark ...

'The mountains aren't safe at night,' she said in an unthinking reflex, and he pulled up an eyebrow, a glimpse of humour returning to his tired face.

'Ah, yes. Imagine we'd run into some vagabond with dastardly intentions.'

Her cheeks turned even hotter. Oh. He was still the Lord Protector, a male powerful enough to survive since the age of the gods. Unless they walked into the Mother or her son themselves, she would be safer than in her own bed.

She swallowed. Safe, yes – except, perhaps, from the ridiculous urges of her own body.

'I'm not dragging you out,' he added, observing her far too closely. She could feel his eyes on her even as she stubbornly stared at the wall behind him – could feel his gaze travel where his hands had been. 'But I'd be grateful if you could answer a few questions, and I don't want to keep Inga awake.'

Oh, damn him. Did he have to be *considerate* about this? She could hardly tell him to figure out his own answers and send him back to the court – not if a single day of his goodwill had saved them all from starving, and there were so many more problems to solve.

'Fine,' she said, and wished her voice sounded a little steadier. 'Let's take a walk. But if any dastardly vagabond puts a hand on me, you'll be in trouble.'

His grin was nothing if not dastardly. 'I didn't live this long by looking for trouble. You'll be fine.'

It sounded like a bad idea – a *terribly* bad idea, really. But he made no move to touch her, didn't even offer her his arm as they stepped into the quiet darkness of the night and took the nearest path between the rugged mountain slopes. By the light of the waxing moon, Allie saw just enough not to step into any pits or on sharp pebbles. Next to her, Agenor sauntered along as if they were walking around in the bright light of day.

Five minutes went by before he finally spoke, his voice low in the rustling darkness. 'So, were these the dozen humans among which I was supposed to find five others like you?'

Thank the merciful gods that it was dark enough to hide any more blushing. Yes. Yes, they were, and it would have been better if he'd just agreed she was nothing exceptional after all. And yet, even the suggestion that he regarded her as more than just the next human – it did some unnerving, fluttery things to her stomach.

Allie cleared her throat and managed a reasonably composed, 'Did you look for them?'

'I did.' His voice was quieter now. 'I certainly did.'

Again they were silent for a moment. On both sides of this narrow path, the mountains towered over them, the rough limestone covered in moss and succulents. The air was fresher at night, without the sweaty heat of the sun to weigh it down; every breath made Allie feel lighter and freer and farther away from home.

Farther away from Inga's quiet, concerned questions. Farther away from Russ's grumbling and the neighbours' nosy gossip.

She was taking an evening walk with the Mother's Lord Protector. And he wanted her.

Desperately.

Again her stomach made some utterly unnecessary jumps.

'That red-haired fellow – Rinald?' He spoke slowly, thoughtfully. 'He seems unusually fascinated by vampires.'

'Oh,' Allie said, and managed a laugh. 'Yes. He's court-born, and your people captured some vampire rebel when he was five years old or so. He's been obsessed ever since. Has rather revolutionary opinions on the whole debate of living dead versus dead-like living, from what I know about the matter.'

'Where does he find the literature?'

'Library.' She threw him a side glance. 'He works as a copyist.'

Agenor muttered a curse. 'Knew I'd seen his face before. I had no idea.'

'Of course you didn't,' she said dryly.

He gave her a pained look. 'How am I supposed to know a simple copyist is—'

'—spending his life doing more than working, eating, and sleeping?'

He came to an abrupt halt, sucked in a breath, then clearly thought better of it before the words could come out. Allie turned so she could watch him wrestle – watch the thoughts wash over his face, annoyance and confusion and, finally, a heavy, resigned acceptance.

He looked away. 'Are you going to kill me if I tell you I never really thought of humans doing anything but working and – well, eating and sleeping, I suppose?"

She snorted. 'Like cattle trotting back into the stables at the end of the day.'

'If you're going to put it like that,' he said with a pained grimace, 'I prefer murder.'

'Oh, no. I can't kill you. I'd have to find another fae lord to listen to my rambling and see sense.' She threw him a wry grin. 'You're too valuable to me to die now, Lord Agenor. I need you to fix the world for me before I quietly stab you to death with a kitchen knife.'

He gave a joyless chuckle. 'And that is all?'

'What?'

'That's your only reason not to kill me?'

'What else did you expect?' Allie said, pushing away yet another sting of misplaced sympathy. She had no use for that feeling. She had no use for *any* feelings where this male was concerned. He wasn't helping her from the goodness of his heart – she had to remember that – he was helping her to fix his own dreary life, to fulfil his own desires. Hell, he still hadn't managed to break the bargain and do a single thing without selfish intentions. So why would she feel like she owed him any affection – like she owed him *anything*?

'You didn't throw me out,' he said quietly. 'You invited me for dinner. You are here now while you could be sleeping soundly in your bed. All because you can't wait to see me die a violent death?'

'It's just politics.' Why did her words come out on such a ridiculous whisper, as if even her vocal chords resisted the truth? 'Everything I do is. Don't look for more.'

'Everything?' he repeated, tilting his head a fraction but keeping his eyes on her. 'Not just running off with fae lords' possessions?'

Breathing became an effort under his gaze. So did standing still and meeting his eyes. Every fibre of her body burned to move, to get away from that intent scrutinising look – or perhaps to do the opposite.

Not just stealing his shirts. Not just inviting him for dinner. *Everything.*

He didn't move, and yet, with her gaze locked on those almond-shaped eyes, it seemed he was advancing on her. Coming too close. Digging too deep. Slipping behind that safe shield of cold ire and distant indifference she kept between herself and the world of the fae, that shield that had kept her from shattering since the day the bastards had dragged her onto their tribute ships and bound her to the island that would one day be the death of her.

'I see,' he added slowly, softly. 'Like managing a host of neighbours. Like marrying a man who—'

'Not a *word* about Russ.' She jerked a step back, biting out a laugh. 'You have no idea what he did for us, no idea what ... Look, when Resa found Inga and took her in, no one wanted shit to do with her for housing a little faeling. And when she died ...' Allie swallowed. 'I'd prepared for years. People owed us enough to keep their hands off Inga – for that moment. But if Russ hadn't stood up for us, I don't know how long that would have lasted. So take that jealousy and stick it up somewhere else, because—'

'I'm not *jealous*.' He let out a befuddled laugh. 'Gods and demons, you're determined to think the worst of me, aren't you?'

'Russ says you've been giving him unhappy looks.'

'Not intentionally,' he said hoarsely. 'And even if you'd been sleeping in his bed ... Allow me to just be glad *someone's* keeping an eye on you, will you?'

Her insides stirred again. Sharp scepticism was all she had to keep that desperate flutter at bay, her only way to keep the shield where it ought to be. 'How *very* magnanimous, Lord Protector.'

Even in the moonlit darkness, she saw the shadow draw over his face, like a door slamming shut – a door she'd slammed shut herself. 'I'm trying to be *decent*. Is that something to be ashamed of now?'

'It's hardly a strike in your favour if you're only being decent to impress me,' Allie said and forced herself to scoff. 'Or do we need to test how the bargain is faring again?'

'Oh, there's no need to,' he said sharply. 'I'll gladly confirm I'm trying to impress you. What else would you have me do? Turn my back on you and continue my past stupidities? Nod along while you call me a possessive bastard and a fool and never even try to change your mind?'

Her heart was beating in the tips of her fingers. 'And what do you want me to do, then? Ignore that you could have spared my people years and years of suffering if you'd just opened your eyes a little earlier?'

'I want you to stop pretending I repel you,' he snapped. He *was* moving, now – advancing on her ever so slowly, closing the six feet of distance between them. She should have stepped back but didn't – couldn't. 'Be furious all you want – I won't pretend I don't deserve it – but do you really think I failed to notice how far from repelled you were by finding yourself stuck in my bed a few hours ago?'

'A matter of biology,' Allie managed, her face so hot she wondered if he'd feel it burning. Her feet still wouldn't move. Wouldn't carry her away from his towering figure, the menacing spread of his flaring wings. *Far from repelled.* The touch of his hands ... She could still feel it, and disgust was the last thing the memory evoked in her. 'It's been a while since I found myself in anyone's bed. Don't take it personally.'

'And if I don't?' His voice was a low, luring siren's call. Too close. Far too close. 'If it's just a matter of biology indeed – then what?'

'Then ...'

Her words drifted off. Floated from her grasp like wisps of morning mist. Barely a foot of empty air remained between them. He was close enough to drag her into his arms. Close enough for her to stretch out her hands and feel the hard ridges of his abdomen under her fingertips again, that trail of hair below his navel, the heat of his skin.

The night cold had become a sweaty fever, the silent mountains a dangerous promise of secrecy.

'Then, Allie?' he muttered.

A shiver ran through her. She dragged a laugh over her lips – a pathetic, unconvincing thing. 'Then nothing.'

If only he wasn't so close. If only he wasn't so insufferably gorgeous – that inhuman beauty radiating from every inch of golden skin, every line of perfectly sculpted muscle. She shook her head, as if that would convince her body to let go of the burning heat rising between her thighs.

'And either way,' she whispered, a last desperate attempt to convince herself, 'you might not even be worth the trouble. Fae are selfish lovers, from all I've heard.'

'I thought I was trying to impress you.' His chuckle brushed over her cheeks as he leaned over, bringing his lips inches away from her ear. 'Do you really believe I'd cease my efforts so easily, little thief?'

'I'd think you'd cease your efforts as soon as you got what you wanted,' she breathed.

'Do I give the impression a single quick tumble is all I want?'

There was a hoarseness to his voice, a shimmer of barely restrained longing, like a wild animal tearing at its chains. Her knees went weak. Too close – he was too close, the warmth of his body enveloping her, the scent of firewood and leather, the whisper of his breath against her cheek. She had to close her eyes. She had to step back and tell him to go bother someone else with his flattery and desires. But her gaze wouldn't move away from the slender bulges of the muscles below his shirt, the promise of smooth skin at his collar, and ...

The key.

Dangling safely against his muscular chest, where he would notice any attempt to steal it.

Her breath caught in her throat. No chance to win that task – not if she played fair. But if he were to be just a little distracted ...

That was different, wasn't it?

There would be nothing personal about it that way. Nothing remotely sympathetic. Just politics, as always. Like everything.

And if it were to be pleasant politics – who was she to complain?

She moved before she could change her mind. Raised her hands and clutched his shoulders as if she'd wilt without the support, knees almost buckling in earnest as her fingers moulded to the rock hard contours of his body. His breath quickened, his lips still at her ear. Yet he stayed there, his face, his hands, his body inches away from hers, and didn't move.

She tightened her fingers. A tremor racked through him, every muscle and tendon tensing under her touch. Twelve hundred years of ancient power bucking against the reins of his self-control – and still he stood frozen.

Her mouth turned dry. The key. She had to remember this was only about the key. About driving him just mad enough to make him forget about where exactly her hands were going and what exactly she was keeping in her pocket.

'So what do you want?' she whispered.

'I want you to keep doing this,' he said, his voice rough. 'Surprising me. Driving me mad. I want you to stop hating me. I want to keep you safe. And right now ...' He drew in a shuddering breath. 'Right now I just want to *taste* you, little thief.'

Warmth pooled in her belly and lower still, sinking between her legs in a hot, throbbing slide of arousal. The key, she repeated to herself. It was all about the key. No other reason to lean just a fraction closer to his tall body and breathe in the smell of him. No other reason to slip her hands up over his shoulders, skimming over silk and then his feverish skin, until her fingers lay against his neck, soaking up his pounding heartbeat.

All for selfish reasons. He wanted her for his own desires. She just played the game – but gods, it was a game worth playing.

'This doesn't mean anything,' she managed. 'Doesn't change anything.'

His laugh was a growl. She could feel it vibrating far too deep inside her, touching some hot, aching part of her – and still his hands didn't move.

'I didn't ask for meaning.'

'Good,' she whispered, knees buckling. She knew what he *had* asked for. 'Then make your point, Lord Protector.'

'Agenor,' he said hoarsely, lowering his face the last inch. His lips brushed over the delicate skin between her neck and shoulder, unbearably soft, unfathomably tender – a touch spreading through her like water ripples. 'Call me Agenor.'

Where had last night's hunger gone? That ruthless, ravenous desire? His hands were nothing like the hands that clawed into her body in that moonlit bed, slipping around her waist now with the gentleness of a feather. And the caresses of his lips, trailing up along her neck, her jaw, the vulnerable spot just behind her ears ... Not a claim. An invitation. Warm breath and velvety lips luring a creature she barely knew from below her own skin, a woman who didn't care about common sense or consequences.

The key. She tightened her hands on his shoulders, fighting her own quickening breath. She had to focus on that key. As soon as she got her hands on her loot, she no longer had a need for this – for his hands drawing slow, lazy circles on her back, for those vexingly soft lips exploring her body as if to map out every inch of her.

All for his own pleasure – wasn't it?

The key. Why was she allowing him to make her lose her mind when he was supposed to be the one mad with longing here?

She let out a shivering breath and realised only then that she'd held it. Agenor's chuckle sent a whisper of warm breath over the shell of her ear. Arrogant bastard – but as she parted her lips to tell him so, he bent over to kiss her neck, then gently clamped his teeth on her earlobe. An acute flare of heat speared all the way to her lower belly. All that escaped her lips was an involuntary moan. Again he laughed, nibbling on her earlobe until she couldn't tell pleasure from pain, resistance from surrender – until she felt every scrape of his teeth all over her body, tightening her nipples, heating the aching flesh between her thighs.

Focus. *Focus.* The thought of his key was the last anchor keeping her from drowning. *He* should be the one to lose his senses tonight ...

She forced her fingers to let go of the tantalising firmness of his shoulders. Trailed them down along his torso, over his hard chest and the ridges of his abdomen, savouring the feel of his body, even if she knew better. His kisses and caresses turned tighter, more desperate – betraying the effort of his restraint as her wandering touches approached the band of his trousers and slowed down.

A grim satisfaction bloomed in her lower belly. Good. Restraint meant a loss of self-control. Loss of self-control meant she stood a chance.

She slipped her fingers below his shirt, below the sturdy linen of his trousers.

Taut muscle waited for her, hot skin and – gods help her – the tight bulge of his erection pressing against the cloth. Agenor's breath caught against her shoulder, and triumph mingled with the desperate need aching in her breasts, her hips, her thighs as she unfastened his first button with deliberate slowness. Let him lose his mind. Let him think about nothing but that hard length begging for her attention and—

Agenor's hands locked around her wrists.

Her cry came a heartbeat too late. He pulled her arms behind her body before the thought of resistance even occurred to her, drawing her tight against him as he pinned her hands against her back. His fingers were a vice, holding her wrists in place with graceful, merciless control, and she had no choice but to stumble into his embrace, against that marble wall of his powerful torso.

'You *bastard*,' she managed, wrenching her hands to escape, to no avail. Pressed so tight against him, helpless and powerless, drowning in the cedar scent of his skin ... She could feel the control trickling from her grip as her attempts to escape weakened. Could feel herself sinking back into the madness of last night, soft blankets and hungry flesh and only the faintest spark of reason to keep her sane.

'I'd better keep an eye on those hands, little thief,' he muttered, encircling both her wrists with his left hand as if he'd barely even noticed her struggling. The fingers of his right hand moulded to her hip. Then slid down, down, down, over her thigh, towards the hem of her dress, far too close to that yearning, throbbing core of her. Far too close to surrender.

Allie bit her lip so hard she tasted blood – it was all she could do not to gasp. 'I wouldn't—'

He tugged up her skirt; his fingertips reached her bare thigh. She gasped anyway.

'Of course you wouldn't.' He pressed his lips to her temple as he trailed his fingers up again, drawing an inevitable line towards the hunger brewing between her legs. Wet, wanton secrets, and she couldn't bring herself to stop him. Not when he reached the vulnerable skin at the inside of her thigh and waited a last moment, then flicked a single fingertip over that most sensitive spot between her lips.

Fire burst through her. Again she tried to wrestle free, not for the key now but because she *needed* to touch him, needed her hands on that gorgeous, tall body even if it were to be the death of her.

'Allie.' A low, guttural plea. 'Let me.'

She forgot to struggle.

Forgot to be quiet. Forgot to think about tasks and thieving and proving herself. Every nerve, every fibre of her being focused only on those desperate fingers slipping between her legs, twisting and teasing, exploring every line and fold of her. She wilted against him, hands relaxing in his grip, and gave in. Heard nothing but his ragged breath against her temple, saw nothing but his moonlit shoulder supporting her. Felt nothing but her pounding heart and her lust-crazed elation and those nimble fingers stroking her, swirling over her drenched flesh until she could scream with the need to feel him closer, *deeper* ...

Another moan escaped her. Far away from everything and everyone she knew, she could no longer hold it in.

'That's it,' he muttered, his voice so hoarse, so tender, that she felt like cracking and melting in his arms. 'That's it, little thief ...'

Again she tugged at his hold, and this time he let her go, releasing her wrists to wrap his hand around her nape. She tilted her head back at his first nudge. Eyes closed, knees weak, she met the demands of his probing lips instinctively, moaning again as his mouth swept over hers and wiped the last clear thoughts from her mind. His fingers continued their blissful exploration between her thighs as she grabbed his shoulders to steady herself. Taunting and soothing. Coaxing and demanding. Igniting some devastating need inside her that couldn't be met by even his touches, that cried out for more, for *better*, at every stroke over her drenched, hankering flesh.

Dazed mews fell from her lips as he kissed her. They seemed to be another woman's moans, another woman's madness to her ears.

'Tell me you want this.' His whisper was yet another caress against her lips, gentle yet intent enough to turn her heart inside out. 'Tell me you want more.'

'I want more,' she breathed. 'I – I ...'

His fingers disappeared from between her thighs.

'*Please.*' It came out as a sob. Her incoherent thoughts could focus on nothing but that sudden emptiness where his touches had been, her nerves crying out in savage frustration. 'I want – I—'

He began hitching up her dress, each brush of his fingers over her thigh another bolt of lightning. Allie stood still as a statue, her hands clenching on his shoulders, her limbs trembling in feverish anticipation. Flutters of cold night air stroked over her skin as he bared her legs inch by inch, his lips still close enough to hers to kiss her.

'More?' he muttered.

She couldn't think. Could only want and plead. '*More.*'

And with a last kiss between her brows, he sank to his knees before her.

One firm hand spread wide over her bottom, keeping her in place. One slipped between her thighs again, fingertips teasing between her wet lips, playing around her slit. And before she could regain her composure, before she could fully fathom what he was about to do, he leaned over the last few inches and teased his tongue over that bundle of nerves where her lips met.

Allie cried out, clutching his hair to keep standing. Blinding heat and power trembled through her, leaving her light-headed and on the brink of fainting – and again he licked her, firmer now, dragging his tongue over every sensitive spot in a slow, luxurious slide. Her knees gave in.

She wavered, her muffled cry fuelled by alarm as much as by pleasure now.

A faint whoosh broke the silence of the night. Taut, strong velvet wrapped around her legs, her lower back, holding her steady as he flicked his tongue over that same spot again.

Wings.

His wings were holding her.

Allie blinked at the dark velvet, her sight hazy with lust. The tight membrane didn't give way as she leaned into it, folded around her in a cocoon of sturdy safety. But the hand on her bottom clawed tighter, drawing her nearer, demanding surrender.

She closed her eyes. And gave in.

He let out a groan of satisfaction as she relaxed in his hold, hands and wings keeping her there for him to devour. His fingers stroked the slippery lines of her body while he licked and sucked and nuzzled, dragging her to unbearable heights but never high enough, never close enough to that point of shattering she so desperately needed.

Perhaps she'd die from this. Perhaps she'd go up in smoke, a whiff of nothing but maddening want, from the bone-shattering anticipation building inside her.

He pressed his fingertip against her slit, then another one. Slipped them half a digit inside, teasing her open, as his lips relentlessly worked her. Every muscle in her body drew tight around him, welcoming the invasion, *craving* it ...

He pulled back.

She heard herself moan for more, pleading, begging. She didn't care. Not when that slender finger returned, filling her slowly and gently. Never had she needed anything as much as she needed that touch, that blissful friction as he slid deeper and deeper, past every barrier she'd ever put up.

'Please,' she whispered. 'Please, Agenor ...'

Like a bursting dam, he broke at the sound of his name. Drove his fingers into her with raw, insatiable force, filling her so deep she could have fainted from the overwhelming sensation of *completeness*. Release slammed over her like a tidal wave, a surge of pleasure that swept her off her feet and flooded her again and again and again until she was nothing but an empty shell of perfect, contented bliss ...

He was holding her when she came to her senses, cradling her like a child against his chest. His face hovered inches above her, a silvery mask of undiluted awe in the moonlight.

For a moment, not even the cold night air creeping over her skin could stifle the warmth swelling through her.

She wanted to reach out and tear his shirt off his shoulders, wanted to cup her hands around his cheek and kiss him until he, too, would be begging for mercy. But as she raised her hands, he bent over, pressed a kiss to her forehead, and whispered, 'Let me take you home, little thief.'

Home.

He wanted her to return *home*?

As she should want, too. The realisation came a little too late. She wasn't supposed to be here. She wasn't supposed to do this. She wasn't supposed to lie in his arms and feel *safe*, as if this wasn't the male who could obliviate her entire village with a single flick of his fingers ...

'Alright,' she whispered.

Her thoughts and feelings were a tangled blur as he carried her back over the narrow mountain road until they came into view of Rustvale's houses – confusion, frustration, a desire she shouldn't be feeling. When he finally put her back on her feet, she couldn't suppress a sting of disappointment, no matter how hard she tried.

Only hours later, lying awake in bed as Inga softly snored beside her, did it occur to her she had forgotten about the key entirely.

CHAPTER 9

How he ever managed to pull his hands off her, Agenor didn't know. How he managed to watch her vanish inside that gods-damned house without tearing down the walls and dragging her out again, into his arms, into his bed ... If not for that single venomous sentence she'd thrown into his face, he wouldn't have been able to.

But her words wouldn't leave his thoughts against the silence of the night. *Selfish lovers, from all I've heard.*

He was not going to confirm her worst opinion of him all over again.

Which was probably selfish in itself, with that warped way the bargain worked – being selfless only for her good opinion of him. He didn't care. Let him be bound to help her; that was the least of his problems. Bargain or not, he wasn't going to give her a reason to accuse him of manipulating her, of seducing her only to get his fill. Not even if the alternative was returning home like this, his mind a hazy mess of maddening want, his body pulsing with a reckless, primitive need he hadn't felt since the War of the Gods started and his life turned into a never-ending song of bloodshed and duty.

His fist would have to make do. At least until he'd figured out where they stood now, what exactly had changed between them with an evening of both too much honesty and not nearly enough of it.

It's just politics.

And yet ... was it?

He flew too fast, too recklessly, and landed on his own small balcony with such speed he nearly sprained an ankle from the impact. Just politics. Which had been true of much of her life, he understood that now – as true as the colourlessness of his own. It was the truth about Russ, the truth about her calculated interactions with her neighbours, the truth about the letters she'd left between his shirts. It may even be the truth about him. Much of what she said and did was easy to explain if he was simply a tool to her, the first and only fae ruler forced to take note of the humans' predicaments on the island.

But he'd seen those glimpses of softness on her face in the few un-guarded moments where she forgot to be furious. Had felt her come apart in his arms.

His arousal flared again, unhindered by even the familiar, colourless sight of his bedroom.

What was she *doing* to him? He'd never been one to lose his mind over anyone. As much as he'd enjoyed his time with some of his past lovers, they'd always come second to work and matters of state – sensible, mutually beneficial affairs that lasted a few years and then dissolved as amiably as they had started. Following all the rules. Meeting all his expectations. Just as he'd thought he wanted, simple and reliable and ...

Tedious.

And now a pair of cold blue eyes was enough to send him spinning like an infatuated youth.

With a joyless laugh he tore off his shirt – like she would have done for him on that silent mountain path, if he hadn't been so stupidly determined to be honourable and selfless. Gods and demons. Time for a bath. Time to soak some of this madness from his pores and figure out what to do next, now that she had once again shattered every plan he'd tried to make that morning.

A folded piece of parchment on his desk caught his eye as he passed – a letter that hadn't been there when he left his room that morning.

His heart skipped a single beat. Then he noted the seal keeping the message shut, and bit out a curse at his own flighty mind – what was he thinking? Of course it wasn't Allie's. The wheels of the court were still turning, people still needed him for their meetings and decisions; it was a miracle he had gotten away with nearly a week of dazed brainlessness. Letters were the least he should have expected. He'd be lucky if no one asked where in hell he had been all night.

And he *certainly* didn't have any reason to feel so ridiculously morose over just the prospect of getting some work done tomorrow.

Some issues with a nymph community on Tolya, the note told him. Melinoë expected him to solve the matter with Creon tomorrow. That really couldn't be too bad. The nymphs had a habit of creating trouble every other year or so, only to quickly withdraw as soon as it looked like there might be consequences. He didn't expect it to take more than—

Expect.

You only ever see what you expect to see. Her voice was clear as a shallow sea in his memory, echoing at him from every corner of his room. *No wonder you're never surprised.*

Oh, fuck.

He slammed the note back down on his desk, then fell into his chair and buried his face in his hands. What he expected to see ... Some sputtering nymphs, no decent reason for rebellion, and an arrogant but efficient murderer to make a quick end to the noise.

Did you ask them?

He had not.

Hell. How had everything become this complicated all of a sudden? His brain felt like a sore muscle, tearing just a little too far in its desperate attempts to accommodate the movements he needed it to make. A nagging strain, just too annoying to ignore – and yet, in a twisted way, an oddly pleasant sensation, too.

Like sore muscles, it was a feeling of growth. Of movement.

He'd meet with Creon tomorrow, he resolved. He'd ask what the uproar was all about. And then he'd see – he'd *see* – what was to be done about it.

And perhaps Allie wouldn't hate him too much by the time he had that behind him.

The emissary waiting for him in the meeting room, half an hour past sunrise, was a pale-skinned, blue-winged lady by the name of Eldoris. Agenor hadn't seen her since just after the end of the War, when she'd been one of the voices proposing to establish fae settlements throughout all of the archipelago. When it turned out most fae were in no hurry to leave their own homes, she had taken an ambassador's post on the nymphs' islands and rarely shown her face at the Crimson Court again.

Agenor wasn't too fond of her, but at least she was more sociable company than Creon, who stood lounging against the windowsill and stared outside as they talked, casually cutting small lines into the back of his hand with one of his daggers. Cut. Blood. A flash of blue magic to heal the wound. Another cut. Agenor wasn't going to tell the Mother's son how to spend his time, but the combination of utter indifference and casual bloodshed in the corner of his eye made him feel significantly more sympathetic towards Eldoris than he normally might.

From the sound of her report, the issue with the nymphs was rather straightforward. Agreed tribute rates hadn't been met for half a decade. At the embassy's decision to take some stricter measures against this, the inhabitants of Tolya had taken to stealing from the fae company residing on the island, and when that hadn't delivered the desired results, fae had started vanishing without a trace at night.

'So at that point,' Eldoris said, and scowled, 'I thought the Mother should be informed that her servants are being killed in their beds by—'

'Not killed, presumably,' Agenor said mildly, shifting his wings slightly to lean back in his chair.

'What?'

'They don't do murder.' Once he'd thought it to be a weakness. Since he'd stumbled upon a nymph prison in the second century of the War, he'd quite changed his mind on that point. 'Your people may be sitting somewhere tangled up in nettle vines as we speak, but I'm quite positive they'll survive.'

Eldoris looked like she'd swallowed a lemon whole. 'Does that make any difference to the core of the matter, Lord Protector?'

It didn't. Not directly, at least. Such an easy point to agree too – such a *self-evident* point to agree to. Even after his resolution of last night, the temptation was almost too strong to withstand, like a storm current pulling him from his course. But sooner or later he'd have to face Allie again, and if last night had changed *anything* about her opinion of him, he wasn't going to ruin it with a moment of indolence.

And if Allie had been here ...

Did you ask why?

Had Eldoris asked?

Agenor closed his eyes, thoughts unravelling, *shifting*, with a sensation as if someone pulled his own brain from his skull and plunked it down in an entirely new head. She should have asked. It was an ambassador's job to ask. But if she'd spent a century on a nymph isle and still hadn't learned one of the most sacred rules of the people she oversaw – the vow not to kill any living creature – then what were the chances she'd thought to enquire what exactly had sparked this sudden rebellion?

'No,' he said, a little too late. 'I suppose it doesn't.'

On the edge of his sight, Creon was still toying with his knife, his gaze stubbornly directed at something in a far, irrelevant distance. Cut. Heal. Cut. Heal. Eldoris stole a glance at him in the silence that fell, an expression on her face Agenor knew all too well when the Mother's son was involved – part fearful unease, part quiet admiration. In Eldoris's case, it seemed to be a rather eager kind of admiration.

Had she requested Creon's help specifically in some vague hope this mission would provide a way into his bed? Agenor wished her good luck, if that were the case. As far as he was aware, the Silent Death hadn't taken a single lover since that embarrassment at the Last Battle, and not because no one had tried.

'Well,' she said, dragging her gaze back to him. Yes, that was definitely too much admiration in her eyes, and not nearly enough healthy caution. Agenor inwardly groaned. 'I suppose you agree with me that something needs to be done about the matter, then?'

Something. Yes. Most days he'd send Creon after the trouble and know it would be fixed. But he knew the other male's methods, and could he really justify those if he didn't know exactly what had caused the uproar?

Blue eyes scowled at him from the back of his memory.

He probably couldn't.

'Please tell me a little more about the cause of the conflict first,' he said slowly.

At the window, Creon's knife stopped circling for the blink of an eye. Barely a falter – but from a male who never faltered, never broke, it was a show of surprise as clear as anyone else's shocked gasp would have been.

So he *was* listening.

That, too, was not what Agenor had expected.

'The cause?' Eldoris repeated. 'I already told you – we took measures after they consistently failed to meet the tribute rates, and—'

'Yes,' Agenor said, waving that aside. 'What measures, exactly?'

'Creating more farmland. Since their own community apparently wasn't able to produce a reasonable amount of food, we took it upon ourselves to—'

To create more farmland. It sounded so sensible, for the first one, two heartbeats – and then the consequences of that innocent sentence came through to him, and his heart stopped dead in his chest for a moment.

'Eldoris.' Too sharp. But gods be damned, what had these idiots been up to? 'Please say you haven't been cutting down any trees for those new fields.'

She stared at him – a blank, violet-blue stare.

Oh, gods and demons.

'You *have* been cutting down the trees?' His voice lowered to a soft, smooth timbre – his deadly politeness, Thysandra would say. 'On a nymph isle, Eldoris? Meaning you have effectively been cutting down their family members?'

Creon didn't turn around at the window, but his knife lay motionless in his hand now.

'They were very normal trees!' Eldoris protested, but her already pale face grew a fraction lighter. 'That wouldn't be a reason to kill – or kidnap, whatever they—'

'There are no "normal" trees on nymph isles,' Agenor interrupted, pronouncing every word with sharp, clipped precision. 'Even the ones without a soul are sacred to them. How exactly did you *not* expect this to escalate?'

She let out a shrill laugh. 'I didn't know—'

'You spent a century in that place and you didn't know? May I ask exactly how you've been spending your time at that post, Eldoris?'

She shrunk half a step away from the desk, her wings flaring out in nervous instinct – like a cornered bird looking for escape. 'I don't see how I am suddenly to blame for *their*—'

'Please get out,' Agenor said.

Eldoris blinked at him and didn't move.

He smiled even more politely. 'Do I need to repeat myself?'

'But—'

'The *door*, Eldoris.' She flinched as he helpfully pointed out the exit for her. 'I'll let you know how we solve the matter. Thank you.'

Her throat bobbed as she glanced at Creon, with a far more reasonable dose of fear in her eyes this time. 'I—'

'*Thank* you, Eldoris.'

She fled.

Only once the door had slammed shut after her blue wings did Creon turn around, a look of faint amusement on his hard face. It took Agenor an effort to suppress a curse. Of course the bastard was amused. Cutting family members – of whatever race – to pieces was how he spent half of his days, after all. But that was never a reply to a first offense – was it?

Perhaps he sounded a tad too accusing when he said, 'Did you know about this?'

Creon shook his head, then shrugged.

'I presume Achlys and Melinoë have no idea of it either?'

Another shrug.

They couldn't know, then, Agenor decided. He would have heard about it if the High Ladies had the faintest idea of this madness – wouldn't he?

'Could you go to Tolya?' he said, feeling suddenly exhausted. For the bloody gods' sake, they were barely an hour into the day. 'Make sure the idiots stop chopping down trees, then make the nymphs give their hostages back in return. If anyone causes trouble over that deal, I suppose you'll be able to handle them.'

Creon's smile could have made a grown warrior shiver.

'And keep an eye on Eldoris,' Agenor added, rubbing his forehead to press back his emerging headache. 'I'm starting to think she may not be the person we need on that post. If you think we're better off replacing her – well, vacate the position.'

There was not a trace of hesitation in Creon's nod. The interest appeared to be entirely one-sided, indeed.

'Anything I'm forgetting?'

Creon pulled a short pencil from his pocket as he sauntered towards the desk and bent over to scrabble his answer down on the nearest piece of scrap parchment. *Want to do anything about the tributes?*

Those damn tributes the nymphs hadn't managed to deliver for years. He was obliged to take measures, Agenor knew. A week ago he wouldn't have hesitated to raise their rates to compensate, as well as issue a few threats in case of the undesirable possibility that those new rates wouldn't be met. After all, everyone knew nymphs and their fleeting minds were incapable of planning more than a week in advance, and couldn't do basic calculations to save their lives. Odds were they'd simply been sloppy and wispy as always and a stern schedule would be enough to get them back on track.

Now ...

We starved ourselves for months, but we had the grain.

The rates were supposed to be reasonable. Proportional. And somehow he didn't think Allie's people had simply misjudged and messed up their planning without her noticing.

'I'll think about the tributes,' he heard himself say. 'Will discuss it with the Mother.'

Creon had to sense his confusion. But the Silent Death turned away with only a last nod, blasting his note to dust with a nonchalant flash of red as he made for the door. No questions. No smug remarks about the Mother's opinion on this sudden mildness. Either the boy didn't care about the unusual course of the conversation and planned to murder a host of people either way, or the matter would be brought up in a future conversation, presumably at the worst possible moment.

Agenor muttered a curse. A worry for later. He had to figure out the issue with those cursed tributes, first.

The archive rooms were a mere few corridors away from this meeting room, and yet he ran into far too many fae within that short distance, who asked him far too many questions about duties he couldn't give a damn about. By the time he finally reached his destination, one look was enough to convince the scribes they were urgently needed elsewhere.

What had Allie said? *Do you think anyone gives a damn about your protocols?*

She had to be wrong, at least about the majority. He'd checked some of this administration himself. Some small irregularities, surely, the occasional miscalculation – but what else would one expect in an administration of this extent?

Expect.

He cursed.

The report of Deiras's last mission still lay where he'd left it after correcting the small errors the First Emissary had made. He pulled out the thick leather folder and spread it open before him. Small errors, yes, but they had been so minor ...

His mind stilled with dread as his eyes slid over the crawling numbers again.

Minor mistakes, perhaps. A few subtotals that were just a fraction off, a few estimates of value that didn't entirely fit the registered weights. Nothing that couldn't be sloppiness in itself. But if he no longer expected it to be sloppiness – if he actually *thought* about the clues and calculations presented to him here ...

Oh, gods.

He spent an hour browsing through that first report, the hollow pit in his stomach opening wider and wider as he took stock of every small oversight, every minor inaccuracy. Put together, taken in earnest consideration, they painted an image not nearly so minor. From the mess of numbers arose a disturbingly clear report – one that underestimated the payments the human isles had made and overestimated the gold and grain delivered to the court; one that miraculously raised the tribute rates by some twenty percent and made that same twenty percent vanish again in a mirage of near-precision.

A report he'd held in his hands. And approved.

In a burst of agonising dread, he slammed the folder down on the nearest desk and grabbed three others from the shelves at random, flipping them open with trembling fingers. The numbers spun around him, elusive and intangible, sneering at his desperate attempts to make sense of them – but he wrestled them down, found the patterns, found the errors ...

They were worse.

They were even *worse*.

The sweat on his back was an ice cold slide down between his wings. More reports. More calculations. More thinly veiled fraud, the signs of it so laughably obvious, now that he knew what to look for – a cheap little trick, and every single bastard bringing in human tributes had been employing it right under his very nose for decades.

And he'd allowed them to. Settled into his new routine, battle-weary and desperate for peace after the losses he'd suffered in the War, he'd decided they *had* their peace, and never looked for anything else again.

While the battles had continued.

His hands were shaking as he browsed, page after page confirming the worst of his suspicions. He should have seen it decades ago. This was his duty to fix. And instead he'd let the burden of his own work fall on the shoulders of the humans he'd thought to be protecting from their own stupidity – had left the battle to those without the power to fight it. Why hadn't he seen it?

And worse – who had?

He wanted to fold into a little ball of misery on the archive floor, wings curled around his head like a little fae boy desperate to fall asleep. Shutting out the world. Shutting out his failures. But these people he'd failed had no way of shutting out his failures, and just the thought of Allie's glare ...

Oh, gods. He'd told her she was wrong. He'd *chuckled* at her accusations.

He wanted to die. Wanted the floor to open up below his feet for the mountain to swallow him. Buried beneath ten feet of solid rock, he could hardly be more useless than he'd proven himself to be so far.

There was no fixing this. There was no convincing her not to hate him – she *should* damn well hate him. All he could do was admit his mistakes to her and promise to do better, not because he wanted to redeem himself or angle for gratitude, but because the very least she deserved was to know what she'd achieved. That he finally saw the courage it must have taken her to challenge him, the male responsible for her people's suffering, that he finally understood a fraction of what she'd been forced to survive for all these years. Keeping her family alive. Keeping her village alive. All the things *he* should have been doing.

He'd tell her. And then he'd do better.

By all the gods, dead or living – he would do better.

Chapter 10

Allie woke with a spinning mind and a swimming stomach and decided today was a good day to be ill.

It was an escape she didn't dare to use too often, for fear of diminishing its usefulness; if she started complaining about headaches every other week, sooner or later even the many favours the village's appointed fae healer owed her would no longer be enough to keep him silent. But she hadn't complained of any illnesses for a year and a half, and she had certainly helped him fix and cover up several instances of incorrect diagnoses or sloppy work during that time.

And she really, *really* didn't want to be at the court today. Not if a certain ancient, handsome, uncannily tender fae lord would be walking around the same building too.

So she made a show of nearly fainting at her supervisor's feet and gagged a bit as she waited in the office antechamber, where she knew the carpet was new and expensive. They were quick to tell her she was excused for the day and that the healer would come to see her tomorrow.

He wouldn't find much, but Allie wasn't particularly concerned about that.

She staggered out and around the corner and then ran the rest of the way home, eager to put as many miles between herself and the court as possible. Or rather ...

Hell. Who was she trying to fool?

Between herself and Agenor. Between herself and that soft, persuasive voice, between herself and those skilled fingers that had somehow made her lose all sense and reason last night. What exactly had happened on that dark mountain path? She could no longer make sense of it. She wasn't sure if she *wanted* to make sense of it.

Why had she let herself be so vulnerable around him? Why had she told him about Russ, about Inga, about the choices she'd made? Why, *why* had she revealed just how much he affected her – how much she couldn't help but want him?

Desperately.

And why wouldn't his voice stop echoing through her mind, for the bloody gods' sake?

Perhaps she should simply stay away from him. Damn that key, and damn the bargain mark at her wrist. There were more dangerous things at stake now than a lost bet. Her sanity, her dignity, her ...

Her heart?

She abruptly halted in the middle of Rustvale's only street. Good gods. Surely that wasn't a thought her mind had in all earnestness suggested?

She'd heard too many of Marette's sappy ballads, it seemed. Hearts had nothing to do with the matter – nothing at all. She didn't *feel* anything where he was concerned, or at least nothing but sensible, justified fury. Last night had been a matter of stupid, primitive lust. A bit of confusion, too. Some surprise at the confessions he'd made at her kitchen table. But certainly nothing else – certainly no *affection.*

It didn't matter how broken he'd seemed in those few moments, how he'd *pleaded* with her. That was his own damn problem, just like her own problems were still her own, too. He wasn't taking them off her shoulders, after all. The bargain still held; nothing he'd done had been done for anyone but himself.

So she was going to stay away from him until she could be sensible. Then she could start thinking about that key again.

And if he came to look for her in the meantime ...

Well, she would be far, far gone. She'd been planning to make the walk to Greyside one of these days; the latest smuggled bags of goods still lay waiting for her there. Now that she had an unexpected free day, she might as well use it. At least that released Russ from the obligation to accompany her, which would have been necessary if she were to make the same walk after work and wouldn't return before nightfall.

She instructed the girls who looked after Rustvale's children not to disturb her in her sleep. Then she got a bag and her sturdiest pair of boots and slipped out of the village without anyone seeing her.

The walk took a little over an hour and a half. This island might be a prison, but it was a sizeable one.

She passed rugged mountain slopes and dusty valleys. Two other human settlements, as quiet as Rustvale was around this hour of the day. The outskirts of a few fae neighbourhoods, even the simplest of their brick and marble houses a sneer at the ramshackle huts in which the human slaves were supposed to spend their lives.

More than once, Allie found herself wishing she was brave enough to set fire to a couple of them.

She'd never been that kind of fighter, though. Never been one to smuggle poisonous herbs into fae meals or to destroy archive folders and name lists behind their winged backs. Even the work of the smugglers, going out onto the beaches at night to receive whatever help the world outside was willing to offer, had always been too physical for her. She kept her eyes and ears open, instead. Knew things and made sure people knew she knew. Stealing Agenor's shirts had been an exception, and ...

Well. Little good had come from that desperate plan, indeed.

And why was she thinking about Agenor again?

She stamped on, determined to occupy her thoughts with *anything* else and failing hopelessly. By the time the gallows and herb gardens of Greyside loomed up before her, she was so sick of it she could have screamed – sick of bloody Lord Agenor, of his selfish games, of this entire gods-damned island and the invisible bars keeping her stuck on its shores. She hated the helplessness. Hated being stuck and having no other dreams than being a little less stuck, hated having to be grateful for a day of decent food, a day of not too much danger, as if *that* was what her life was supposed to be.

Hated having to use these smuggled goods, further proof of having to rely entirely on the mercy of others.

But Rustvale needed any help it could get, and she hadn't made the walk for nothing. So she stamped on until she found Russ's cousin between the workers in the fields, the woman's hair bound in a messy bun, her hands covered in earth and weeds. Clara only noticed Allie at the last possible moment, squinting a warning at her the moment their gazes met.

'Oh, Al,' she said, a little too loud. 'Here for Russ's new shirt?'

The meaning was clear. There were unfriendly ears around. Unsurprisingly so – Russ, the wives and mothers of Greyside all agreed, was far too good a man to find himself shackled to a woman housing some little faeling. Of course, they weren't aware Allie was the one who had on several occasions smuggled extra food and candles into their village. The network's members stayed very, very quiet. Even in Rustvale, only a handful of people knew she was responsible for the bags and crates that would sometimes, discreetly, appear out of nowhere in someone's living room.

So she chatted out loud about work and mutual acquaintances until they were well out of hearing distance and Clara quietly said, 'It's some flu medicines this time, Al.'

'Oh, thank the gods. We'll need that this winter.'

Clara nodded but remained silent as they walked on – more silent than usual. They passed the gallows, some half-eaten human remains still dangling from their nooses. Allie had gotten used to the sight years ago, and yet her stomach turned this time – did Agenor know?

And then it turned again, because why was she thinking about Agenor?

As if she could smell her thoughts, Clara chose the same moment to break the silence. 'There are rumours about some fae male visiting your house.'

The distrust was thick as butter. Allie suppressed a curse and repeated, '*Some* fae male?'

'Someone said it was bloody Lord Agenor himself, but—'

'Right. It was.'

Clara's face contorted into a grimace of the purest spite – an expression so sharp it could have cut steel. Which was reasonable. More than reasonable. And yet Allie found herself hurrying to explain, hurrying to *defend* him – 'Did you get more food delivered here in Greyside as well?'

The suspicion didn't soften. 'We did, yesterday.'

'He's been looking into mismanagement by our supervisors.' The same lie she'd told her own neighbours, the safest option. 'Had a few harsh words with them about their neglect, apparently.'

Clara scoffed. 'Well now. Isn't that admirable, after *decades*?'

The right reaction – the only right reaction – and yet Allie had to fight the objections on her tongue. But he didn't know. But he *wanted* to have known. An idiot, yes, but an idiot with good intentions ...

She kept quiet.

Clara handed her the bags with herbal preparations in silence and walked her out of the village with more loud, innocent conversation to draw the attention away from the smuggled wares. But as they approached the silent mountain paths, Russ's cousin lowered her voice again.

'Al?'

'Hmm?'

'Please be careful with his lordship.' A scowl. 'I don't care much about his pretty words. They're all the same selfish bastards in the end.'

Yes, greedy and self-centred, all of them – a week ago she wouldn't have hesitated to agree. She still shouldn't hesitate. If anything, the bargain had proven her point more convincingly than ever before.

And yet it took her just a moment too long to smile her most reassuring smile and say, 'Don't worry. I know.'

She made detours past two more human villages on her way home, where she hid little bags of medicine in the designated locations – empty flowerpots and tool sheds, where they would be found by other members of the network within a day. She didn't know the identity of those other members, of course. It was the way the network functioned; the less anyone knew, the less they could betray.

The sun was far past its highest point by the time she finally returned to Rustvale with the remainder of her loot safely in her backpack. The rest of the village hadn't yet returned from work, which made matters much easier. She slipped into Farran's hut through the back door, which she knew he usually left open, and put the medicine on his dinner table. No links to her; no links to anyone else.

Then she snuck back to her own house and hastily slipped inside before any of the girls or children could see she'd left her bed. A good enough alibi if anyone in the village wasted time wondering where in the world the sudden gift had come from this time.

'Allie?' a voice said from the shadows of her living room.

She shrieked, snapping around so fast she nearly sprained an ankle.

'Please!' He jumped up from his chair at the table, hands stretched out to catch her, wings flaring out in alarm. Oh, gods, those hands. Those *wings*. At once, last night's madness burned through her again, tired feet and sweaty skin be damned. 'I'm sorry – I didn't want to frighten you. I—'

'What in the world are you *doing* here?' she snapped. Spitting fury was the best defence she had against that treacherous feeling of relief welling up inside her. That ridiculous tingle of pleasure at the sight of him. *All selfish bastards.* She should know better. Glaring at him, she added, 'I know I don't technically own this house, but that doesn't give you the right to come bursting in whenever—'

'I know,' Agenor interrupted, staggering back again as if she might swing a fist at him. He looked paler than yesterday. *Smaller* than yesterday. 'I know, I'll be out in a moment. I just ...'

He fell silent, his breaths too shallow.

Allie realised she'd clenched her fists. She unclenched them and kicked off her boots, feeling dangerously tempted to kick them into his face. At least with a broken nose he wouldn't be so insufferably *gorgeous*.

'Just?' she repeated sharply.

'Just wanted to tell you you've won the game,' he muttered.

She stared at him – at his dull eyes and sagging shoulders and wilting wings – and felt her violent urges seep away like sand between her fingers.

'Are you – are you alright?'

'I laughed at you.' He sounded like he wanted to throw up. 'You told me what was going on, and I *laughed* at you.'

'Yes,' Allie said, blinking. 'You're a prick. I assume you were aware of that before today.'

'I thought I knew what I was doing.' Like a drunk blurting out words. 'I really thought ... Well, you know what I thought. I've been blathering about it enough, I suppose.'

She let out a mirthless laugh. 'What in the world made you—'

'Seeing,' he said quietly.

The air abruptly left her lungs.

'The tribute administration.' He was speaking faster now, thoughts bursting from his lips like confessions. 'It's a mess. It's been a mess for decades. I should have seen. Our ambassadors, they've been' – he swallowed – 'fucking up, frankly. And I never noticed – I barely even *thought* about it, and ...'

Again his words drifted off. There was no need to finish the sentence. She knew the conclusion – she'd lived in the conclusion for twenty-four years.

'I'm so sorry,' he whispered, his voice hollow. 'I'm so very sorry.'

She staggered a step forward, unable to look away from the plea in his eyes. Not a plea for reassurance, for her to tell him it was all fine and forgiven. If anything, it looked like a plea for her to start throwing stones.

All selfish bastards.

But could it still be selfishness dulling the life in his voice like that? Was he breaking apart on her kitchen floor to appease her or to soothe his own guilty conscience?

She opened her mouth. Closed it again. Suppressed the ridiculous reflex to step forward and wrap her arms around his sagging shoulders.

'I'm getting to work tomorrow,' he added, averting his face. 'Time to cause some trouble over those tributes. If you have any other suggestions – I know it won't undo the damage done – but at least ...'

His throat bobbed. Honest, vulnerable agony. Allie parted her lips again and still couldn't find the words, or even the thoughts to put into words.

'Oh,' she said.

'So.' He cleared his throat. 'That's what I wanted you to know. And – and I wanted to ask ...'

There was something unnerving about hearing a fae male of twelve centuries stumble over his words. She didn't move.

'Is there anything I can do for you?' he finished quietly.

'For *me*?'

Selfish, her thoughts droned. Trying to make an impression. Trying to sway her opinion of him, even now. And yet, the despair in his eyes ...

'You've been fighting so hard,' he muttered at her floor. 'I know I can't make that right, either. But at the very least, you deserve *some* help – whatever I can do for you – and—'

The words were out before she could stop them. 'The best thing you can do to help me is to help my people.'

'Yes, of course you're saying that,' he said with a joyless laugh. 'You're the real protector between the two of us, aren't you?'

'That ...' Fuck. She really shouldn't have told him *anything* about herself – those words wouldn't hit her with such sledgehammer force if they weren't based on so much truth. 'That's not for you to decide. Help them to help me. You—'

'Allie,' he said hoarsely, 'I'll save the entire damn world tomorrow if you ask me to. Let me put you first for a few hours. Please.'

Please.

And no sign of pain. No sign of a burning bargain mark. He was refusing her explicit request for help, and the magic didn't stop him.

Did he even realise it? Did he even understand what it meant?

No hidden intentions, for once. No attempts to win her over or to make him feel better about himself – just that offer, plain and simple. A few hours. Whatever he could do. What had he said last night? *Allow me to be happy someone's keeping an eye on you.*

She swallowed. Her throat was dry as sand.

Last night ... He had held her so tenderly. Wrapped his arms and wings around her and taken that terrible weight off her shoulders for those few blissful moments, freed her from some cage she'd started believing a part of herself after all these years. Was it bad to want more of that sudden, quiet peace? To trust someone else to carry her just every now and then? If there truly were no hidden attentions, if he was here just to *help*, and nothing else ...

'Allie,' he said again.

She wanted to drown in the sound of her name. Wanted to drift off on it and forget, just for a moment, who she used to be.

Who she used to be ...

Quiet, little Al, curled up on the windowsill of Father's office with her books and her blankets – and at once, she knew what she wanted. Craved it, suddenly, with such violence that she would have taken *anyone's* hand to bring her back to that place.

'I ...' She hesitated a last moment. Vulnerable – far too vulnerable. But then again ...

So was he. And so damn dutiful, so ridiculously tender, and perhaps not so very selfish after all ...

So she straightened her shoulders, shoved her doubts aside, drew in a last breath, and said, 'I'd like to read a book again.'

CHAPTER 11

Agenor should have known she would surprise him.

He'd braced himself for many things – cruel revenge and bland indifference and outright mockery, all of which would have been equally reasonable. And instead ...

A book.

That was all?

She wasn't going to tell him that he could keep his helping hands to himself? That he was probably just attempting to redeem himself in her eyes and that she wasn't going to be his crutch to make him feel better over his pathetic failures? He found himself faltering as the expected impact of her retort failed to come, his prepared defences useless against the unusually mild scrutiny in her bright blue eyes.

There was no attack in that look. Not a trace of the suspicion he'd grown accustomed too.

He made a good attempt to reply – yes, of course. A book. He'd get something for her immediately. Did she have any specific wishes? But the words lost their way long before they could reach his lips, his mind dazed and disoriented by that look on her face – an expression he'd almost call *gentle*.

What in hell was going on?

'You seem stunned,' she said, tilting her head a fraction. 'Are you in need of more detailed suggestions?'

Gods and demons. Stunned indeed, but at least he could *talk*. He scraped a few last shreds of composure together and managed, 'If you have them?'

'Of course I do,' she said, one corner of her mouth curling up a fraction. A *smile*? Since when did she *smile* at him? 'I won't have more than five minutes of reading time in this place once the neighbours return from work, and your court library doesn't allow humans access unless they're scribes. So ...' She shrugged, and again that disconcerting smile flashed over her face. 'Your rooms?'

Agenor blinked. 'What?'

'You could bring me to your rooms.' She turned away, making for the bedroom as she pulled pin after pin from her hair. 'I suppose no one will harass me there.'

'No, of course not,' he said, no less bewildered, 'but you'd have to be in my rooms.'

She paused at the bedroom door, glancing over her shoulder. 'So?'

'Last time you stepped into my bedroom you told me you hated me.'

'Well, you *were* being an arse.'

He closed his eyes for a heartbeat. 'And I'm not being an arse now?'

'No,' she said, vanishing into the backroom. 'Not at all. Let me write Russ a quick note and put on something a little less sweaty.'

The sound of rustling clothes really didn't do his sanity any good. He shouldn't be imagining the sight of her lithe body as it emerged from that tunic – shouldn't be thinking of the quickness of her fingers and the softness of her skin. If she was still willing to come anywhere near him after last night, he needed his restraint. Needed to stop thinking about the way she'd moaned his name, the way she'd collapsed into his arms ...

Needed to stop *immediately*.

He hadn't made nearly enough progress cleansing his imagination when she reappeared, in a clean tunic and slippers, her hair in loose chestnut curls over her shoulders. He'd never seen her with her hair down. This was probably the worst possible moment to stretch out a hand and curl one of the strands around his finger – but gods be damned, he wanted to.

'So,' she said, raising her eyebrows at him. Still no glares. His spinning head couldn't make sense of it – couldn't make sense of anything anymore. His world was a lie, and his coat thief didn't hate him. What should he expect next – for Creon to fling his knives into the ocean and take up a healer's life?

'So?' he repeated with some effort.

She gave him a smile, and there was no sharpness in it. She seemed oddly *cheerful*, if anything. 'Are we walking or flying?'

Agenor nearly choked on his own tongue. 'You want to *fly*?'

'I've never done it before,' she said. 'They brought me here by tribute ship, and it looks like it might be fun.' A chuckle. 'Although, you're looking like I just suggested burying you alive.'

'Allie ...' He had to be misunderstanding something. Likely he was misunderstanding *everything*. 'If you want me to fly you up there, I have to hold you, alright? I ...'

She quirked up an eyebrow. 'I didn't expect you to pull a spare set of wings from your pocket, no.'

'But—'

'And since when do you have a problem with touching me?'

'I don't!' he burst out. '*You* should have!'

'Oh, you finally realised that too?'

He closed his eyes. *Oblivious.* Guilt mingled with shame and frustration in his chest – yes, he finally realised it, and wasn't it far, far too late to start realising anything?

'You're being dramatic, Agenor,' she said, a hint of impatience in her voice now. 'None of this is new to *me*, do you realise that? I already knew exactly how much you fucked up. Now you know it too, and that's frankly an improvement – so could you stop pretending I should suddenly spit on you just because your tardy fae brain finally caught up with the state of affairs?'

'Why in hell didn't you just punch me in the face last night?' he said hoarsely.

'I considered it.' The smile that curled around her lips was one he hadn't dared dream he'd ever see on her face – mischievous, almost *flirtatious*. His heart forgot how to beat for a moment. 'But not punching you seemed to have its advantages.'

He didn't dare to open his mouth. He wouldn't be able to utter more than loose, meaningless syllables if he did. *Advantages* – and suddenly he wondered if she was inviting herself to his rooms because she trusted he'd restrain himself or because she suspected he wouldn't.

Asking, though, might well end with a kitchen knife between his shoulders.

She interrupted his feverish thoughts before they could reach a conclusion, turning for the door with that unsettling smile on her face. 'Time to get on our way, then?'

To hell with it. He scraped his wits together and followed her out into the village, silent except for some child's whining and the rustling sea in the background. Allie's glance through the empty street was unusually cautious.

'Are you in hiding?' he said wryly.

'They think I'm ill.' She locked the door behind her, then tiptoed towards him, a small grin on her face. 'I was just fleeing you, of course. How do you want to hold me?'

'*Fleeing* me?'

'You're very confusing.' Her gaze trailed down over his shoulders, his arms, his hands. He could feel it move over him – a tantalising tingle just below his skin, aching for more. 'Get me out of here first, Lord Protector. This is not the place to talk.'

At least he wasn't the only confused one between the two of them, then. He held out a hand, still not entirely reassured she wouldn't set her nails into his eyes if he touched her – but she stepped into his hold without hesitation and didn't protest as he scooped her up, her body still mind-bogglingly light in his arms. Her scent wrapped around him, something salty and floral and altogether divine. It was far too close to the taste of her – far too close to ...

'Agenor?'

He bit down a curse and flared his wings.

It had been ages since he'd last flown with *anyone* in his arms, and never had he been so excruciatingly aware of the person he was carrying – her small squeak as they ascended and her fluttering hair stroking his shoulder and the way she cautiously relaxed in his arms as they flew. Her eyes were wide with wonder, gaping at the dark blue horizon surrounding them, the small green flecks of islands in the distance.

'I never thought I'd see that far again,' she whispered against his chest.

His heart cramped up. Oh, gods. Achlys or Melinoë had bound her at her arrival, magic barring her from ever leaving the island's shores again. A sensible safety measure, he'd thought a week ago. Now, confronted with the wistful longing in her blue eyes …

Cruel indifference. Or perhaps indifferent cruelty. He wasn't sure which option was worse.

'It stops me from flying out, too, doesn't it?' she added, resting her cheek against his shoulder as he flew. 'That binding?'

'I'm afraid so,' he said hoarsely.

She sighed. 'A shame.'

Agenor swallowed. There had to be more he could say now. There had to be more he could do. In a spurt of desperation, he added, 'I could ask if … They've been known to reverse it under certain circumstances. If I put it as a personal favour …'

She peeled his shirt from his collarbone and pressed her lips to the bare skin below.

He almost dropped her as a sting of burning arousal surged through him, drawing a straight line from that kiss to his crotch and leaving every other spot in his body utterly redundant. Her lips were warm and soft and just a little wet, and they lingered against his skin long enough for him to imagine entirely different places, entirely different kisses …

She flicked the tip of her tongue over his skin.

A curse fell over his lips as every muscle in his body tensed for a fraction of an instant. No. He had to keep flying – had to focus on the motions of his wings, the muscles in his back straining and relaxing, and not on this soft, warm, reckless little creature *licking* him …

Allie giggled. That sound, too, could have sent him plummeting to the ground.

'Do you want to *die*?' he ground out. Focus. Wings. Beat after beat after beat. He had to shut out the sensation of her slender hands creeping over his chest, of her warm breath brushing his shoulder. But the harder he tried to shut her out, the more greedily his body clung to every caress, every sound – his own flesh and bones taking revenge for the state in which he'd left himself last night. His cock stirred, not caring about this morning's shattering discoveries or the empty air below them. Did she notice? Her chuckle came out far too amused for his comfort.

'I'd expect fae with centuries of experience to be more level-headed than this, Lord Agenor.'

'You should know I'm all but level-headed about you.' He sucked in a sharp breath as she kissed his chest again. 'And weren't you trying to flee me?'

'I was,' she muttered, soft lips still pressed against his skin. 'But you're undermining all my attempts to consider you a selfish bastard, and you taste so good. I can't help it.'

Fuck. He all but crashed onto his balcony, holding on to her for dear life, every fibre of his body screaming to press her back against the wall and take her right here, right now. Somehow, he put her down. Somehow, he pulled his hands off her. Somehow, he managed to force out the words – 'And what about the books?'

She folded her hands behind her back as if to challenge him. 'Are you trying to *avoid* touching me now?'

'I'm trying to avoid you hating me again.' He let out a laugh and stepped around her to open his door. 'It's rather unnerving, this change of mind coming out of nowhere.'

'Out of nowhere,' she repeated, amused. 'I see. Well, let's talk about books, then.'

Mere days ago he'd still believed he was outwitting her. Now he felt like a witless idiot as he followed her inside – maddeningly but gloriously ignorant, challenged and frustrated in equal amounts. He was missing something. He had no idea what exactly had taken that sharp edge of distrust from her heart so suddenly. But then her amusement suggested there *was* a reason – which meant something significant had changed indeed, didn't it?

Barely a victory, if he had no idea what he had done to deserve it – but the heat brewing in his body cared very little about victories. It focused rather on her graceful movements as she tiptoed towards his desk and ran a glance over the few books he kept there, on the small sound that escaped her as she recognised one of the titles. Hell, he wanted more of those sounds. More of those kisses. More of that addictive gleam of *affection* in her eyes.

'You don't have a lot of them,' she said, running her fingers over a leather-bound spine with a tenderness that made Agenor wish he was a pile of parchment. 'Considering that you had twelve centuries to collect your personal library.'

He took the decision in a single, reckless heartbeat, his hand already halfway to the key around his neck before the words had reached his lips. 'Do you want to see the rest?'

'There's more?' She glanced over her shoulder, eyes narrowing as they noticed the hand on his key. 'Oh. It's a *forbidden* collection?'

'The books in themselves not so much,' Agenor said, tugging the thin chain over his head as he turned for the narrow door beside his bed. She followed without question, her footsteps light taps against the floor. 'But the rest of that room ... well.'

'Guilty secrets?' she suggested, her eyes shining as she caught up with him.

'No. Just ...' He hesitated for a moment, realising only now how long ago it was that he'd opened this door for anyone. 'Just memories.'

Her smile stilled. Her eyes darted from the lock to the key in his hand and then up to his face, examining him with a curiosity that seemed to contain at least a dozen other feelings, too.

'Show me,' she said.

He unlocked the door without another word, slipped the key into his pocket, and opened the room for her.

She tiptoed in as if she was afraid to wake a hibernating bear, eyes wide as she took in the objects staring back at them from the shelves and chests and cabinets. Books. Letters. Portraits. Weapons. Clothes. Maps. A mismatched collection of curiosities to anyone else, but Agenor couldn't lay eyes upon a single item without seeing the face it had belonged to, the place it originated, the wars it had seen – most of them long dead, long gone, long forgotten.

'Oh,' Allie whispered, her hand wrapping around his left wrist. 'Is that your sister?'

He followed her gaze. Emeia's portrait stood on one of the central shelves, next to it her ring, her healer's bag, the pile of letters she'd written him in the decades they were both campaigning on opposite sides of the archipelago. The grief had long since numbed, her absence no longer a sore spot that always lingered in the back of his thoughts – but the tone of Allie's voice made his throat catch for the first time in decades.

'Yes.' He saw the question in her eyes before she could ask, and added, 'She died in an alf ambush some three hundred years ago.'

Her fingers tightened around his wrist. 'I'm glad I didn't touch those shirts she gave you.'

'Oh,' Agenor said wryly. 'Don't worry, they were always in here. I was just curious whether you would be reckless enough to take those shirts I mentioned.'

A laugh escaped her, sounding relieved more than anything. 'How very fae.'

'Can you blame me?'

'Not at all,' she admitted, releasing his arm to take a single, hesitant step forward. Then another one when he didn't stop her. Slowly, almost reverently, she made her way around the room, examining his past, his *life*, blue eyes taking note of every name and face and place. He saw her falter every now and then at mementos of the war, of human casualties, of battles won or lost – but she didn't speak, and he could have kissed her senseless for that alone.

'So many dead warriors,' she eventually muttered, scanning the name list of the full regiment he'd sent out on an exploratory mission in the second century of the War. The Alliance had expected them, it turned out; the list was all that remained of the group.

'I know,' Agenor said quietly.

She looked over her shoulder, her eyes cautious. 'Friends of yours?'

'Many of them, yes.'

'And they all ...' She drew in a shivering breath. 'They all died.'

Agenor closed his eyes for a moment, a familiar heaviness sinking onto his shoulders. The weight didn't feel as dark, somehow, as it usually did.

'I didn't enjoy fighting that war,' he said, his voice croaking a little. 'Frankly, I abhorred every moment of it. And I never would have taken up a single sword if I hadn't been truly convinced it was for the best.'

She stood silent when he looked up, her eyes full of shadows. 'You feel guilty.'

'Yes.'

'For still being alive.'

He didn't reply to that. He couldn't.

Allie turned away from the shelves, away from the names and faces. 'I shouldn't have dragged you in here, should I?'

'It's alright.' He managed a smile. 'If it makes me look a little less like a murderous maniac in your eyes, I'm glad for it. And there are some good memories between the bad ones, too. The peaceful periods ...' He sighed. 'I've been happy enough during those.'

'And bored.'

'They rarely lasted long enough to get bored,' he said wryly. 'I was quite content in the first two, three decades after the Last Battle, too. It's just that life gets rather tedious if no one runs off with your clothes for a century.'

Her face broke into a grin as she took three steps back to him and lifted her hands to his chest, pinching his shirt between thumbs and forefingers. 'It's been a while since I ran off with any of your shirts, hasn't it?'

'I'm *wearing* this one.'

'So?' She looked up at him, eyes shining dangerously – a light in them that wiped the shadows from his mind at once. 'What are you going to do – complain to the Mother about it?'

Agenor choked on his own sudden laughter. 'I think this is an issue I'd rather solve myself, little thief.'

She wrinkled her nose at the nickname. Even that scowl had lost its sharpness, leaving only playful annoyance behind – the kind of annoyance that invited him to do far, far worse. He locked an arm around her waist and pulled her closer. Her exaggerated gasp set his loins on fire, more so than even the warm, soft feel of her, the arousal tensing his thighs and heating every spot where their bodies met.

'Better to keep you very, very close,' he muttered, lowering his face into the hollow of her neck. She squirmed as he brushed his lips over the skin just behind her small, round ear. 'I'm thinking I need to keep a good eye on those quick hands of yours.'

She breathed a laugh, trying to wrench free of his grip. 'Agenor ...'

'Still trying to flee me?'

She ceased her wrestling at once. The flutter of her breath brushed over his chest where she'd unbuttoned his shirt, shallow and irregular.

'No,' she whispered.

'Are you sure?' A coil was tightening within him, starting in his chest, winding tauter and tauter as it spread down. Ten more heartbeats breathing her scent and he would lose control. Like some savage, some reckless youth – and yet he craved it, *needed* it. 'Are you very damn sure—'

She wrapped her cool, slender fingers around his face and kissed him.

Twelve hundred years of restraint evaporated. A low animal groan wrestled free of his throat as he buried his empty hand into the mass of her brown curls and yanked her closer, submerging himself in the salty, lusty taste of her, begging for more ... Her lips opened at the first demand of his tongue, and he swept into the warmth behind. She moaned as their tongues tangled together, pressed her slender body even tighter against him, rubbed herself against the hard bulge of his arousal.

Every nerve in his body seemed to explode in a firestorm of want. He lowered the hand around her waist and grabbed her hips, crushing her against his aching erection. This time there was nothing theatrical about her gasp.

'Keep making those sounds,' he growled against her lips, 'and I don't think I'll make it to the bed with you, little thief.'

Her laugh was half-moan. 'Planning to have me on the floor?'

'I'm planning to have you *everywhere.*' The tiny tremor that racked through her was enough – more than enough – for his burning senses. 'Floor, desk, wall – every damn surface I can find – but if you want it civilised—'

She lowered her hand, slipped it around his torso, and flicked a fingertip over the onset of his wing.

Restraint became a distant memory.

He whirled her against the closed door, back pressed to the wood, and clawed into her hips, her bare thighs, in his hurry to yank her tunic aside. Cursed against her lips as she caressed his wing again and pleasure set its barbs into every inch of him, tearing him inside out with need.

'So civilised.' She trailed a longer line along a thin wing bone. The sensation of her cool fingers against that vulnerable, sensitive membrane sent sharp flares of lust straight into his groin; his cock twitched with every brush, desperate for more. Her other hand was everywhere – his side, his back, his hip, his thigh. He only felt those fingers on his wing, and the deadly, desperate *need* she was stroking into him.

'Allie,' he ground out. Fuck. One more moment of this and he'd be pounding her senseless against a wall, damn all intentions of slow and tender seduction. Did she have any idea what she was doing – that it took *weeks* before most fae lovers would even touch each other's wings? 'Keep doing this and I—'

Her fingers vanished from his wings.

She laughed.

Agenor sucked in a lungful of cool air, his mind clearing a fraction. That laugh – yet another surprise. Husky and hazy, but it sounded *triumphant*, too ...

He pulled back his face to meet her gaze, unease stirring in his gut. She beamed back at him with a grin broad enough to swallow him.

'Looks like we're even again, Lord Protector.'

'Like we're ...' And then he saw her clenched hand, a small silver chain dangling from her fist. The unblemished skin of her wrist, the bargain mark gone.

His key.

He'd stuck his key into his pocket.

Her wandering hands, his lust-hazed thoughts ... His stomach started falling. Oh, hell be damned – her sudden amiability. Her request to see his rooms again. Her eagerness to see what he kept behind this closed door. Had it all just been part of a ruthless strategy, a ploy to finally get him where she needed him?

His burning lust turned to clammy dread. Her soft skin under his hands – he suddenly felt embarrassed touching her, wanting her.

'Are you just a sore loser?' she said, her voice far too light to his frantic thoughts. 'Or is there another reason to look like death is knocking on the door?'

'Did you ...' He looked up. Her eyes shone bright – far too clever, far too triumphant, and so gods-damned beautiful he could die just looking at her. 'Was this just ...'

'Just politics?'

He couldn't breathe. The remainders of his past were turning, blurring, mocking him from their shelves. Defeated by lust and a pair of pretty blue eyes, and could she at least just stop *smirking* at him?

'You still don't realise it, do you?'

'Realise what?' he managed. 'That you played me? That—'

She leaned forward, nuzzling her nose against his chin. '*Even*, I said, Agenor.'

Only then did that part of her words sink in.

Even. By fulfilling her part of the bet. But he hadn't even *thought* about tasks and winning since he'd woken up that morning, and ...

'You refused to help,' she muttered. 'Shouldn't have been able to do that unless your offer was actually a selfless suggestion indeed. Not just an attempt to get me into your bed or to win my good opinion.' A chuckle. 'Which, incidentally, did wonders for my good opinion.'

Oh.

Oh.

He didn't even feel victorious as the realisation came through. Just ... relieved? *Grateful?* His heart was a pounding drum in his chest, a feeling like the first time he'd jumped off a cliff as a boy and prayed his half-grown wings would hold him. The words fell from his lips like that same prayer now—

'Should I conclude you *weren't* just playing the game, then?'

Her lips brushed over his, light as butterfly wings. 'If you aren't.'

'Allie,' he said hoarsely. He barely heard himself over the rush in his ears. 'I'm falling in love with you. I've been falling in love with you since I found that first bloody letter, and I haven't stopped plummeting since. And ...' His heart was pounding free from his ribcage. 'I can't deny I want to fuck you until neither of us is capable of walking, but that's secondary to ... everything. I want you to be safe. I want you to be cared for. If you'll allow me to take a little of that weight off your shoulders ...'

He hesitated. Her gaze lay fixed on his face, blue eyes soaking up every word that came from his lips.

'Let me do better for you,' he whispered. 'Let me change the world for you.'

She moulded her hand to his side again without taking her eyes from his. Soft, cautious touches, as if to prove he was not some figment of her own mind.

'You're ... so very persuasive, Lord Protector.'

His breath rushed from his lungs. 'Say you don't hate me.'

'I don't hate you.' She tightened her fingers on his hip, giving him a small, foxy smile. 'You're growing on me, frankly. I think I might end up liking you quite a lot, if you give me some time.'

The twinkle in her eyes was enough to slow his rattling heart. With a quiet chuckle, he brushed his lips over her forehead, feeling like he could breathe free for the first time in hours.

'Cruel little creature.'

She snorted a laugh. 'You'd be disappointed if I fell to my knees to worship the ground you walk on.'

'Perhaps,' he admitted, kissing her temple, then nipping her ear-lobe. She gave a satisfying hiss, body stiffening against his. 'Although I wouldn't particularly mind seeing you on your knees.'

Her glare was barely convincing. 'For a fearsome lord of respectable age, you're surprisingly shameless, Lord Protector.'

Some last string snapped within him. He yanked her into his arms and lifted her as she clutched his shoulders, her entire slender body shaking with unrestrained laughter – a sound of life, of light, and he couldn't help the grin that grew on his face as he carried her back into his bedroom. The snakes had courteously vanished. He still checked the blankets before dropping her into the fine linen, her tunic bunched up at her hips, her curls a messy chestnut crown around her head.

A perfect little treasure, his to desire, his to devour ... Something uncannily growl-like escaped him as he fell down to his knees beside her and slowly ran his fingers up the inside of her bare thigh until her chuckles became moans.

'Agenor ...'

'Call me respectable one more time,' he muttered, slipping his hand below her tunic, 'and I *will* show you something fearsome, little thief.'

She parted her lips to reply, then gasped as he reached the drenched fabric of her underwear, her retort forgotten. With a hoarse laugh, he traced the contours of her body below, watching her eyes flutter shut in his pillows – so, so close to that delicious surrender. Her fists clenched in his blankets. Her thighs tensed around his hand. Her moans climbed higher, higher, higher, a soft melody of impending release ...

He teased her underlinen aside. She gasped as he stroked his fingertip across her drenched lips, her entire body tightening with need.

'*Agenor.*'

He could no longer hold back.

Yanking her closer, he tore her underwear down, tugged her tunic over her head as she wrestled with his buttons, their bodies reduced to a mess of limbs and clothes and panting, heaving breath. She emerged from the chaos like a goddess triumphant, her pale breasts and hips marble in the indigo twilight, her nipples small, perking rosebuds – a sight so gloriously beautiful that he could have believed he was dreaming after all.

But there was nothing dreamlike about her small hands wrapping around his cock. Searing arousal burned through him, reducing all but the thought of her to ash and cinders – all but the overwhelming, all-consuming need to have her *now*.

'Lie back,' she whispered, clambering into his lap, and every nerve in his body roared in confusion.

'What are you—'

'Lie *back*, Agenor.' Her firm nudge against his shoulder was enough to overrule his stunned reflexes. He sank back in the silk and linen, wings splayed out over the bed – suddenly feeling so vulnerable as she straddled him, beaming at him like she was the hunter and he was the day's catch.

Perhaps he was.

He should have known she would surprise him.

He stopped thinking. Stopped expecting. Just watched in stunned, silent reverence as she came up on her knees and took his cock in her hands again, holding it up between her thighs. His straining tip slid against her tight entrance as she slowly lowered herself over him, and it took every grain of self-restraint he possessed not to thrust up and bury himself inside her.

She sank down another inch, and he let out an involuntary curse as he pressed into her warm wetness, her body stretching and clenching around him. Gods help him, she was tight. Her breath came in hoarse little gasps now, mirroring his own; her eyes gleamed with triumphant hunger in the falling darkness. And yet she took him in slowly, so excruciatingly slowly, until he was whimpering for every inch she gave him and that delirious torment was all his mind could still contain.

'So very fearsome,' she whispered, and drove herself all the way down.

The world became a blur of sensations. Her hips under his hands. Her nails clawing into his chest. Her moans and her scent and her perfect, hot softness, tight as a fist as she rode him, claimed him, conquered him ...

He tried to fight his climax. There was no use to it. The need for release built in him like a tidal wave, a force far stronger than any magic he'd ever wielded – she had him undone and unravelling, barrelling towards the edge, and he had no choice but to give in.

'*Allie ...*'

The sound of her name became a final, desperate growl of abandon as he surrendered the last of his sanity. His release tore through him like a curse, blissful wave after blissful wave of pleasure as he spilled his seed into her again and again ...

She rode him all the way through. Whispered his name as he shattered and came to life again, holding him, kissing him, until the world pieced itself back together and he found himself empty and exhausted in a darkness unlike any other night he'd ever known.

Her slender body lay curled against his chest. Her hair was a tickling cloak over his arms and neck and shoulders.

'Allie,' he whispered, his voice cracking.

She nuzzled his neck, then his jaw, then kissed his cheek. A quiet giggle broke the silence, soft enough that he doubted for a moment whether he'd truly heard it.

'Yes,' she murmured, her voice laced with suppressed laughter. 'I think I could grow to like you, Lord Protector.'

He burst out laughing.

And, with a single ravenous movement, flipped her over in the blankets for a fitting retaliation.

CHAPTER 12

Little thief,

Hope you slept well. You'll be pleased to hear I certainly didn't – I spent most of the night rereading Phyron's Treatises in an attempt to refute your interpretation of his ideal distribution of power. Still not sure if I managed, but you'll find some interesting passages underlined in chapters 6 and 7. One in chapter 13, too, for entirely different reasons.

A practical matter: please don't drop by my office today. Much as I appreciated yesterday's visit (I don't think I'll ever look at a quill the same way again), I'll unfortunately be buried in meetings for most of this afternoon.

Will the Greyside gathering indeed take place tonight? In that case, I might not see you at all today, which I will probably survive, although I'd rather not take the risk. Let me know whether anything can be done about it.

Sleepily yours,
  A.

Allie chuckled, sitting cross-legged on his broad bed with two leather-bound volumes on Divine Era philosophy, a dozing snake, and the letter she'd plucked from the usual spot in his wardrobe. Penning down the answer on the back of the parchment took no more than a few minutes.

My dearest Lord Protector,

It will be a consolation to you that I, too, have lain awake for a significant part of the night, for slightly less intellectual reasons. Our office encounter left me – how do I put this in a ladylike manner – quite unable to find a comfortable sleeping position. Walking, as a matter of fact, is not entirely pleasant either. Perhaps the third time was overdoing it a bit? One lives and learns.

The Greyside meeting is happening, and I'd like to be there – there's a chance I'll finally get their elders to accept your help on the new housing regulations. The way there will be long and dark, however, and considering my current physical predicament, who knows if anyone might make use of the occasion to ambush me? A fearsome fae lord to accompany me would not be unwelcome. I'll wait at the rose creek after work hours.

Sorely devoted,
  Your thief

She folded the letter, then curled up next to Coral on the sun-streaked bed and winced as her backside hit the mattress. Thank the gods she was in no hurry to move again. Since Agenor had told her supervisor that he needed her, specifically, to take care of his rooms – using the reasoning that he wanted a servant without a fear of snakes – she got a good few hours of free reading time every day. The supervisor didn't need to know she didn't actually spend the time cleaning, as the Lord Protector took care of his own living quarters well enough.

She appreciated that about him. No leaning on servants. No carelessness with his hard-won wealth. So reliable and dutiful and *responsible* ...

If only he would stop defending that damned Mother of his, he would be quite perfect.

Allie breathed a slightly crabby sigh as she opened the first volume of the *Treatises on Power and Privilege* and browsed to the chapters he'd mentioned. Centuries and centuries of loyalty to the High Ladies he served; of course, it had been laughably optimistic to expect she'd erase that history within the six weeks she'd been trying now. But it boggled the mind, how a male of high intelligence and good intentions still managed to look straight past the truth of the Mother he served – how he could so staunchly insist there was still a way to fix this fae empire, a way that didn't start with burning it all down to the very ground.

Of course they'll be willing to reconsider the current tribute system once I show them my overview of the troubles it's led to …

Even if that were the case, Allie had pointed out, would that really change anything as long as the power imbalance remained and the humans were still at the Mother's mercy if she ever changed her mind again?

His answer to that point was, presumably, to be found in the book she was holding. Phyron's sixth and seventh chapter dealt with taxation in the history of the archipelago and discussed the concept of the benevolent dictator. The thirteenth … She frowned. What did a discussion of negotiation skills have to do with the matter?

On the third page, Agenor had underlined two short sentences:

More powerful than those who wield swords or magic are those who wield a perceptive eye. A sharp mind is a more dangerous weapon than even the sharpest of blades.

Warm, fuzzy happiness bloomed through her, softer still than the silk and the golden rays of the sun.

Stop it, some old, calloused part of her chided, even through the smile that grew on her face, you're being sappy and sentimental and altogether senseless. But that part was rapidly losing its power over her. Life had become so oddly easy, these weeks. So very busy, too, the days filling up with town meetings and nightly debates and illicit meetings in court offices – but *lighter*, now that half of her worries concerned the state of her underwear rather than whether her neighbours would survive the month.

So she smiled. And then browsed back to chapter six, preparing to prove him wrong.

The worst of the soreness was finally fading when she made her way back to Rustvale in the late afternoon, working out her argument on power imbalances as she walked down the rocky road. Soon she'd have to get on her way to Greyside – the third time in the past ten days alone. But she'd have company this time, and the way there wouldn't be nearly as long in the arms of a helpful fae lord.

Russ wasn't home yet, she found as she arrived – likely off somewhere with Farran. The splashing behind the house suggested Inga had already returned and started with the week's laundry.

Allie yelled a greeting around the corner and disappeared inside to take off her apron. As she took out her braids, quick footsteps rattled around the house; Inga burst into the living room the next moment, her arms wet to the elbows, her blonde hair pinned up in two messy buns that hid those treacherous pointy ears from view.

'*Allie.*'

Impulsiveness wasn't unusual for her little sister. Neither was running around leaving chores unfinished. But the shrillness in her voice – that was a sign of true alarm. Allie stiffened, her hairpins still in her hand, and imagined a dozen distinct catastrophes at once. Dead neighbours? Wounded children? The Mother herself coming for a visit in ten minutes?

'What is it?'

'My monthlies started today,' Inga burst out, with a vague, fluttering gesture at the laundry tub outside. 'I was washing out my linens, and then I realised – Al, we're usually bleeding in the same week, but last month I think you didn't?'

Allie stared at her. 'What?'

'Last month,' Inga repeated, her high voice even more breathless, 'I remember thinking as I was washing that it would be the first time in years your monthlies came later than mine. And then I don't think they did. I haven't seen any blood linens in the entire past month, Al.'

The room cooled to a chilly, clammy cell around her.

Had she bled? She must have. A busy month – perhaps Inga had just forgotten. Perhaps she'd bled *earlier* rather than later last month. Perhaps she'd taken care of her linens herself – there had to be an explanation. A harmless explanation. A misunderstanding and no more than that – because the alternative ...

Inga stood panting in the doorway, her eyes too wide, her face too pale. One of her buns sagged loose, revealing the tip of her ear – that single innocent fae trait that had made her life such a dangerous living hell.

The alternative ...

No. That couldn't be. She'd been taking her herbs so very loyally for six weeks now, every single evening, because this *wasn't* going to happen. She *wasn't* going to bring another child into this war-torn mess of a world. The herbs were a fae preparation, the best quality money could buy – Agenor had promised her when she'd asked. So she had to be safe. Every single time had been safe ...

Except that first night.

Six weeks ago. Two weeks before she should have bled. Oh gods, but it had just been one night, and what were the chances of that?

'Al?'

A month and a half without bleeding. And she had been so very busy, running all over the island and kissing fae lords in every spare minute, that she hadn't even noticed.

The room was spinning – spinning and shrinking.

'Allie, *could* you be pregnant?' Inga's voice lowered to a haunted whisper. 'I mean – not from Russ, obviously, so ...'

They stared at each other in the house's dusky, dusty light. No, Allie wanted to say. No, it really is impossible. I've barely touched a man in my life. Do you think I wouldn't have told you if I was up to anything? But it would all be lies – dirty, dangerous lies – and what if the truth ...

'Is it *his*, Al? Is it – is it Agenor's?'

There was an edge of accusation to those words. Agenor's. Another little faeling, another child that wouldn't see a day of peace in its life. Not on this island, not with these people ... Oh gods, what had she *done*?

Her lips were moving. She felt them move, and yet not a sound came out, not even the faintest shred of a half-baked thought.

'Oh, for fuck's sake,' Inga said.

Hearing her little sister swear in that quiet, young girl's voice – it was enough to break the paralysis. Allie staggered half a step forward, uttering something that could be a laugh or a sob or a panicked shriek. She had to get herself together. She had to fix things, manage things, even if she had no idea of what there was to be managed.

'Al?'

'I'll handle it.' The promise fell from her lips without a single thought of how she would keep it. 'Don't worry – I'll deal with it. Just don't tell anyone. Not a living soul, understood? I'll—'

'What are you going to *do*?' Inga said shrilly.

'I'll figure it out.' Was she trying to reassure herself or her sister now? 'Please, don't worry. I won't be stupid – I'm not going to – to ...'

To bring another child onto this island of sharp divides and mutual hatred. Another *half-blood* child. Into this hell of turning backs and sneering glares and venomous hisses that had ruined her sister's life – oh, no, no. She couldn't do that. She could *not* do that. Not even if part of her clung to this shock with eager gratefulness rather than justified distress – because what was her eagerness worth against the agony of spending a lifetime chained to these treacherous shores?

A half fae child would be bound to the island like any human would, those were the Mother's rules – unless Agenor ...

Unless Agenor would agree to break the rules.

But he never did. He *still* never broke the rules. And if she told him and he refused – oh, gods. What if he disagreed?

And she was running, hair half-loose and dress half-buttoned, ignoring Inga's shocked cries behind her – out of that cursed little house, down those cursed dusty roads, all the way to the cursed, silent beaches of the court where no human soul would be mad enough to follow her.

CHAPTER 13

'Lord Agenor?' the emerald-winged messenger in the office windowsill said. 'The Mother asks for a word with you, my lord.'

Agenor barely suppressed a muttered curse as he fumbled Allie's latest letter back into his pocket. The Tolya business, presumably. He *should* have finished reading Creon's report of his second visit to the nymphs by now. Instead, he'd wasted an hour and a half this afternoon sneaking back into his room, reading the notes Allie had left behind in his book, and desperately trying to find something to disagree with in her arguments.

He'd have to claim yet another unexpected emergency distraction. It had become far too much of a habit these weeks.

And yet he couldn't keep down a glimmer of a smile as his fingertips brushed over the outline of Allie's letter again.

The Mother's hall was still silent as he walked in a few minutes later. Not for the first time in the past month, he found himself swallowing some new and rather unpleasant feelings as his gaze ran over the bone-covered walls. A rather sensible choice, he'd once thought, for a court built by a god of death – and then Allie had beaten him over the head with a couple of rather pointed remarks on using human bones as decorative accessories, and he had rather shamefully admitted he was, once again, an oblivious idiot.

He needed to have a word with the High Ladies about that point, he reminded himself as he made his way to the high throne on the other side of the room. And about the tribute rates and the handling of rebellions and the island bindings and that nasty little law that, if one did the math a little more carefully than he'd bothered to do in the past century, declared one fae life worth about ten human lives …

Basilisk stirred in his chest pocket, and Agenor drew in a deep breath. One thing at a time. There was this conversation to be dealt with, first.

He found a pair of dark eyes watching him as he finally looked up at the throne – Melinoë, awake already, at this time of the day?

'You're up early,' he said, crossing the last few feet to the spot where he could comfortably speak with her without having to squash his head into his neck to look up at her. She gave him a rather cold smile. Ah. Not happy, then.

'It's been ages since I last had a word with you, Agenor. You seem to be terribly busy in the evenings these days.'

Oh. Fuck. He *was* terribly busy most nights, indeed, flying a little human thief around the island and enjoying their quiet hours together just a little more than he probably should – so much so that he hadn't realised he hadn't spoken to one of his High Ladies in weeks. If Melinoë was annoyed enough to wake up during the day now, he had really neglected her too much.

'Apologies,' he said, steeling himself. 'Some trouble with the tributes took more time than expected. Speaking of which—'

'Tolya,' she interrupted before he could get to the subject of tribute rates in general. 'Yes. I presume you read Creon's report?'

'Most of it,' Agenor said, which was almost true, if you ignored half of the text. 'Did you speak with him already?'

'Achlys did. He just left.' She waved at the entrance behind him. 'Seemed a little curt about something. Either one of the little bitches stabbed him in the thigh and he won't admit it, or he's unhappy you didn't tell him to burn the entire island down.'

The first option was unlikely enough to be impossible. Agenor grimaced, not sure if she was sharing her amusement at her son's more bloodthirsty preferences or reproaching him for his apparent mildness in the dragging issue of the nymph hostages. Perhaps she'd have preferred for him to order half of the island killed, rather than to take out only the nymph queen who had come up with the entire hostage plan in the first place. Then again ...

He'd explained the situation to her – the missing tributes, Eldoris's idea to cut down trees. She couldn't want him to resort to general massacres under those circumstances, could she?

'It might have something to do with Eldoris,' he suggested cautiously. 'Heard a rumour that she didn't survive this last mission.'

'Oh, she didn't,' Melinoë said, a smile quirking up her doll face. Amusement indeed, then. 'I should have known you'd hear.'

'Only shreds. The report didn't say anything about it.' It was the first thing he'd checked. 'One of my people said something about her drowning, which seemed rather odd.'

'Well, she was found washed up on the beach.' She let out a high, tingling laugh. 'With her throat slit, though. I'll have to appoint a new ambassador, it seems. One who *can* keep the reins tight on those damned nymphs, because next time someone makes us barter for weeks to get my people back alive—'

'Look,' Agenor said, sucking in a deep breath. 'In all frankness, I'm not sure if loose reins were really the problem with this situation. I've been looking into those tributes—'

'Oh, yes, you mentioned it.' She waved it away. 'There's no problem with the tributes. They're lower than the human tributes, even, so—'

'Yes, but nymph isles aren't generally used for agriculture,' Agenor interrupted her, a little louder than he should have. Why hadn't she thought of that? Why hadn't Achlys thought of it, either? As far as he knew, the sisters always thought of *everything* – it was nothing like them to overlook something so glaringly obvious, even if *he* had been oblivious enough to miss it for decades. 'The nymphs are foragers. If we want them to produce the rates we're currently asking, they'd have to overhaul their entire lifestyle, and that's hardly the idea, is it?'

Melinoë leaned forward from the black velvet and silk of her pillows, pursing her lips a fraction. 'Are you doubting my decisions now, Agenor?'

'No!' Too fast. Too much like the lie it undeniably was. Doubting her – yes, he *was* doubting her. Then again, telling her so to her face ... She would hardly be more open to his line of argument if she stopped trusting him, would she?

'You sound doubtful,' she said, with that silvery, tingling laugh he knew to be a warning. 'You do realise, don't you, that your apparent weak-hearted feelings towards our subjects will directly result in a decline of our comfort? That it is those well-considered tributes which have allowed us to live at the court in peace in the last decades?'

'Of course I realise,' he said sharply. *In peace* – holding lavish banquets, wasting the food for which others may have paid with their lives. She *had* to see that, didn't she? She *had* to care. 'I'm not suggesting we waive the tributes entirely. Just saying we might want to take another look at those rates, if they're a cause of so much trouble for us all.'

'If we lower the rates in response to this madness,' Melinoë said coldly, 'everyone and their mother will be abducting fae officials next month. *You* should know, Lord Protector. Where has your common sense gone?'

His common sense. Gods and demons, he *was* being a fool – why was he antagonising her like this, butting head-first into his argument like a faeling with not a century of life behind him? The High Ladies didn't appreciate abrupt change – they never had – and with the horrors previous changes had brought, he could hardly blame them. Fae politics required patience. Time to gather his data, to plant the first seeds of doubt into the right minds, to test the waters and make sure he would bring forth the right arguments to the right people at the right times – so why was he behaving like something was chasing him at his heels, growling and snarling at him as he made his slow, necessary steps to change the course of an empire?

He almost cursed. Allie.

But she had to realise that an administration this large, this heavy, did not turn around within a day and a half. She had to understand that he ought to be moderate and reasonable and, most of all, *subtle*.

'You're right,' he heard himself say. 'I'm not thinking with my sensible mind. I'll see if I can think of some capable replacement for Eldoris – we must make sure to re-establish law and order as soon as possible, indeed. I suppose you want to make a choice quickly?'

'Before the end of the week. Thank you, Agenor.'

Her voice had mellowed again. Enough sensible words – they *were* sensible words – and yet they felt so very dirty on his lips.

Allie would be most unamused to hear of this encounter, he realised as he bowed and left the hall again.

See? She doesn't want *to fix it.* He could hear her say it – he'd heard her say it so many times before these months, always with that same scowl of furious disgust. A scowl that drove him to defend the High Ladies every time, because of course they'd want to fix it – wasn't that how he'd always known them? They'd landed in his ravaged little village all those centuries ago and comforted the crying children, healed the wounded elders, and promised peace. And they'd kept their promises – time and time again, through wars and loss and years of utter destruction, they'd *always* kept their promises to him ...

Didn't he owe them some patience now, to make them see how this path led away from everything they'd sworn to achieve all those years ago? Shouldn't he know better than to – gods help him – turn away from them after all they'd done for him?

And what if you can't save everyone, Lord Protector?

A curse fell from his lips as he flung out his wings and launched himself through the open window arches.

'And what would you have me do, then?' he muttered to the marble terrace far below him. What else *could* he do? Privately declare that he thought the Mother unwise and incapable of taking the right decisions, and find himself swiftly and efficiently removed from any position of influence? Publicly make the same declaration and be thrown before the hounds? Little good he would be able to do with his wings torn off his shoulders by those monsters' teeth.

Good gods, he needed patience. It really was disconcerting how Allie's more radical tendencies were rubbing off on him, the urge to set the entire place on fire and reduce his life's work to ashes. It wasn't that he didn't *understand*. But throwing faekind into a senseless war would only cause more suffering in the grand scale of things, and wasn't that exactly what they were trying to prevent? The empire wasn't perfect, no. But it was certainly better than nothing, and improving what they had made far more sense than starting again at the very beginning and praying that somehow the new state of affairs would look better than the current.

He'd put some thought into the new ambassador's candidates, he resolved as he descended towards the burbling creek where Allie had told him to wait for her. He'd have to get that right, at least, find someone who appeared properly stern, but who would also be open to milder perspectives on the situation. Someone who'd make sure the nymphs wouldn't starve or lose their trees in the years to come.

And if that worked out well, he could slowly start replacing emissaries in other outposts too.

Still not fast enough for Allie's taste, of course; she'd likely suggest to quietly murder the most aggravating fae representatives in their beds. But he really couldn't resort to those methods habitually. Eldoris had offered him the convenient tool of Creon's irritation. Some of the others may show comparable ways out, but for those who didn't ... Again, there was no sense in dramatically breaking the rules. All it would do was anger the people he still needed to fix the empire's problems.

Slow, diplomatic change. Allie had to see that was really the best of their options.

And yet he didn't feel very confident about her understanding as he sat by the crystal clear water and waited for her to show up. The longer he spent mulling over his own thoughts, the more he began to suspect she'd find some fault in them within a minute – an unpleasant, unexpected fault that would overhaul all his sensible thoughts and force him to new, even more unpleasant conclusions.

And shouldn't she have been here half an hour ago already?

He eyed the sun, squinting against the burning light. Her work day had ended over an hour and a half ago. Even if he included the time it would take for her to walk home, have a quick meal, and change her clothes, she should have shown up by now.

Had he understood her letter incorrectly?

He pulled the parchment from his pocket and ran his eyes over her familiar handwriting again – no, rose creek after work, there was no misunderstanding that. They'd met at this same spot a dozen times, no chance he had somehow found the wrong part of the creek.

So what had caused her delay?

For the first time, a different nervousness stirred in his guts. Had something given her trouble, enough so that she'd forgotten about this appointment entirely? Was she still at home, dealing with some troublesome neighbour or the newest of Leander's stupid ideas?

How long had it been since he'd last shown his face in Rustvale? Was it long enough that he could afford to fly by without raising anyone's suspicions?

He bit down his nervousness for ten more minutes, then gave in to his roaring anxiety. Damn it. She was never late. He was allowed to worry under these circumstances; he'd come up with some quick lie to appease the gossiping neighbours.

Half of his mind still expected to find her on the road between creek and village as he made his way to Rustvale, faithfully following every bend in the mountain path. She was nowhere to be seen. By the time the black brick houses loomed up before him, surrounded by playing children and the occasional housewife hauling laundry baskets around, only the steeliest self-control withheld him from tearing down the walls to find her.

He left the houses standing. But he really didn't have the patience to wait longer than half a heartbeat after knocking, and flung open the door with far too much force.

'Al?' Inga's voice rose from the backroom. 'Are you—'

She stumbled to a halt in the doorway as soon as she caught sight of him.

Her eyes were red, Agenor realised a moment too late. Her hands were trembling. Something twitched in her face as their gazes met – something not nearly so timid as the glances he usually received from her. It looked suspiciously like ...

Hate?

What in hell was going on?

'What's the matter?' His voice sounded too loud in the small living room. 'Is Allie—'

'She's not here.' She was clutching the doorway with her small hands, all but spitting out the words. 'What do you want from her?'

Agenor stared at the girl before him. Fifteen years old, thin and trembling and powerless, and yet she'd thrown that question into his face like an elderly matron looking out for her ward's respectable reputation. Gods and demons, she'd barely ever spoken two words in a row to him until today – and now this?

Now *what*?

'I want to know where the hell she is,' he said, unable to stop himself from glancing over the girl's shoulder. The room behind seemed to be empty indeed. 'And if you could tell me what's upset you like this, that would be—'

'I don't know where she is,' Inga said stiffly. 'So leave us alone, yes?'

'Leave ... Gods' sakes, Inga, what's going on?'

She threw him a glower he could never have imagined on that young, timid face. 'Can't tell.'

'You mean you don't *want* to tell me?' He was grasping for straws now. No one had magically bound her to silence, had they? *Had* they? 'Or—'

'Promised Al not to tell you,' she interrupted, folding her arms. 'Are you getting out?'

'What? Inga, please, I—'

'Get out or I'll scream.' Tears were welling in her eyes again. 'You bastard – I thought you *understood*. I thought you were *helping*. And all this time ...' A half-sobbed scoff. 'You're all the fucking same, aren't you?'

'All the ...' He had to stop repeating her. Had to stop blinking at her like some half-wit caught in a play far beyond his mental capacities. All the same ... Had she somehow figured out what had been going on between Allie and him in the past few weeks? But then why in the hell would Allie tell her and suddenly insist on secrecy towards him – what was there to keep quiet?

'Get *out*,' Inga whispered, and somehow it sounded like a threat.

He got out.

The sun was a blinding, burning hellfire as he staggered back into the light, struggling to make sense of the world – not here. Promised not to tell you. Leave us alone ... Had he somehow caused them trouble? Set another bastard like Deiras on their trail or accidentally infuriated Leander to the point he'd retaliated and taken his anger out on the village? But Allie should know he could deal with the likes of those males, so why wouldn't she come straight to him if the issue was anything external?

Why would she avoid him? Vanish without a trace? Instruct her sister not to tell him anything? That really only made sense if—

If he was the problem.

He stared at the now empty village road with empty, unseeing eyes. The day really hadn't been that extraordinary. A few meetings, a handful of letters, and of course Melinoë – but Allie couldn't know much about that last conversation, could she? And either way, would it be a reason to disappear on him like this?

Leave us alone.

Did she *want* him to leave her alone?

For what had to be the twentieth time today he fumbled her letter from his pocket and unfolded the worn parchment. *My dearest Lord Protector ...*

Something hardened inside him.

She did *not* hate him. She did *not* fear him. For the past six weeks she'd trusted him with her dangerous secrets and her neighbours' predicaments and every fae bastard trying to harm her – so if she was now fleeing him all of a sudden, something was wrong. Terribly, terrifyingly wrong, and he was not going to sit back and wait for the threat to reveal itself.

He'd spent enough time looking away from trouble.

Three quick wingbeats and he was high enough to see all the way down to the towns in the north, the wilderness and beaches in the south, the endless rows of rugged ridges separating him from Greyside in the west. She *had* planned to go to Greyside. As a first place to look, it was as good as any other.

But the anxiety wouldn't stop churning in his guts even as he flew — that nameless, instinctive dread that told him the world was once again slipping from his hands entirely.

CHAPTER 14

The first thing to be done, Allie decided as she hurried over the mountain roads with her heart in her throat and her thoughts a swirling, whirling mess, was to pull herself together.

The second thing to do was to make decisions and make them *fast*.

Memories were crowding her, merciless in their razor-sharp clarity – of little Inga sobbing in her bed, of the backs turning wherever the girl showed her face, of Resa's pleas in her very last moments. Of her own first night on this island, when her captors offloaded her from their ship and forced her to sit in that gods-damned bone hall until the Mother's magic left her feeling cold and hollow, no longer able to leave these shores.

And now there was to be a child?

She barely knew where she was going. Out. Away. *Safety.* A tidal wave of fury was seeping through the panic, an instinctive anger so deep it could have swallowed this entire cursed court up to the very last tower – a child, a dream she'd thought long dead and buried, and even *that* had to be ruined by this living hell of a place. There was no bearable life to be found here, caught in the divide between peoples. Either she had to smuggle her little half fae out of this place somehow, breaking the Mother's rules and the heinous bonds that kept them here, or ...

Her guts cramped. No. She didn't want to think about the alternative.

The sweat ran in chilly cascades over her back by the time she left the mountains behind and ventured into the olive and cypress woods of the south side of the island. No safe place for humans, she knew. The hounds were rumoured to stalk these parts, and the one glimpse she'd caught of those monsters in the distance when she was sixteen years old had convinced her she didn't need a second encounter. But it was the only area of the island that was always deserted, and right now she'd rather be torn apart by hounds' teeth than make small talk with innocent passers-by.

No hounds showed up as she stumbled through the tangled labyrinth of myrtle and wild grapes, closer and closer to the heavy briny scent of the sea. Perhaps they slept during the day. Or perhaps she still smelled of fearsome fae lord.

Oh, gods help her. Agenor.

She wanted to talk with him. She *needed* to talk with him. She craved the safety of his arms around her, the reassurance of his almost limitless devotion – but there *was* a limit, she knew, and it consisted of the Mother's rules. Those same rules she desperately needed to break.

He would tell her not to be reckless. Promise her all would be well. *I'll take care of it, little thief*, she could already hear him say, *I'll just ask them not to bind this child.* And then the vicious bitches would do it anyway, and he would make excuses for them and promise he would change the High Ladies' mind if they just gave it some time, and their child would grow up in a never-ending nightmare of scorn and loathing and probably die from a knife in the back before Agenor would admit the world wasn't fixable.

And if that was the price of telling him ... she couldn't.

She reached the beach, somehow. By the time she stumbled barefoot into the lukewarm, frothing water, she could no longer remember how she had ended up there or where her shoes had gone. Pearly white sand stretched out to her left and right, making such a deceptively good effort to look like a paradise rather than a prison wall.

Allie sucked in a deep breath and waded deeper into the sea.

The water reached to the hem of her servant's frock when the magic caught her, an invisible punch in the midriff that sent her gasping and staggering back. Salty sea foam came soaking through her skirts, sticking them to her skin like clammy hands. She gritted her teeth and stepped forward, bracing herself for the impact this time; if she gave up so easily, she'd never find out if the binding could be broken at all. Perhaps it was just a single barrier to crack. Perhaps if she ignored the pain for long enough, just continued going forward, it would fade eventually and leave her free of these cursed magic-forged binds.

She drew in a deep breath, promised herself it would just be a few minutes, and struggled on.

The magic didn't fade.

The painful punches became a burning, chafing sensation as she wrestled farther into the crystal-clear sea, grating on her chest and stomach until she gagged with every inch forward. By the time she stood hip-deep in the water, the magic was pulling at her heart, driving it to rattle and slow and rattle again. Her feet turned numb and limp and wouldn't take another step. Her hands tingled and burned, disobeying her mind's commands as she tried to swim. Sobbing and suffocating, she stood waist-deep in the azure sea and tried to make herself admit defeat – but admitting defeat meant admitting *she* would never be the one to take her baby off this island, and that—

The loud whoosh of a wingbeat broke through the monotonous rustling of the surf behind her.

Agenor?

She wasn't sure if it was fear or relief that made her heart jump as she jerked around in the sparkling water – oh gods, he'd found her. Thank the gods, he'd found her. All would be well. All would be lost. He'd figure it out. He'd ruin everything. He—

The fae male on the beach wasn't Agenor.

Her eyes made sense of the sight a little too late. Long black hair ruffled by the breeze. Cold eyes staring straight into the most dangerous depths of her mind. Scarred hands on the silvery knives at his belt ...

The Silent Death.

Allie stood frozen as her thoughts slowly, patiently drew their conclusions. The Mother's son. On the beach behind her. Watching her
pathetic attempts to escape like a predator ready to strike – ready to slit
her throat or skin her alive or whatever his preferred method of murder
was today ...

Although, he did not look particularly murderous right now.

Really, he looked rather *ill*.

Allie blinked, limbs numbed by fear as much as the magic now. Even
in the late afternoon sunlight, his copper skin shone pale, almost grey-
ish; the fingers clutched around his knife hilts were shaking lightly. Like
a flu patient just crawling out of bed. Good gods, had those nymphs
Agenor told her about sent him back home with a marsh fever or two?

She cleared her throat, holding his hard gaze despite every fibre in her
body screaming at her to flee. Fleeing would only hasten her untimely
demise. And perhaps if he was dealing with cold sweats and twisty
guts, killing rebellious servants would not be the first thought on his
mind for once in his life.

'If you'll excuse me?' she said, and tried to do it politely despite the
fear clenching her throat shut. 'I'm currently quite busy running from
the consequences of my own actions, my lord, and I'd hate to die in the
process. Should I move my efforts elsewhere?'

The Silent Death didn't move. Still no flashes of deadly red magic.
Still no knife diving at her chest.

Allie drew in the slowest of breaths and added, on barely more than
a whisper, 'My lord?'

He sank to his knees, scribbled something into the wet sand with
quick, rash gestures, got up without giving her so much as a glance, and
turned away before she even opened her mouth to ask her questions.
His steps as he stalked off were oddly jerky, nothing like that supple
predator's gait she'd seen from a very safe distance at the court.

What in hell? *Was* he ill?

She drew in a next, shivering breath, suddenly feeling her feet again.
Only one way to find out, presumably.

The pain of the binding magic vanished as soon as she wobbled onto the beach, leaving only a violent nausea behind. The message scratched into the wet sand was short but left nothing to the imagination.

You'll die that way.

And that was all.

Allie blinked at the lines in the sand, and then at his winged, black-clad back, somehow already dozens of feet away from her. A *warning*? The Mother's loyal murderer found a bound human servant making obvious attempts to escape the island, and instead of turning her inside out and painting the sand with her guts, his only reaction was to *warn* her?

She swallowed. If he dared to leave her alone after such evident rebellion, the message was likely true. With the way she'd felt the magic tearing and tugging at her heart, she shouldn't be surprised.

Which meant Creon's unexpected mercy and mysterious illness were not the worst of her problems by far.

She felt her shoulders sag as she glared back at the sparkling sea, managing only with the greatest of efforts to keep a frustrated roar down. *You'll die like that.* It didn't matter if she found a boat or built a raft or smuggled herself on board of a tribute ship. The magic would keep her here or kill her.

And neither option would save her child.

She sank down in the sand, soaking wet and cold to the bone, and closed her eyes. The obvious solution was clear – so mercilessly clear. She could get the herbs from Heloise in a heartbeat. No child would ever be born to suffer a life at the Crimson Court; no one but her and Inga would ever even know what could have been. A clean cut. A sensible decision.

But she didn't *want* it.

She'd lost hope in her dream of children since those nights on the tribute ship, given up on it altogether when she and Russ decided to marry. It was better this way, she'd told herself. It would be selfish to get a new, vulnerable soul stuck on this island. She had Inga to take care of, and that was enough. And yet ...

A single careless night and the impossible had happened. Didn't that mean *something*? The old gods were dead – she refused to believe otherwise in this broken world – and yet for the first time in her life, she found herself wondering if perhaps fate was trying to tell her something after all.

So what were the weapons it had placed into her hands?

She sat on that beach as the sun slowly sank towards a horizon that may forever be out of her reach and considered her options. Her assets. Her arguments. Her pleas and, if all else failed, her threats. She had Russ. Through him, Clara and the network. A fae healer who owed her his silence, and neighbours who *probably* wouldn't rat on her.

Which meant she might stand a chance, if not for the single biggest obstacle ...

Agenor.

What game, in hell's name, should she have him play?

She'd have to tell him *something*. At some point, she'd start showing, no chance he'd overlook her pregnancy entirely. There was no avoiding him for months on this island either. So unless she was willing to tell him the child was Russ's after all – a lie that made her feel dirty just thinking about it – he'd have to know.

But if he knew, he'd have to know about the laws she was planning to break, too. And if he knew that much ...

She shivered. Would he stop her? He very well might. His loyalty had always been firmly with the Mother. Shoving centuries of history aside for some mortal woman he'd known for weeks and a half-blood child that would never be accepted as his heir in the first place – it seemed a lot to ask.

And yet, what else could she do? Lie about the child's paternity, after all? She may be wrong about him. Was she really going to betray him like that if there was a chance he *would* see what had to be done?

But if she told him and he didn't—

'*Allie!*'

She jerked around.

It *was* him, this time, hurrying towards her over the sand, his wings folding in like he'd called out her name before even landing. Dark trousers and polished boots, wine red shirt with the sleeves rolled up, every inch the Lord Protector of the Crimson Court – but his eyes clung to her soaked, sweaty form as if he barely even remembered the cruel red castle walls rising up behind him.

'Thank the gods,' he said hoarsely. 'I've been looking for you everywhere – what in the world are you doing here, Al? Why weren't you at the creek?'

Al. She shivered. He'd started doing that in recent weeks, shortening what was already an abbreviation – like only family members did, although she wasn't sure if he realised that. It sounded so familiar from his lips already. And yet, now, with the weight of this brand new secret on her mind ...

Was it real, this uncanny sense of safety she felt around him? Real enough for what she'd have to ask of him?

Her lips parted. No sound came out.

'What *happened*?' He fell to his knees in the sand beside her. His breath was coming too fast – as if he'd run all the way from his offices to this quiet beach. Even now his eyes wouldn't hold still; they kept shooting from her to the peaceful sea and the dunes behind, looking for a culprit to blame, looking for someone to tear to shreds over the state she was in. 'Who did this to you? If anyone put a hand on you—'

'No!' she blurted out, and then suddenly she was crying – heavy, ugly sobs of pain and confusion and exhaustion and everything in between. 'Nobody – nobody ...'

His strong, safe arms wrapped around her. She curled against his chest, smearing sand and seawater all over his clothes, blubbering unconvincing attempts at reassurances she didn't even believe herself as he stroked his fingers through her messy hair and held her even tighter.

'Little thief ...'

There was a slight crack in his voice, and she cried even harder at the sound of it. At the lies she'd considered telling, the excuses she'd wanted to make.

'I'm sorry, I'm so sorry ...'

'Al,' he whispered. 'Stop it. What's going on? Tell me what you need – tell me what I can do. I don't want to see you like this.'

'But I can't—'

'Yes, you can.' His hands tensed around her in a reassurance stronger than anything words could express. 'Please, little thief. I promise I'll help, but you *have* to tell me what you need.'

She had to know better. She had to know how little this illusion of safety truly meant, had to know how little weight that promise would hold as soon as it put him on the opposite side of the Mother herself. But she was hurting and exhausted and she needed the sincerity in his voice to be true so, so desperately ...

'You promise?' she sobbed. 'You really, really promise ...'

'Anything, Al. Please.'

And that last word – the despair in his voice, the concern, the tenderness – was just enough to make her suck in a deep breath and bawl, 'I'm *pregnant*.'

CHAPTER 15

It took Agenor a good five heartbeats to make sense of the words she'd sobbed out against his chest, the syllables barely recognisable through the blur of her crying.

Pregnant.

Pregnant?

The word seemed to slide off the surface of reality like raindrops off a wing's membrane, too utterly impossible to stick. Of course she wasn't pregnant. No one ever got pregnant within a year of trying, let alone within a month. Hell, they hadn't even been trying – she'd been taking her herbs faithfully, hadn't she? So she had to be mistaken. She had to be confused. An innocent misunderstanding, nothing more ...

He parted his lips, then paused. Somehow, with her soaked, sandy, shivering body in his arms, those words on the tip of his tongue no longer sounded nearly so reassuring.

Unlikely or not, she did not make a habit of being confused, did she? But if she wasn't ...

His pounding heart stilled in his chest as the thought finally punched through. If she wasn't confused, then she was indeed pregnant. With his child. After all those decades of war, all those centuries in which even the *thought* of a family was too much of a distraction from the armies to lead and fights to win.

Oh gods.

Allie had gone still in his arms. Waiting for him to speak. Waiting for him to figure out what words were again.

'Little thief ...' He cleared his throat. Sensible. He had to be sensible more than anything, now; the only alternative was screaming, and he had *some* pride left. 'That does seem a little improbable, doesn't it?'

'That first night,' she muttered, her face still buried in his shirt. 'When I stole your key. I didn't have my herbs yet.'

'*One* night,' Agenor said with a breathless chuckle. 'Nobody's ever gotten pregnant from ...'

'Oh, you ...' She jerked up her head, something like a laugh breaking through the sobs. 'Don't be oblivious again, Agenor. Humans are much more fertile than fae. We don't have centuries to wait for progeny, remember?'

He blinked at her. Humans. Who somehow produced families of fourteen children within two decades. Yet another difference he'd never given more than a moment's thought.

Gods and demons. He *was* an idiot.

Allie sniffed before he could speak, averting her tear-stained face. 'And the timing checks out, too. And I didn't bleed for two months. So as sure as anyone can be with these things ...'

He dropped farther back into the sand, so gracelessly he had to swing out his left wing to keep his balance. Two months. Too long – far too long. Which meant they could be sure, indeed, and he was an oblivious fool, and she was ...

Pregnant.

The rustle of the sea swelled into a roar in his ears, drowning out even the sound of his pounding heartbeat.

'Did you not realise until today?' he brought himself to say.

'I stopped keeping track of my cycles years ago.' A joyless chuckle against his chest. 'There really was no use for it after I married Russ. But Inga realised it while she was washing out her own linens.'

The first pieces of the puzzle finally shoved into place through the mist of shock and confusion. No bleeding, and Inga knew Russ hadn't been the cause of the issue – which left few contenders for the honour and even less honour for the contenders. Of course the girl had drawn her conclusions. *All the same …*

But he *wasn't* like that, one of the honourless bastards who violated human women left and right and vanished when matters became pressing – he wasn't like the anonymous male who had fathered Inga and left her to the world's mercy after she was born. Allie should *know* he wasn't. And yet it didn't seem she'd defended him against her sister's accusations. Quite the opposite …

He glanced down again at her slender body in his lap, at the wet frock sticking to her thighs, the sand on her bare feet. The rustling sea beside them, so deceptively peaceful.

Oh gods.

'Allie,' he said, and his voice came out hollow. No. She couldn't think *that* ill of him, could she? 'You – you weren't trying to flee me again, were you?'

She sat frozen in his lap, gaze stubbornly fixed on the sunset shrouding the horizon in brilliant pink.

'Allie.'

'Not *you*,' she whispered, squeezing her eyes shut. 'But everything else – this island, the humans on it, the Mother, everything that would turn a child's existence into a living hell—'

'You … Al, please.' The sound that escaped him was half laugh, half groan, and entirely baffled. 'What do you think of me? If I'm – gods and demons – if I'm to have a child, I'll make damn sure their life isn't—'

'A child that's half human?'

Half human. His firstborn heir would be *half human*. The irony of it was almost too painful to be true – but hell, he could think about the odd games of fate later. A child wouldn't be here for months. Right now, there was the cold, drenched woman in his arms and, worse, the unbearable distrust in her voice.

'You really think I'd cast my own child aside for being half human?' he managed. 'For being half *you*?'

'No!' At once her tears were flowing again, violent, frustrated sobs. 'No, but you don't get it. Do you think that whatever the hell you could do would make their life pleasant in this place? That you could shield a child from the mockery and the—'

He let out a bewildered laugh. 'I'm the bloody Lord Protector of this court! If that's good for anything—'

'That will only make your child more of a target! And it may not even have magic to defend itself!'

'Little thief,' Agenor said, closing his eyes, 'you're very much assuming the worst now.'

'I'm not assuming the *worst*,' she burst out. 'I'm assuming reality! Remember last time you tried to tell me the world wasn't as bad as I thought it was?'

He stiffened. With a sharp laugh, she crawled from his lap, brushing the sand off her legs with short, snappish gestures.

'It's not that I don't understand your concerns,' he said faintly. 'But do you really think—'

'I don't *think*, Agenor. I *know*.' She grabbed his hand, fingers pressing into his palm as if to press her thoughts into the marrow of his bones. Her eyes were burning embers in the falling twilight. 'And of course you think I'm exaggerating, but *you* haven't heard ten-year-old Inga crying in her bed because she'd rather not have existed, and—'

'But she didn't have her fae parent to protect her! She was surrounded by humans who—'

'Do you think the fae are better?' she snapped. 'You don't know how many of them are still going out of their way to call her a blemish on their pure-blooded ideal world – hell, even *Leander* realised he had to give her a job away from the court to keep her safe. Does that tell you how bad it was?'

Even Leander. His thoughts wavered. Even that bloody fool who cared more about his pretty clothes than the humans' lives or the duty he was paid to do ...

'People will hate a half-blood child for just *existing*, Agenor.' Her harrowed whisper twisted through the tangle of his thoughts. 'Even if you can offer the protection we would need, it would be a life of constant danger, constant vigilance, constant fear. Is that really how you want any child to grow up, let alone your own?'

He buried his face in his hands, mind spinning. Too many questions. Too many new thoughts. For the bloody gods' sake, he could barely make sense of the news of her pregnancy – and now he was supposed to have ideas on *parenting*?

'What other option do we have, then?' he heard himself say.

Her answer came so intimidatingly fast he knew she'd prepared for it. 'I want my children to grow up somewhere else. Anywhere else.'

'Oh gods. Al.' He rubbed his face. 'The law is that all the court's human and half-human children are to be bound to the island at birth.'

'Yes,' she said defiantly, 'I know. I want to break the law.'

He stared at her. Fierce blue eyes glared back at him, a challenge and an unspeakable fear fighting for dominance in the hard lines around her lips.

Break the law – the rules he'd made himself, the rules that had kept his world together as long as he lived. Gods and demons, there really was no need for such drastic plans, was there?

'You seem to be racing ahead of the situation a little,' he said, forcing himself to stay calm as he folded his hand over hers. 'If I ask Achlys and Melinoë to make an exception for this situation, there will be—'

She made a small, wailing sound. 'Oh, gods help me. I knew you were going to say that.'

'Then what is the problem?'

'They might refuse.'

He gave a bewildered chuckle. 'Why would they?'

'Why wouldn't they?' she retorted sharply. 'Did you convince them to leave those poor nymphs alone yet?'

'That ... Al, that's an entirely different—'

'That's a no, I presume?'

He rubbed his face, letting out another joyless laugh. 'The Tolya situation is a matter of general governance. You can't compare that to a simple personal favour.'

'So what should I compare it to?' Her scowl was back – an expression he hadn't seen for weeks and hadn't missed. 'Do you have any recent examples of other bindings they've undone for personal reasons? The only examples you ever mentioned to me were for *their* benefit.'

'I – gods – of course they don't do it for just anyone who asks, but—'

'And you have never asked them before,' she interrupted, 'and you have never discussed a similar case with them, and you don't know anyone else who ever got them to pay a comparable favour, meaning that we don't know anything. So they can say no. And if you ask them and they say no, they'll know about the matter, meaning that the alternative option would no longer be possible either.'

'What alternative option?' he said a little too loudly. 'Smuggling out an entire damn child?'

'Well, yes. Exactly that.'

He blinked at her. 'Allie.'

'Yes?'

'That's ... not how these things work. It's a half fae child. There's a chance it has magic. There'll be a fae physician around at birth to make sure that magic is bound immediately, and—'

'They don't have to know it's half fae,' she said.

Again he fell silent. Next to them, the sea continued its steady rhythm – such an oddly constant sound to accompany a conversation tugging at every pillar of his life's foundations. They didn't have to know ... because she was a married woman. Because all but the few aware of her arrangement with Russ would assume the child was her husband's, and Leander and his people *certainly* didn't know any better.

'No,' he muttered. 'No, they won't know, but—'

'Which means,' she interrupted, faster now, 'that they won't be around when I give birth. I know they've shown up with unmarried human women, just in case, but they're not nearly so strict with married women. They come to bind the child sometime during the day after the birth, but the Mother isn't sticking her nose into the delivery room if there's no magic involved. So that should give us time.'

Agenor closed his eyes. 'Time for *what*?'

'Time for you to take the child elsewhere while I tell the world it was a stillbirth.'

'Impossible,' he said hoarsely. 'There's a chance that child *does* inherit my magic. We'd have an unbound mage on our hands, and that breaks the very first law we—'

'Do you think I give a damn?'

'You should—'

'Agenor, *listen* to me.' Her voice rose to a near-shout. 'Your child's life will be a living hell if you allow her to bind it. That's not speculation. It's a damn fact. Are you really so far gone that you'd put some tyrant's laws above your own blood?'

He muttered a curse. 'We've had this conversation. They may not be doing everything perfectly, but calling them tyrants is—'

'They're idiots at best and cruel oppressors at worst,' Allie snapped, even louder now, 'and I don't *care* what ideals they claimed to fight for a millennium ago, do you understand? Whatever they did for you then is not going to make anything better for a half-blood child born today, and your misplaced loyalty isn't going to—'

'Al, *stop* it!'

She slammed her mouth shut as if he'd slapped her in the face, glaring at him in the darkening twilight. Agenor heard his own voice echo back at him from the forest shielding the beach from the rest of the island. Too loud, too brusque – but his heart was in his throat and his mind was a blur and her blue eyes were so painfully cold again.

What was this wall between them, suddenly – this battlefield?

At once he was the enemy again. As if she hadn't spent weeks in his arms. As if she'd never written him that morning's letter. As if his loyalty was a matter of shame, foolish pig-headedness, rather than a carefully considered choice.

He closed his eyes. The sand was clammy and cold beneath him, the sea breeze a chilly hand stroking his cheeks and wings.

'You promised.' Thinly veiled accusations shimmered beneath the surface of her words. 'You *promised* you would do whatever I needed.'

'I was not expecting you to make plans to send unbound mages out into the world!' he fell out. 'You're asking me to break the one law that's been the basis of their reign, of—'

'And why do you still give a damn about their reign, if you know what it's led to?'

'It's all we have!' His voice cracked. 'Al, I'll beg them on my own bloody knees to release you from your bindings if that's what it takes, but I *cannot* betray them, do you understand? I owe them too much. We need them too much. If we start unravelling the foundations of the empire, we'll have bigger problems at hand than—'

'I'm not asking you to declare war on her!' She was nothing but fire and rage in the darkness now, only her pale face still clearly visible in the deepening indigo of the night. 'It's *one* child. It may not inherit your magic. We're not creating an army of unbound fae. All I want is for this baby to be safe, and—'

'And I *will* keep it safe,' Agenor snapped, 'but without breaking the law. Is that such an impossible compromise?'

She scoffed. 'I'm not looking for compromises. Halfway to happiness is still unhappiness.'

'I'm not—'

'Agenor.' She sucked in a terse breath. 'My child is not staying at this court. That's a fact, not a request. I'd rather die than see a second Inga live through this hell. So ...' She pressed her lips together, a look in her eyes he knew all too well – the look of warriors about to enter a fight they might not survive. 'So either you accept that and work with me, or you try to stop me and prepare to never see me or that baby again. It's your pick, Lord Protector.'

A razor-sharp, blistering silence fell – a silence that was barely a silence, the foot of empty air between them filled with panting breath and desperate fury and glares that could cut through solid rock. His fingers had dug themselves into the sand, Agenor realised, as if to squeeze the life from the earth itself. His wings had spread themselves wide behind his back. Every muscle in his body had tensed to the point of tearing.

He sank back into the sand, folded his wings, drew the cool air deep into his lungs. Allie didn't move, a small bundle of slender limbs and dark glares against the backdrop of dunes and trees and the night sky beyond.

'Al ...'

Her throat bobbed. *'Please.'*

'You ... you can't do this.' More sensible words abandoned him. He was wading through quicksand again, and this time there was no pleasant challenge to it, no game to win. Losing meant drowning. Losing meant death. 'You can't reduce all of this to a question of you or them; you can't—'

'So what are you going to do?' She scoffed. 'Stop me?'

He stared at her. She scowled back, shivering and out of breath, and not a trace of doubt in her defiant blue eyes.

Prepare to never see me again.

His stomach turned. No. She couldn't be serious, could she? She couldn't believe this was a choice he was capable of making, breaking the first law of faekind. Couldn't think she would win anything by pitting herself against the entirety of the Crimson Court – against *him*. Hell, didn't she need him as much as he needed her? At the very least, she could never smuggle any child off the island without his help, so this really was a senseless ultimatum; she *had* to see that much.

'Listen.' His words came out hurried and jumbled. 'You're being too rash. We need to take some time to figure this out – to figure this out *together* – to work out all the options we have and—'

'And if we work out all the options we have,' she interrupted him, wrapping her arms around herself, 'and you still find yourself forced to make the choice between my wishes and their laws, what will you do?'

'Little thief, please ...'

Her lip curled up. 'What will you *do*?'

'You can't ask this of me!' he burst out, voice rising again. 'I love you, Al, I really do, but you don't understand what's at stake here; you don't understand that I can't—'

'Take a stance for once? Draw your own gods-damned conclusions, rather than running after the same old commands for the rest of your life?' She uttered a sharp, mirthless laugh as she scrambled to her feet. 'Don't worry, Agenor, I *do* understand. And I really hoped you'd be better than that. I really thought you had *some* sense left in that shadowy heart of yours, but if this is how you want to play the game—'

'And where do you think you'll be going?' he snapped, getting to his feet in a single, furious motion. 'Do you really think I'll let you run off with my child without—'

Her voice was a jeer from the darkness. 'Is that a *threat*, Lord Protector?'

'I don't want you to get hurt!'

'So it's a threat.' Another one of those furious laughs. 'Well, that makes the matter easier. Enjoy sacrificing the last of your morals to please a couple of bloodthirsty bitches who'll never see you as more than a tool, and—'

Agenor lurched forward in the direction of her voice. Burning pain seared up his arm in the same moment, fierce enough to draw a cry from his lips.

Oh, fuck.

The bargain.

The night sky spun around him as he staggered another step after her and his entire arm burst into flames, the chafing sensation spreading to his shoulders, his chest. *Fuck.* Not a step farther, the magic told him. One more attempt to follow her against her wishes and he might find himself passing out on the cold sand.

'Allie!'

No answer.

His breath came ragged from his throat now. No. This could not be happening. He couldn't lose her like this – he couldn't lose his gods-damned *child* like this. She had to come back. She had to see reason. He would *make* her see reason, if he had no other option—

The bargain fire flared through his wrist again, blazing and biting. With a roar of frustration, he clutched his hand around his lower arm, stumbling back until the pain subsided.

'*Allie!*'

His breaking voice echoed over the empty beach, and no one but the sea moved to answer.

CHAPTER 16

Allie made it to the edge of the forest without crying.

Then he shouted her name a second time behind her, his voice so full of agony she could feel it writhing in her own guts, and the tears broke free despite all her good intentions not to give a damn about him. How dare he feel hurt – how dare he feel hurt about *her*? The fool, with his warped priorities and his wilful blindness and his threats ...

She stumbled between the trees, her tears blurring what little sight the darkness left her. Vines and branches swung into her face and shoulders as she blindly found her way through the vegetation, wrestling down her shrieking breath. She shouldn't have told him. She should never have told him. Why had she believed for even a second that he'd keep that throwaway promise as soon as he found out what the price of his word was?

I love you, Al, I really do ...

Her heart cramped – a violent, painful cramp of undiluted rage.

She'd *wanted* to believe him. Had wanted him to be that best version of himself, the gentle, dutiful male who'd so tenderly peeled layer after layer of distrust from her heart in these past weeks – the one who took her seriously, who believed her, who called her brilliant and the saviour of his sanity. The Lord Agenor she'd so stupidly fallen in love with. And instead ...

Instead she got the loyal Lord Protector of the Crimson Court. Who would hand over his firstborn child to the Mother and make excuses for her while she skinned it alive.

Another sob broke from her lips as she struggled on, pushing brambles and vines aside to make her way north, away from the beach. So much for his devoted admiration. What had he said, that night weeks ago? *If you'll allow me to take a little of that weight off your shoulders ...*

She'd wanted him to, *craved* for him to make the world just a little easier – and then it turned out it was all politics after all.

A supple branch whipped across her face, missing her eye by a hair's breadth. Allie cried out, stumbling blindly through the night until she bumped into a broad tree trunk and stayed there, resting her forehead against the rough bark as she blinked the tears away and tried to calm her wheezing breath. So much for her attempts to rely on anyone but herself. Now she'd told him and lost him and only made everything twice as complicated.

Do you really think I'll let you run off with my child?

Her knees were shaking. She should just have told him it was Russ's after all. This entire affair would be over anyway, and at least if Agenor believed she'd simply been unfaithful to him, he wouldn't be looking for ways to stop her.

Would he stop her?

She let go of the tree and staggered on through the darkness, barely even feeling the thorns and nettles anymore. He would *try*, presumably. But the bargain was still there, and by the sound of his pained cries, it had not become any less effective after weeks of inactivity. As long as he was going against her wishes, as long as his intended actions would cause her grief, she should be safe. The bargain wouldn't allow him to betray her to the Mother. It wouldn't allow him to show up at her home and burst in to drag her baby from her arms.

She shivered. Would he even *want* to?

She didn't want to think of him that way, hateful and vengeful. She wanted him to still be his mild, playful, occasionally shameless self –

hell, she still wanted him to *love* her. But after she'd called his beloved Mother a pair of bloodthirsty bitches to his face ...

She'd lost him.

Lost those blissful mornings in his room, surrounded by books and sunlight. Lost the thrill of his letters, their office trysts, the pleasant tingle of shared secrets whenever their gazes met in public. Lost the safety of his strong arms around her, his deep voice muttering promises of protection into her ears as he held her.

Her heart was cracking in her chest, leaving a hollow, gaping hole the shape of him.

She should not have told him, not like this. If only she had kept her secret – if only she had taken a little more time to make her request ... Would he have listened?

Did it make sense to wonder?

Somehow she reached the edge of the forest and the slightly more familiar mountain paths. A first sliver of moonlight peeked over the horizon now, shrouding the rugged slopes and twisting paths in a mesmerizing pearly glow; in that eerie, unearthly light, she found her steps with a little more confidence, glancing up at the sky every other heartbeat. No winged silhouettes soared by to eclipse the stars.

He couldn't follow her, she reminded herself whenever the rustle of a bird's wings made her jump aside and hide. Not if he came after her with the intention to thwart her in any way. Of course, if he changed his mind – if he decided he would help her after all ...

She shook her head so violently the last of her hairpins slipped from her braids. No sense in hoping for the impossible. She'd spoken a few too many unforgivable words; he'd made a few too many unforgivable threats. This would be her own problem to handle.

As she should have realised from the start.

And she *would* find a way. As soon as the shock waned, she would be sensible, so very sensible – tell the right people, close the right deals, find the right leverage if she needed to. Getting her baby to safety wouldn't be the hardest part. If the smugglers' network could bring goods to the island, it should just as well be able to take something *off* the island every now and then – she should be able to arrange that. The main question ...

How would she be able to follow?

But she'd figure it out. She'd pester Rinald to look around the library for more information on those bloody bindings; she'd interrogate the recently bound newcomers to get all the details on the process she no longer remembered herself; she'd have a few more innocent chats with Leander and other fae mages to see what they could tell her. *You'll die that way*, the Silent Death had written. Which might as well mean there were other, less lethal methods to achieve her goals. Highly illegal methods, perhaps – but without Agenor to worry about, that at least wasn't much of a problem.

The slow, methodical considerations of planning and scheming distracted her from her withering heart for now. She clung to it, to every little detail and every little problem she could solve, glad for a way to think of *anything* other than the heart-wrenching anguish in his voice as he'd cried out her name.

Not her problem. Not her pain. It was him or her child now, and he wasn't the one with the world stacked against him for nothing but his blood.

She felt like she'd been walking for three full nights when finally the familiar shapes of Rustvale loomed up from the darkness – most of the houses dark, but a candle was still burning behind the one small window of her own.

Inga.

Somehow, her tired bare feet managed to run the last steps as guilt set its fangs into her heart. Oh gods. How long had it been since she'd run out like a madwoman, with no message about where she was going or when she'd be back? Hours? For all her sister knew, she'd thrown herself off a cliff somewhere like one of the dramatic heroines from Marette's ballads.

She threw open the door and all but stumbled into the living room, apologies flowing from her lips before she'd even closed the door behind her – she was back and she was fine and she was sorry, so sorry, for leaving here in such a state and—

'Al, that's *enough*.'

Allie fell silent at once, staggering to a halt against the kitchen counter. Her little sister sat at the table with her single candle and a small notebook that Rinald had probably pocketed from the library – looking so oddly calm and so oddly *composed* that all thought of hysteria fled Allie's mind at once.

'I'm sorry,' she breathed again. 'I—'

'You look like shit,' Inga told her, unnervingly matter-of-factly.

Allie glanced down – her feet raw and bloody from the walk back, her dress soaked and sandy, her hair a tangled mess over her shoulders. Like shit. Like a woman in deep, deep trouble. Like a walking, breathing broken heart. Her knees buckled ... No, don't think about that now.

'I tried to escape,' she said hoarsely, 'just to see if I could.'

Inga's shoulders stiffened as she got up from her chair. 'Should just have asked me. I've tried every single bay on the island.' An unusually wry grin. 'No luck, so please save your time for better solutions.'

'I – I didn't know that.'

'Didn't tell you. You were worried enough already.' She waved at the chair she'd just left as she tiptoed towards the bedroom with her usual, light-footed movements. 'Sit down. Let me get you some water and soap for your feet. I'll reheat dinner for you.'

Allie no longer had the heart to object. She sank down on the ramshackle wooden seat and pulled her knees to her chest, staring at the wall as Inga rummaged around with washcloths and soap. The familiarity of the room washed over her like a warm bath, soothing the worst of the exhaustion and panic still sending tremors through her limbs, reminding her with unexpected reassurance that this at least was *real*. Home. Family. These dreamlike six weeks had been nothing but a fanciful dream indeed, far too good to be true – a short respite from the misery of life, but nothing that could ever last. But this ... broken and cruel and devoid of handsome fae lords as it was, it was *hers*.

Only when she shuffled back into the room with a small tub of soapy water did Inga say, 'So it was Agenor, then.'

Allie nodded. One more word and she suspected she might burst out crying again.

'Is he going to be useful, at least?'

She shook her head, even closer to tears now. But Inga just sighed, a crabby sigh sounding far too mature for the timid fifteen-year-old Allie was used to, and turned away with a fluttery gesture at the tub.

'Take care of your feet. I'll make you some food.'

Allie scrubbed the blood and sand and salt off her feet and shins, then limped to the back room to get her hairbrush and take off her stiff, sticky dress for a more comfortable tunic. Behind her, the smell of grilled peppers and strong broth filled the house. Her sister was just filling a soup bowl when she returned, still ominously silent until they'd both sat down.

'I've been thinking,' Inga said.

She said it very calmly. But there was a tremble in her voice, a hint of a crack, that made Allie pause her spoon halfway to her bowl.

'Hmm?'

'You really are the best sister I could ever wish for, Al.' Somehow, in that unusually thoughtful tone, it didn't sound like a compliment. 'And I don't think I can ever thank you enough for all you've done to protect me these years. You know that. But ...'

A short silence fell. Inga stared at the table, fidgeting with the tips of her blonde hair. Allie didn't dare move.

'But?'

'But if you make another child go through this,' Inga said, looking up with wide grey eyes, 'I'll never speak to you again.'

A mirthless laugh fell from her lips. 'Don't worry. Not going to happen.'

'Even if Agenor doesn't—'

'Agenor can go to hell,' Allie said and ignored the twinge in her guts that said something entirely different. 'I'll just do this by myself.'

As always.

Like everything.

CHAPTER 17

His bedroom was dark when Agenor finally staggered inside through the balcony doors, the warmth of the day's fire still lingering in the air. His hands were shaking. His wings were shaking. Had his heart been able to, it would have shaken, too. Dazed, incredulous dread churned through his guts, his mind still spinning to make sense of the world ...

She was pregnant.

She was gone.

And she was absolutely, lethally furious with him.

His hands didn't seem to know what to do with themselves after he'd slammed the door shut behind himself. Somehow, he got his clothes off. Somehow, he swept the sand from his floor with a quick flash of red magic. Somehow, he found his way to his wardrobe to put his shirt and trousers away – and then his eyes fell on that one pile where he'd found that last letter, that pile where he may never find her letters again, and the world once more sank away below his feet.

'Fuck,' he muttered, turning away, and then again, 'Fuck, fuck, *fuck,*' as if his lips could think of nothing else to say anymore. Damn the composure. Damn the common sense. He crashed into his bed, nearly twisting his wings as he landed, spitting curses at the world, at his loss, at her incomprehensible human mind ...

Cold leather slithered over his bare thigh. Coral.

Agenor abruptly swallowed the last of his curses, knowing what she'd think of them, and blankly muttered, 'Evening, girl.'

She hissed a question. He hauled himself up on his elbows and found his three snakes staring at him – Oleander from the floor just beside his desk, Basilisk curled up on the seat of his chair, Coral half-buried between his blankets, all three of them looking like they might do him a favour by just setting their fangs in his neck and at least offering him the pleasure of a quick end.

He heard a groaned laugh fall from his lips. 'Don't worry. Bit of a rough night.'

They looked no more reassured – if anything, the opposite.

'It's just ...' Agenor sucked in a deep breath, trying to piece some of the puzzle together from the tangled mess of his bewildered thoughts. Trying to find some reassurance between the knots. 'It's just because she's human. She's not looking at things in the long-term. She'll come to her senses soon enough, and ...'

Coral tilted her thin head at him, looking thoroughly unconvinced. He swallowed another curse and glanced at the other two, just in time to catch the even more sceptical glances they exchanged between the two of them.

Oleander and Basilisk agreeing? Perhaps he was being too optimistic, then. He cursed anyway.

'Well, fine. I'll wait until she's calmed down a bit and explain the situation to her, and—'

His bargain mark flared again.

'Oh, *fuck*.' He fell back into his blankets, glaring at the black gemstone lodged into the skin of his wrist. 'Fine! If she doesn't want to understand I'll figure something out – something ... something else...'

Coral slipped away from him, and his thoughts started spiralling again. Something else. He had to do *something*. She was out there with his child, and he wanted her back, wanted her to talk to him again, wanted her to see sense. He'd have to talk to her, and—

A searing flare of pain shot through his wrist.

Not talk to her, then. Fine. He'd be more subtle. Figure out some grand gesture, anything that would clearly show her that he was still as much in love with her as he'd ever been, and wait until she would come to him to—

Another flare.

He groaned. Alright, perhaps that was a little manipulative. He'd just write her a letter, in that case, and—

Flare.

'Oh, for fuck's sake,' he snapped, shooting upright with an exasperated glare at the bargain mark. 'I don't want to *harm* her! I only want to make her *see*! If she just understood—'

Coral hissed another warning from between his pillows.

He jerked his head towards her, finding her body curled around the familiar shape of a book in the darkness. Phyron's *Treatises*. He'd been reading it yesterday, he recalled through the bewildered haze of his thoughts. Allie must have been reading it this morning. What was that sentence he'd underlined for her again?

A sharp mind is a more dangerous weapon than even the sharpest of blades.

Coral's glare, too, was deadlier than the sharpest of blades he'd encountered.

A sharp mind. He sagged in the blankets as his thoughts seemed to tilt, twist, turn inside out. He'd thought of her as soon as his eye had fallen on that part of the text – because she *was* painfully, dangerously brilliant. Because mere hours ago, he'd still been in utter awe of the way her quick mind dissected his view of reality and made him notice an entirely different world behind the charade he'd always seen.

So why was he thinking of her like some dense student of life now, then?

He swallowed yet another curse. Coral held his gaze like an impatient teacher waiting for her student to figure out his own mistakes.

'But—'

She hissed.

'But she called them tyrants and bloodthirsty bitches,' Agenor said weakly. 'That's not very reasonable, is it?'

If snakes could have rolled their eyes, she would have.

'I know they're not doing everything perfectly!' How often had he spoken those words in the last few weeks? 'But I can make all of this better – I can fix everything. All I need is a little more time to play my pieces …'

And time was what they didn't have. Eleven months – or wait, human children were born even sooner, weren't they? Nine months, perhaps. Which *was* very little time to do all he had to do, admittedly. He'd never aimed to change anyone's mind within a year. In a decade, perhaps – but he likely wouldn't manage before his child was born.

Was it so unreasonable that Allie didn't want to wait ten years if an innocent child would be caught up in the mess in the meantime?

He groaned. But he *would* handle it. He could keep a child safe for ten years, half-blood or not. Or fifteen years or however long it would take …

A life of constant danger, constant vigilance, constant fear.

The room chilled around him. Perhaps he could. But Allie – he didn't think she would ever forgive him.

Fine. He tried to scoff. If loyalty didn't mean a damn thing to her, perhaps she didn't understand him so well after all. Then again, she *was* loyal. She'd defended Inga even though no one had ever obliged her to. So if she didn't understand *his* loyalty …

Who'll never see you as more than a tool.

That was oversimplifying matters, wasn't it? He worked for them. It was what he had always been – their loyal servant, but one they respected, one they trusted.

Did you convince them to leave those poor nymphs alone yet?

A curse fell from his lips. No, he hadn't, because he needed time. The same circles over and over again. He needed time, and they didn't have it, and she wasn't willing to wait for him. And that was her problem, the loyal part of his mind said. He'd clearly set out his stance; it was a sensible, reasonable stance, and if that wasn't something she could accept, perhaps it was best they go their separate ways.

But the thought of that solution, of accepting that she'd walk away and stay away …

Dread stirred in his guts again, heavy and sickening.

He'd wake up to the endlessly familiar sunrise tomorrow and the day after tomorrow and the day after that, and the prospect of her smile would not be there to pull him from the blankets. He'd walk these endlessly familiar corridors and never feel his heart jump at a glimpse of her; he'd sit in these endlessly familiar offices and never look up to see her slip in with that brilliant twinkle of desire in her eyes. He would return to his rooms after meetings and dinners and boring conversations and never again find her letters waiting for him in his wardrobe to lift the weight of the centuries from his heart.

And the years would go by. The decades would go by. And one day he'd lose her forever.

An agonised moan escaped him as he fell back into the blankets. The knowledge had slumbered at the back of his mind over these past weeks, always there but never urgent enough to warrant conscious thoughts or conversations – her lifespan was shorter. She *would* die. Wasting a decade angering her – wasting even a minute angering her …

He did not have the time.

His breath quickened. Already the image of her absence was a boulder on his chest, leaving him wrestling for air, for life, for even the slightest sliver of relief from the years crawling up on him. Hell, he *needed* her. Needed the delight of every unexpected word she spoke, of every thought she challenged, of every safe assumption she twisted and turned around until he was scrambling to find his footing again.

As she'd just done.

And instead of turning with her, instead of taking the justified challenge she offered, he'd pushed back. *Slammed* back. Called her a naïve fool rather than taken another look at his own foolishness, and all but threatened her when she didn't give way.

Was it a surprise she'd run?

He should have thought twice. Should have doubted himself. Should have listened to what she was saying, rather than what he was hearing – she wanted him to break the law, yes, but she knew as well as he did that he'd prefer not to. And yet she'd asked him to, *begged* him to. Heard his counterarguments and refuted them. She was still the same sensible person, still the woman who would never make a melodrama out of nothing – so if she was willing to go this far, should he not consider for a moment that she may be *right*?

He closed his eyes. But he could deal with this, the loyal side of his mind insisted. He could keep his family safe. He could convince the court to overlook his child's human blood, because it was *his* child, and they would know better than to defy him, wouldn't they?

Just like they should have known better than to mess with the tribute intake. Just like they should have known better than to cut down trees on nymph isles.

His throat was dry as ash when he swallowed. Well, fine. If matters became dire, he could find an exception to those laws, convince Achlys and Melinoë that there was no need to bind this little half fae to the island. They'd listen, wouldn't they? Why *wouldn't* they listen?

Did you convince them to leave those poor nymphs alone?

Oh, fuck.

His hands clenched themselves into fists in the soft blankets as his thoughts spiralled out of control. He couldn't start breaking rules. He could *not* start breaking rules. He'd fought for the damn things, *lived* for them – they were all that had kept his world from unravelling for centuries. He should know better. But yet again his little thief had caught him on a battlefield he'd never faced before, and knowing better was not going to do him any favours now.

He didn't have time to be stubborn, to slowly figure out which of his age-old habits were worth keeping and which were merely remnants of a world he no longer wanted to live in. If he wanted her ...

He wanted her.

Certainty solidified in every fibre of him, the first thing feeling firm and fixed in this spinning new world. He wanted her. Ached for her. Craved her with a passion that made him feel on the brink of dying and yet so very alive, a need so much stronger than the wish to be loyal or lawful or a pinnacle of fine fae breeding – and if those were his desires, if those were his priorities, then why in hell was he focusing on his own oblivious perspective rather than relying on the one person who had never failed to see things sharply?

His heartbeat rattled against his ribs as he drew in a slow, deep breath. But the mist cleared in his mind. The weight on his chest vanished. His fists unclenched themselves, the fight reflex soothed, the battlefield gone.

Was this happening?

He felt like he was being sucked into an eddy, the water drawing him farther and farther along into some deadly, inevitable outcome. He wanted her. Such a small, innocent certainty, and yet the implications ...

This was to be the start of it, then. This was where he became a traitor. The Lord Protector of the Crimson Court, right hand of the Mother herself, defeated by a little human thief of barely two dozen summers.

But she was *his* little thief. And if she wanted a traitor ... hell, then a traitor he would be.

A mindless laugh fell over his lips. He felt drunk on it, suddenly, the world around him swimming with newness and lightness and delirious relief. Damn the rules, then. Perhaps it was that easy after all. Allie was right, they weren't building an army of unbound fae or any such ridiculous thing – this was just a single harmless secret, a single hidden source of joy, and he could indulge himself a *little* after twelve centuries of unwavering duty.

Coral hissed, slithering back to him in the blankets, her scales gleaming like blood in the light of the waning moon. The way she flicked out her tongue at him looked like a warning.

He groaned and rolled towards her. 'What is it, girl?'

She cocked her head at him – ready to bury her fangs in his neck, it seemed, if he spoke one wrong word too many. The gesture oddly reminded him of Allie, of her looks in those first days when only the fear of consequences had kept her from planting a kitchen knife between his shoulders.

Oh, right. Allie.

He groaned again, the pressure on his chest drawing tighter. At this point, he was probably lucky if she limited herself to kitchen knives.

And the bargain wouldn't let him come anywhere near her, wouldn't let him talk to her, wouldn't let him apologise or tell her he'd do better.

Or at least, not as long as whatever he'd do would hurt her.

So he had to be clever, now. He had to think very hard and understand very well and be very damn honest with himself – and if he managed all of that ...

'I'll find a way,' he muttered to Coral. 'I'll make sure she knows.'

She hissed again but lowered her head onto his shoulder. A reassuring gesture, steadying him, comforting him, until finally the whirl of his thoughts became a clear line again and the first shreds of plans and ideas slowly stuck themselves together.

He knew what he had to do, indeed.

The eastern horizon was already paling by the time he finally got up from his bed, wrapped Coral around his shoulders, and made his way to his desk. Basilisk lay waiting for him, his small body curled around the inkpot. Oleander showed up moments after Agenor sat down, slipping from behind a row of books on his bookshelves, her expression as apologetic as any snake could look.

'Thanks,' Agenor muttered. 'I'll need your help.'

They didn't glare or hiss now as he reached for his pens, smoothed his parchment, and closed his eyes to gather his thoughts one last time. And when he finally dipped his pen in the ink and scribbled down the message, his wrist mark didn't burn.

CHAPTER 18

Allie closed the archive door behind her, threw a quick look around, and, finding the room deserted, dropped her cleaning materials in the nearest corner. Judging by the thick layers of dust on the floor and shelves, it was unlikely anyone would interrupt her here.

Good.

With three quick steps, she was at the first cabinet and rose up on her toes to reach the upper shelf. The lists should be somewhere in here, if Rinald's information was correct. Updated every month, he'd said, so it couldn't be buried *too* deep below the unravelling leather folders and crumbling parchment. Holding her breath, she browsed through the piles and books – not the village administration of long-forgotten decades, not the marriage certificates of couples long dead ...

It took her three shelves and fifteen minutes to find what she'd been looking for, in a large felt folder that felt dusty and dry in her hands when she pulled it out – a list of children the Mother had bound.

Finally.

It had taken her five days to get to this point. Not too long, all things considered, but even with her due date still a good seven months away, she could feel the days ticking away like little steps closer to death – closer to a failure that would be hers, and hers alone, to bear. She had so much to do and so little time. The only advantage, although she refused to be grateful, was that her old arrangement with Agenor left her free to roam about the court during the hours she'd spent in his rooms before; she hadn't returned to that part of the castle since their falling-out on the beach, and he hadn't complained to her supervisor about it. He likely couldn't, considering that angry employers would without doubt be harmful to her general wellbeing.

He hadn't complained to *her* about it either. Hadn't bothered to communicate a single word to her, really. Perhaps he simply couldn't; if all he was planning to do was tell her once again how she should just trust the Mother's benevolence to take care of their child, the bargain was likely keeping him away.

For which she was glad, she reminded herself as she sat down on the cold floor with her loot and tucked her feet beneath her thighs. Really very glad. She barely missed him. She *certainly* didn't think about him in the quiet moments just before she fell asleep or during the long discussions and conversations with her family or – well, any other time. She had better things to do than coddle a broken heart, after all. She was too sensible for that nonsense.

With a firm headshake, she pushed her thoughts aside and opened the heavy folder. Page after page of scribbled names and dates, and—

A sheet of folded parchment slid out.

She muttered a curse, scrambling to shove it back where it had come from. Had it been sitting at the back of the folder? Or somewhere in the middle? The parchment looked relatively new, so likely closer to the back, but she should probably check if it wasn't some very specific addendum that had to be included with a particular page.

With a quick glance at the door, she unfolded the sheet, then turned back to run her eyes over the writing.

Little thief.

Allie froze.

No. She had to be seeing things now. That greeting, that infinitely familiar handwriting ... She squeezed her eyes shut and sucked in a deep breath, willing her own mind to behave – of course this wasn't a letter he'd sent her. Why would he be leaving her letters *here*? Clearly she just hadn't had enough sleep last night or – or ...

She swallowed and opened her eyes again.

Little thief,

I don't doubt you'll find this archive without my help before the week is over. Once again, I'm finding that you manage without me far more easily than I can stand your absence – you probably won't be surprised to hear that.

I'm a bloody fool. That won't be news to you either.

You likely have little need for elaborate promises and apologies (although if you'd like to get them, I could compose you several books of them – just say the word). To make myself slightly more useful, I've taken a look at the Mother's personal library and found a small handful of works on binding magic. I'm somewhat hesitant to bring them elsewhere, as I'm not technically allowed to have them in my possession, but you can find them in my rooms whenever you wish.

Let me know if there is anything else I can do. I'll be here.

Yours,
  A.

Allie stared at the letter for five minutes, her fingers shaking violently enough for the words to blur before her eyes. Then, with a curse, she flicked the parchment around and scrabbled her answer on the back.

Go to hell.

In a fit of panic, she shoved it all back into the folder, back onto the shelf where she'd found it, too agitated now to care about leaving no trace behind. The bastard – how dare he show up like this, all mildness and considerate helpfulness? How dare he make her heart jump all over again when she was still supposed to be so very angry with him?

How dare he make his offer sound like something she would be so, so glad to accept?

She fled the archive room without another glance at the valuable information gathered on those shelves, and spent the rest of the day scrubbing floors as if her life depended on it – as if she might scrub *him* from her thoughts too, if only she exhausted herself to the point where he would finally leave her heart and mind alone. She had to get rid of this sentimentality. She couldn't trust him. He'd broken a promise once before; who was to say he wouldn't do it again?

In the end, she was the only person she could rely on. She wasn't going to put herself in danger of more heartbreak for some fanciful dream of love.

And yet ...

She tried to stay away from that bloody archive room, away from his dangerously persuasive letter, away from the shelves where he, too, had been looking for a solution to a problem she'd thought he wouldn't want to solve. There was nothing there for her, she told herself time and time again over the course of an endless, sleepless night. Either he hadn't yet seen her message, in which case nothing had changed, or he *had* seen it and surely understood that there was nothing salvageable between them at this point.

And yet ...

She found herself wandering closer and closer the next day, tempting corner after tempting corner, bad decision after bad decision. Perhaps he hadn't yet given up on her – even though he should, of course, even though she wanted him to, of course ... What if he *had* answered her already? What if somehow his reply solved everything, this burning ache in her heart and the smothering fear and the days passing far too fast for her to handle?

Just one look. If she didn't reply to whatever message he'd left this time, he'd never even know she'd seen it.

The folder had moved; she knew it as soon as she slipped into that grey room and found the rows of documents significantly neater than she'd left them yesterday. Her hands trembled as she pulled out the felt folder again, too focused on the contents to even double-check the door behind her.

He'd been back indeed, and left another message below her *Go to hell* of the previous day.

Seeing as you probably won't be there to keep me company, I'll politely decline. Unless you were suggesting an afterworld rendezvous, of course, in which case burning in the flames of death for eternity sounds like a small price to pay to see you again.

I miss you, Al. Come tell me I'm an idiot to my face. Come tell me you hate me. Bring the kitchen knives for all I care, steal every single shirt I own and parade around the court with them, leave me scathing letters in every corner of my room. Even the deadliest of you is better than your absence.

Yours,
  A.

It was only when she lowered the letter that Allie realised a small smile had grown on her face.

She quickly wiped it off, cursing her treacherous facial muscles and her treacherous heart and her treacherous feet itching to give in to his pleas. She knew better, of course. She could perfectly well tell him he was an idiot from a very safe distance, far away from those smouldering eyes and unexpected smiles and vexingly irresistible wings.

But perhaps she could at least grant him a few more words to make her point.

Last time I stopped hating you, it took you six weeks to start breaking your promises. How long would you need if I put the kitchen knives away this time? Until you disagree with my opinions on baby names? Until your darling Mother threatens another one of my family members? You've been a fool twice; I prefer not to follow the example.

Entirely my own,
  A.

She shoved the letter back where she'd found it and spent the next two hours doing the work she'd come for – counting names. How many people had been bound every year since the Last Battle? How many had died on the island, according to the separate list Rinald had found her? Any mismatch might be relevant; those who had been bound but not lived at the court until the end of their days could be the answer to her questions.

With a pocket full of notes, she eventually left the archives, rushing the rest of her tasks for the day, her thoughts never straying from that note she'd left behind. The longer she worked, the more unbearable the thought of waiting another full night for answers became – another twelve hours of lying awake and staring at the ceiling until she'd know what he thought of her latest point.

Good gods, why was she allowing him so much power over her mind again?

But he had her defeated, or perhaps she'd defeated herself; just before the end of the working day, she found herself with her hand on the archive room's doorhandle again, unable to step back, unable to resist the magnetic pull of whatever might be waiting for her inside.

The books had once again shifted. He'd been back in the meantime.

She gave up on her attempts to be unaffected and pulled the folder from its shelf so brusquely that some of the surrounding books and piles of parchment almost followed. The letter was stuck loosely in the back.

You are the furthest from a fool I've ever known anyone to be. But for your consideration – as I have never even felt tempted to betray them for twelve centuries, and just changed my mind for you and you alone, I don't think the chances are great someone will show up tomorrow to pull you down from the spot of my top priority.

And I know this wasn't your point, but ...

Tell me about your name opinions. All of them. Just in case you need a point to start, no, I am not at all opposed to human names, unless you were planning to call the child Herbert. My love for you is well-nigh limitless, but I think Herbert would be a limit. I'm most open to all other ideas, though.

Allie chuckled.

Then quickly shut her mouth, threw a quick glance around – as if anyone might have heard that embarrassing moment of lost control – and glared back at the letter. She *almost* wanted to tell him Herbert was the name she'd dreamed of for most of her life; it was a damn shame she hated the sound of it, too.

Crouching against the cabinet, she scribbled her reply on a last empty corner of the parchment.

I confess I didn't yet spend much time thinking about names. If you must know, I'm not necessarily opposed to fae names either, although some carry unpleasant connotations for me. But if you know of any names with meanings such as "great destroyer of empires" or "blessed puncher of noses", I could be persuaded to consider them.

How much longer are you going to continue this charm offensive? Until I either give in or manage to properly infuriate you? Or is it a matter of who first runs out of writing space on this poor sheet of parchment?

She felt uncannily giddy as she returned the letter to the spot where she'd found it. A feeling far too close to the blissful excitement of all these past weeks, to mornings of reading in his bed surrounded by snakes and afternoons spent in various positions on desks and office sofas ...

Which was the *last* thing she should be thinking about now.

But that annoyingly warm feeling in her chest wouldn't stop glowing, no matter how often she told herself she was being nonsensical. She shouldn't be *hoping*. She most certainly shouldn't be *wishing*. And yet ...

Changed my mind for you and you alone.

'You're smiling,' Inga told her over dinner, squinting at her with suspicious grey eyes. 'Did you find anything useful today, then?'

'Oh, yes,' Allie said and quickly folded her face back into an expression reflecting the seriousness of her situation. 'I might have a way to get my hands on some books on binding magic, actually.'

Inga nodded but didn't look any less suspicious as she shifted her attention back to her plate.

Once again, Allie spent a significant portion of the night awake – mulling over senseless old memories and dangerous new dreams, her mind never quite strong enough to squash the latter but never weak enough to give in and sprint back to the court in her nightgown either. Was she really so silly to hope? Or would it be silly by now *not* to hope, to cling to this anger even as her heart was desperately begging her to let go of it?

What if he could be who she'd hoped he would be after all? What if he kept his promises and helped her escape this place after all – helped their child escape this place, too?

If she wanted to do what was best for their baby, shouldn't she be taking all the help she could get?

She got up too early and left for the court before the sun had even fully risen. Armed with a bucket and a mop, she made her way to the same old archive room in a straight line, unable to keep up the pretence of patience even with herself.

A few more lines of ink had been added to the overcrowded sheet of parchment during the night. In the dusky light, she had to squint to read them.

Perhaps we should be fair, abandon both human and fae traditions, and simply name the child after a snake. That way everyone can be equally outraged. Oleander does have a nice ring to it, don't you think?

As to your other question – I'm glad to hear you still consider me charming, and I wish you good luck in your endeavours to enrage me to the point of giving up on you. How many full sheets of parchment is it going to take before you accept I'll do no such thing? Speaking of which, the current one is running out of available space indeed. Either we get ourselves a new sheet, or we'll have to continue the conversation in person. You know where to find me.

P.S. I left you something in the pen tray.

She blinked at that last sentence, then gave the silver pen tray on the room's small desk a suspicious glance. It was probably too small for Basilisk to fit in, she concluded after a moment. There could be no harm in taking a look, then, could there?

Still, her hands trembled as she lifted the lid off the tray and carefully studied the contents.

Pens and pencils, as expected. A snapped quill someone hadn't bothered to throw away. Two bronze coins, a red ribbon bookmark. And below all of that ...

A key.

A key she knew a little better than she wanted to admit.

With shaking fingers, she plucked it from the mess, holding her breath as she examined it in the light of the early morning sun. No doubt about it – it was his key indeed, the one she'd once stolen from his pocket, the one he kept so carefully close at all times. The key to his *life*. Lying here waiting for her, as if to tell her he'd rather forget about every single memory of those long-gone centuries than lose her.

A laugh escaped her.

The bastard. The charming, tempting, persuasive bastard, with his promises and pleasantries and proofs of loyalty – so what was she supposed to do now, then? Tell him to go to hell once again? Fling that key into the sea just to see if that, finally, would make him lose his patience? But she didn't even *want* to anger him, didn't even want to hurt him.

If she was entirely honest, she just wanted to see him again.

She muttered a curse, running her eyes over their exchange again. She'd been testing him, hadn't she? Prodding and poking, hoping for him to prove her right about him – and clearly he knew it as well as she did. Clearly he was prepared for worse. Which meant there was really very little chance he would suddenly decide she wasn't worth his time and effort after all.

Which meant he would stay.

She swallowed, clenching her fingers around the key. Be reasonable, she told her heart swelling against her ribcage. Be sensible. But if she *was* reasonable and sensible about the matter, did she really believe he was making all this effort, taking all these risks, just to drop her again in a few more weeks?

You know where to find me.

Oh, damn him.

She shoved the letter into her apron pocket and ran.

No one ever noticed a human servant at the Crimson Court. Even as she came sprinting up stairs and barging through doorways, none of the fae she encountered gave her more than a glance; she reached that familiar tower unhindered, her heart in her throat, her knees on the brink of giving in. At last, there was the door that either concealed her downfall or her rescue.

She gave herself ten heartbeats to gather her breath. Ten more to reconsider what she was about to do. Then she pushed down the doorhandle and slipped inside before she could change her mind after all.

Golden sunlight welcomed her, red-veined marble and rich mahogany and the lingering scent of parchment and firewood. Straight back into the dream. Back into those weeks of impossible safety and unspeakable pleasure and ...

Agenor.

She stood frozen at the door, drinking in the sight of him in that fraction of a heartbeat before he realised her presence – sitting at his desk, shirtless in the smothering warmth of the fire, his wings folded loosely over his back. His fingers hovering over an old scroll on his desk, a sheet full of notes under his other hand. Oleander's black body draped around his shoulders, drawing all the more attention to the bronze skin and solid muscle below. A surreal, ageless beauty that made her heart stop dead in her throat for a moment – gods, how dare he *look* like that when she was still nowhere near ready to forgive him?

Then he jerked around, pen clattering to the floor, and all she saw was the flare of harrowed panic in his green-gold eyes.

"*Allie?*"

She couldn't bring herself to move, clutching his key so tightly the edges cut painfully into her skin. Couldn't bring herself to tear her gaze away from his, the shadows in the depths of his eyes, the fear, the remorse, the exhaustion.

'Allie,' he said again, his voice softer now, hoarser, trailing down her spine like a single tender fingertip. 'Allie, you ...'

His words drifted off on an inaudible whisper. He turned a fraction in his chair, then froze again, as if the slightest movement would send her running again. Oleander slithered from his shoulders, taking up position between the books on the desk, peering at the both of them like a spectator at a dramatic play.

Allie didn't move. Her tongue seemed stuck to the roof of her mouth, her words lost somewhere between dangerous hope and fearful anticipation.

'You just insist on surprising me, don't you?' he finished softly.

'You ...' She uttered a chuckle, although it didn't come out nearly as confident as she'd hoped. 'You're the one who invited me.'

'I didn't assume you'd be forgiving enough to show up already.'

'Well,' she managed, straightening her shoulders a little. 'I *am* still furious.'

A faint, joyless smile played around his lips. 'Good. You should be.'

She blinked. 'What?'

'I broke a promise,' he said, cocking his head at her, challenging her to remember. 'Started explaining the world to you again as if you were a bloody child. Got fixated on my loyalty, even in the face of your rather harmless requests. Anything else I—'

'That ...' She let out another laugh, staggering half a step forward. 'Those are *my* lines, Agenor.'

'I know.' His wry smile broadened a fraction. 'I'm still quite determined to save you some effort whenever possible.'

Only then did her eyes take note of the rest of the room. The books on the shelves behind him, the piles beside his bed, the long list of notes on his desks. She swallowed, suddenly unable to meet his gaze again.

'You've really been looking into her bindings.'

'Yes.'

'Even though that's ...'

'Quite forbidden?' He sounded oddly cheerful over it. 'Yes.'

'Oh,' she said numbly.

He sat silent, waiting. She stared at his hands, his knees, the tips of his wings – anything but his vexingly handsome face, anything but those yearning green eyes. If she met his gaze again ...

She swallowed again. She wasn't sure what she would do.

'I really am still furious, Agenor,' she reminded him.

'Yes,' he said, his voice suspiciously grave. 'That's crystal clear, don't worry.'

She narrowed her eyes at the floor around his feet, clenching her fists even tighter. Focus, Allie. *Focus.* 'Really *very* furious.'

From the edge of her sight, she could see him nod sagely. Gods damn him, why wouldn't he defend himself? Already she could feel the fieriest edges of her anger sizzle out against his mild composure, and how was she going to keep control of herself without her justified fury to keep her grounded?

'I could probably ... punch you or something,' she added through clenched teeth, and this time he had the gall to chuckle.

'Wouldn't it be a shame if you did?'

She snapped up her gaze to scowl at him, annoyed enough for a moment to ignore her stomach's somersaults. 'What would you do if I actually hurt you?'

'Al, please,' he said, his deep voice brimming with an intensity that made her knees quiver like twigs. 'You're here. You're talking to me. If you tried to chop off my hand and set your nails into my eyes in a minute, I would still be having a pretty fine day on average.'

The quivering became an uncontrollable shaking. 'Do you have to be like that?'

'Like what? Madly in love with you?'

'You're doing it *again*!' She swung out a hand at him. 'How am I supposed to be angry with you if you insist on being so – so ...'

'Ah,' he said mildly, folding his hands behind his back. 'I'm very sorry. If you prefer for me to blurt out some unforgiveable insults or throw some false accusations at you, of course I'll be glad to oblige. Whatever makes you happiest, little thief.'

She tried to glare at him – tried to ignore the way her insides melted at the sound of that nickname, at the sight of the twinkle in his eye. She was angry, she desperately reminded herself. She was *very* angry. He ...

His lips were trembling.

So were hers.

Here they were, in this beautiful golden room, surrounded by evidence that he hadn't cast her aside after all, that he *would* help, that he *would* defy the Mother for her – and then she was laughing, unable to help herself, shrieks of hysterical relief shaking through her body as she stumbled towards him. He was standing in the blink of an eye, ready to catch her. So safe, still so safe, as she flung herself into his embrace and he wrapped his arms and wings around her, burying his face in her hair.

Her laughter faded as his scent washed over her. His turned breathless, almost choked.

'Little thief ...'

'Don't you *ever*,' she managed, knees finally buckling at the crack in his voice, 'do that again, Agenor. Don't you ever—'

'Never,' he whispered, pulling her even closer. 'For all my promises are still worth to you, I promise. On that shadowy heart of mine, I'm not going anywhere ever again. I can't lose you, Al. I'm an utter mess without you.'

She rested her face against his bare chest, clutched her arms around his muscular torso. Too good to be true – far, far too good to be true – and yet the words were there, the apologies, the promises ... How could she *not* believe him when his voice cracked so painfully, when his hands held onto her so desperately?

'Say you're with me,' he said quietly, a plea in his voice. Warm air caressed her forehead, her temple. 'Angrily, lovingly, I don't care. Just be with me. Please.'

'I'm with you.' She closed her eyes, held him closer, revelling in the nearness of him. His body was so perfectly powerful under her fingers, his bronze skin so unfathomably soft – warrior's strength, mage's power, and somehow he was still *hers*. 'I – I missed you, too. I ...'

His fingers tightened around her neck, tipped her head back, forced her to meet the wild, stormy whirlpool of his eyes. 'Say that again.'

'I missed you,' she breathed. 'Angrily. But missed you all the same.'

He bent over until his breath brushed her cheek, holding her still with the hand at her nape. A smile hovered around the corners of his lips. It looked nothing like his usual smiles, those mild, composed creations – this smile escaped him like a predator escaping its cage, all savage wickedness, all untamed need.

'And how angry are you now, little thief?'

'Still angry,' she managed through the palpitations of her heart, the haze of sensations. The sweet, musky scent of him. The trails of his roving fingers on her back and shoulders. The warmth of his body, so familiar and yet so dangerously enticing, and that *smile* ... 'Still impressively angry, really.'

His smile became a ravenous grin. 'Everything about you is impressive. I'm unsurprised. And no less determined to do something about it.'

The breath eddied from her lungs. Desperate to keep standing, she clawed her nails into his lower back, digging into satin skin and rock hard muscle, answering the claim of his hands on her. He groaned her name against her temple, and her knees gave out in spite of all her good intentions to control them.

'That's it, little thief,' he muttered, pinning her tighter against him, keeping her on her feet. The bulge of his erection pressed hard into her stomach, and whatever sensible thoughts still populated her mind fled to places unknown and unreachable, leaving her at the mercy of only the molten heat spreading just below her navel. His hands brushed their way down over her hips, her bottom, leaving goosebumps wherever they passed. 'That's it ...'

'No ... less ... angry,' she forced over her lips, and he let out a chuckle as he pressed his lips to the spot just below her ear, clawing his fingers into the inside of her thighs. A moan wrestled from her throat; she didn't seem able to stop it.

'You're so beautiful,' he whispered, kissing her jaw, her neck. 'Did I tell you how beautiful you are, Al? I could look at you for a lifetime and never grow bored of it ...'

She barely held in another moan. 'Were you always such a flatterer?'

'No, and it's haunted me.' His heavy breath stroked over her shoulder as his left hand slipped below her skirt. His touch rippled through her from all sides now: his lips on her shoulder, his fingertips on her thigh, the hard length of him prodding into her stomach with every shallow inhalation. 'I've lain awake over all I never told you, all I might never have the chance to tell you – how gods-damned brilliant you are. How desperately addicted I am to the sound of your laughter. And ...'

His hand crept up below her skirt, his other arm tight around her waist. She yelped as his exploring fingertips reached the hem of her underwear, and he shuddered.

'And those sounds,' he said hoarsely. 'The sounds you give me when I make you come, little thief – I would die and return to life just to hear them again.'

She parted her lips, then whimpered as he stroked a slow, languid path over the linen separating his fingers from her drenched flesh.

'Still angry?' he murmured.

'Perhaps ... perhaps a little less.' She could barely recall what anger was supposed to feel like. Burning, yes, but all of her body was burning now, every fibre of her being focused on the slow twists of his fingers over her hankering core. 'Perhaps if you go on like this ...'

'Like this?' He slipped his fingers below her underwear, and she arched against him, unable to suppress a ragged cry.

'Like that,' she breathed, and he chuckled. His arm locked around her waist, and he slowly moved forward, leaving her no choice but to stumble along until her back hit the wall and the breath once more rushed from her lungs. His wings rose on either side of them, eclipsing her view of the room. Only his face was still clear before her, eyes narrowed in feral need, sharp jaws clenched with self-restraint.

'Anything else I should do to earn your forgiveness?' He swirled his fingertips through her wetness as he spoke, his voice a rough purr. 'You don't *feel* so very angry anymore, little thief.'

She didn't care about anger. She didn't care about forgiveness. Hunger set its claws into every fibre of her, urgent and painful; all her mind could still comprehend was the agonising *emptiness* inside her, her body clenching and yearning around a nothingness she couldn't endure for a moment longer. His fingers were close, so excruciatingly close, and yet not even near to close enough ...

'I'll be very angry—'

He slowly slid a single slender finger into her, just the first digit, and words abandoned her. If not for the marble wall behind her back, she may have fainted at his feet as tendrils of need spiralled from her core to the very tips of her toes and fingers.

"*Agenor* ...'

'Very angry?' he muttered, probing just a fraction deeper.

A sob of frustration welled from her lips. 'I'll be absolutely furious if you – *oh* – if you don't properly fuck me *now*.' She moaned as he pulled back his finger. 'A full week of celibacy, Lord Protector. Did you apologise for *that* already?'

'I don't believe I did,' he admitted, spearing his finger back into her, so deep she saw stars for a moment. 'Did you suffer?'

'You're lucky I didn't die. I would have been even angrier if I'd died.'

He gave another chuckle as he pulled out and teased a second finger into her, stretching her open for him. 'I wholeheartedly apologise for denying you the company of my cock for a full week, little thief. Have a little patience and—'

She shot forward and hooked her fingers around the band of his trousers, snapping open the first button before he had time to react. His erection was scorching steel against the cloth of his underwear. She rubbed her thumb over the rim, and his exhalation became a groan, then a curse.

'Very nasty word you're using there,' she muttered, blinking up at him as she traced the full length of him with her palm. '*Patience*.'

His lips tensed into a strained, wild grin. 'Not so angry anymore, then?'

'Sometimes, Lord Agenor,' she told him, her voice cracking as his cock twitched in her hand, 'we must set our personal feelings aside when there are greater matters at stake. Such as my current, very urgent need to be fucked senseless on whatever the nearest surface is. Once those broader issues are taken care of, we can reassess—'

With another curse, he pulled her into his arms, then turned and swung her over his desk in the same motion, shoving off books and pens as he pinned her down against the wood. She let out a breathless laugh, clutching the edges of the tabletop to restrain her shaking hands.

'Weren't those books—'

'Absolutely invaluable,' he growled, yanking up her skirt. The sound of a button snapped behind her, and a second. Her toes curled in her shoes in maddening anticipation. 'Monetary considerations will have to wait for the broader issues, too, I'm afraid. Fuck, Al, you're beautiful – so very beautiful, and ...'

He tugged her drawers down, then pressed a finger against her entrance again. She twitched, gasping for breath.

'And so very wet.' His voice sank to a hoarse whisper. 'Did you think of me these days, little thief? Did you dream of me?'

'I tried not to,' she grumbled, and he laughed as he laid his tip against her slit, rubbing himself through her wetness. She whimpered, clutching the desk even tighter, and again his laughter shook through him.

'Let's put an end to your suffering, then ...'

He buried himself inside her with such force that she nearly followed the books over the edge of the desk. Allie cried out, holding on for dear life as he pulled back and plunged into her again, the sheer size of him enough to wipe every last trace of the week's hurt and despair from her mind – filling her deep and even deeper, until there was not a fibre of her body that didn't burn for him, ache for him. He clasped her hips, rode her hard, each thrust a claim and a surrender at once. Hers. Still *hers*.

'You,' she managed through the haze of bliss and blinding lust, 'you feel ... so ...'

His hand slipped around her hip and found that little core of her pleasure. She lost the last of her words as his thumb rubbed the spot, so rough it was almost painful and yet enough to drive a frenzied cry from her lips. In unthinking ecstasy, she tilted her hips, and he slammed into her even deeper, his cock a glorious, ruthless promise.

He moaned a laugh behind her. 'How do I feel?'

She was beyond answering now. She didn't recognise the sounds that rose from her at every savage thrust, could no longer tell if they were hers or his or something else entirely. He thrust and stroked, stroked and thrust. His free hand clamped down on her hip as he fucked her faster and faster, driving her to some edge, some *wonder*, that even the rising madness inside her could barely begin to imagine.

'Allie,' he grunted, a wild animal's groan. 'Come for me.'

She burst.

Release barrelled down her spine like a strike of lightning, filled her with sizzling power down to the very tips of her fingers. She heard herself cry out his name. Felt her body clench tight around his pounding cock. Two, three last thrusts and he followed her over the edge, flooding her with his warm seed, making a mess of her thighs, her dress, the desk

...

She sagged against the wood, out of breath and out of thoughts to think. The world shrunk to his slowing movements inside her, his hands on her back, the blissful, peaceful calm of her own mind.

'Little thief,' he whispered, wrapping his arms around her and lifting her against his chest. 'You miracle ... you ...'

She locked her arms around his shoulders and didn't let go until he lowered the both of them into his sun-soaked bed. He stripped her dress off her, she his shirt; they curled up between the blankets together, bare skin on bare skin, limbs entangled until she barely knew where she ended and he began.

He whispered, 'Still angry?'

Allie closed her eyes, snuggled up even closer to his muscular chest, breathed in the salty, lusty scent of him, and muttered the only answer that seemed even close to relevant.

'I'm going to have your baby.'

His arms tightened around her. 'Yes.'

'We can fight about names,' she added dreamily. It seemed the most joyous prospect in the world, suddenly. 'And places to live. And the right age to put a knife in a child's hand for the first time. And you're not going anywhere.'

'I'm not going anywhere.' He chuckled. 'Also, twelve years old.'

'Five years old at the very latest,' she grumbled into his chest, 'and we should teach them to always aim for the wings.'

Laughter rumbled through him. 'You *are* a very bloodthirsty creature, little thief.'

She hummed a content confirmation and huddled even closer against him, holding onto him with all her strength. The world slowly soaked through her conscious thoughts again, with all its inevitable cruelty and danger. Soon there would be books to read. Plans to make. Bindings to break.

Now, though, in this soft, simple moment ...

One last moment, she hesitated. Then, her lips against the satin skin just below his collarbone, she whispered, 'But I'm *your* bloodthirsty creature.'

His breath caught. 'I'll try my hardest to be worthy of that.'

She held him even tighter.

For minutes, they lay there in silence, his strong arms a shield around her, his lips against her forehead the sweetest, tenderest reassurance. Perhaps, Allie considered, dozing in the sunlight, this was how one changed the world after all. One not so rule-abiding fae lord at a time. One safe child at a time ...

Perhaps, in the end, this was how empires fell.

The end...
for now

Allie and Agenor's story continues in the main Fae Isles series, which tells the story of their daughter Emelin, her fight against the em-

pire, and her dangerous, tempestuous romance with Creon, the Silent Death.
Get their first book, *Court of Blood and Bindings*, via mybook.to/cobab.
Want to get all the latest news? Sign up at www.lisettemarshall.com /sign-up to receive my bi-monthly newsletter with release alerts, free bonus books and other fun bookish stuff.

About the Author

Lisette Marshall is a fantasy romance author, language nerd and cartography enthusiast. Having grown up on a steady diet of epic fantasy, regency romance and cosy mysteries, she now writes steamy, swoony stories with a generous sprinkle of murder.

Lisette lives in the Netherlands (yes, below sea level) with her boyfriend and the few house plants that miraculously survive her highly irregular watering regime. When she's not reading or writing, she can usually be found drawing fantasy maps, baking and eating too many chocolate cookies, or geeking out over Ancient Greek.

To get in touch, visit www.lisettemarshall.com, or follow @authorlisettemarshall on Instagram, where she spends way too much time looking at pretty book pictures.

Made in the USA
Coppell, TX
18 May 2024

32530488R00125